THE PENDERWICKS ON GARDAM STREET

Also by Jeanne Birdsall

The Penderwicks: A Summer Tale of Four Sisters,
Two Rabbits, and a Very Interesting Boy

THE
PENDERWICKS
ON
GARDAM
STREET

JEANNE BIRDSALL

ALFRED A. KNOPF
NEW YORK

THIS IS A BORZOI BOOK PUBLISHED BY ALFRED A. KNOPF

Visit us on the Web! www.randomhouse.com/kids

Educators and librarians, for a variety of teaching tools, visit us at
www.randomhouse.com/teachers

Library of Congress Cataloging-in-Publication Data
Birdsall, Jeanne.
The Penderwicks on Gardam Street / Jeanne Birdsall ; [illustrations by David Frankland]. — 1st ed.
    p.   cm.
Summary: The four Penderwick sisters are faced with the unimaginable prospect of their widowed father dating, and they hatch a plot to stop him.
ISBN 978-0-375-84090-6 (trade) — ISBN 978-0-375-94090-3 (lib. bdg.)
[1. Sisters—Fiction. 2. Single-parent families—Fiction. 3. Dating (Social customs)—Fiction. 4. Family life—Massachusetts—Fiction. 5. Massachusetts—Fiction.] I. Frankland, David, ill. II. Title.
PZ7.B51197Pen 2008
[Fic]—dc22
2007049232

The text of this book is set in 12-point Goudy.

Printed in the United States of America
April 2008
10 9 8 7 6 5 4 3 2

First Edition

For David, Amy, and Tim

CONTENTS

PROLOGUE

Their mother had been here in the hospital with the new baby for almost a week. Though the three little Penderwick girls had been to visit her every day—sometimes twice a day—it wasn't enough. They wanted her to come home.

"When, Mommy?" asked Jane, the youngest of the three.

"You've asked her five times already, and she doesn't know." Rosalind was the oldest and felt the responsibility of it deeply, though she was only eight. "May I hold Batty, Aunt Claire?"

Aunt Claire, their father's sister, carefully handed the baby over to Rosalind, who thought that holding babies was one of the great joys of life, even when the baby was asleep and didn't know she was being held.

"Mommy, can you at least come home for a visit? You don't need to bring the baby with you." Skye was the sister between Rosalind and Jane, and the only one who had inherited their mother's blond hair and blue eyes. The other two had their father's—and Aunt Claire's—dark curls and brown eyes. And while the baby so far had only fuzz, it looked like she was going to be dark, too.

"When I come home, honey, I'm afraid Batty's coming with me," said their mother, laughing. Then she stopped laughing and pressed her hands to her side.

"The gift shop!" said Aunt Claire, jumping out of her chair. "Why don't you three go to the gift shop and get yourselves treats?"

"We don't have any money," said Jane.

"I'll give you money." Aunt Claire pulled a bill from her wallet and handed it to Skye. "Rosalind, better leave Batty here. She's still too young for the gift shop."

"Maybe we can get her a present, anyway." Rosalind reluctantly laid the baby into the white bassinet beside her mother's bed.

"There's not enough money for her, too," said Skye.

"Manners!" said her mother.

But Aunt Claire smiled and handed several more bills to Skye. "Now get going, my greedy pirates!"

Aunt Claire was that most perfect kind of

relative—she loved and understood children but had none of her own to take attention away from nieces. So the sisters didn't mind when she called them names. Indeed, Skye seemed proud of being called a pirate, heading off to the gift shop with a bold, seafaring strut. Rosalind took Jane's hand and followed less boisterously, saying hello along the way to the many nurses they'd befriended during the week.

The shop was just up the hall and around the corner—the girls knew the way, for they'd been there many times, but never with so much money. Aunt Claire had been generous. There was enough for each girl to get at least a small treasure. Skye went straight to the watches, for she'd been yearning for a black one. Jane looked at everything—she always did— then ended up at the dolls, just as she always did. Rosalind picked out a stuffed black dog for Batty, then headed over to the jewelry case. Her best friend, Anna, had just gotten a new turquoise ring, and Rosalind thought nothing would be better than to have one like it.

When she got to the jewelry, her eye was drawn not to the rings, though, but to a delicate gold necklace with five dangling hearts—the largest one in the middle, with two smaller hearts on either side. She looked at the price, did a quick calculation on her fingers, did it again to make sure, then called her sisters over.

"We should buy that necklace for Mommy," she said.

"It would take up all of the money we have." Skye had already strapped a black watch onto her wrist.

"I know, but Mommy would love it. The big heart is her, and the four little ones are us three and the baby."

"This one's me," said Jane, pointing to one of the small hearts. "Rosalind, is Mommy still sick?"

"Yes."

"Because of Batty?"

"Because of the cancer," answered Rosalind. She hated that word, "cancer." "Remember how Daddy explained it to us? But she's going to get better soon."

"Of course she is," said Skye fiercely. "Daddy said the doctors are doing everything they can, and they're the best doctors in the universe."

"All right," said Jane. "I vote we buy Mommy the necklace."

"Rats." Skye disappeared, then came back without the watch and with a saleslady who put the necklace in a box with a bow on top.

Rosalind was now anxious to get back to her mother and Batty. Skye and Jane, though, had spotted their favorite nurse, Ruben, who always had time to give them a wheelchair ride. Knowing they'd be safe with Ruben, Rosalind hurried back down the hall, slowing down only when she got to the right room.

But instead of going in, she hung back, for she could hear her mother and aunt murmuring together—and it sounded like one of those conversations grown-ups had when children weren't supposed to be around. It wasn't bad manners to listen, Rosalind knew, because the murmuring was too low to be understood. But then the two women raised their voices, and Rosalind couldn't help understanding every word.

"No, Lizzy, no," Aunt Claire was saying. "It's too soon to talk about this. It sounds like you've given up."

"You know I'll never give up until there's no hope left, Claire. Please just promise me that if I don't make it, you'll give Martin my letter in three or four years. You know he's too shy to start dating without encouragement, and I just can't bear to think of him being lonely."

"He'll have the girls."

"And someday they'll grow up and—"

The sentence was broken off, for Ruben had arrived with Skye and Jane squashed into a wheelchair, squealing and giggling. They tumbled out and ran into the room while Rosalind followed more slowly, trying to puzzle out what she'd heard. What did her mother mean about not making it? And why would her father be dating? She felt so cold inside she was shivering, which only got worse as she saw Aunt Claire sliding a blue envelope into her pocket. Was that the letter her mother had mentioned?

Skye and Jane were so noisily excited about the wheelchair ride and about handing over the necklace, and then their mother was so pleased with the necklace and looked so lovely wearing it, that no one noticed that Rosalind was off to one side, pale and quiet. And then, too soon, a nurse arrived with a frightening-looking cart and made it clear that mother and baby both needed their rest. Reluctantly, the girls kissed their mother good-bye.

Rosalind took her turn last. "I'll see you tomorrow, Mommy," she whispered. Maybe by then she'd have the right questions to ask—about hope, about Daddy being lonely, and about that scary blue letter.

But Rosalind never got to ask her questions, and soon they'd been pushed aside and forgotten, for when tomorrow came, her mother was suddenly getting weaker instead of stronger. Despite the best efforts by the best doctors, within a week hope ran out altogether. Elizabeth Penderwick had enough time to say good-bye to her husband and girls one unbearable evening, but only just enough. She died before dawn the next morning, with baby Batty nestled, calm and quiet, in her arms.

CHAPTER ONE
Rosalind Bakes a Cake

F OUR YEARS AND FOUR MONTHS LATER

Rosalind was happy. Not the kind of passionate, thrilling happy that can quickly turn into disappointment, but the calm happy that comes when life is steadily going along just the way it should. Three weeks earlier, she'd started seventh grade at the middle school, which was turning out not to be as overwhelming as rumored, mostly because she and her best friend, Anna, shared all the same classes. And it was late September, and the leaves were on the verge of bursting into wild colors—Rosalind adored autumn. And it was a Friday afternoon, and although school was all right, who doesn't like weekends better?

On top of all that, Aunt Claire was coming to visit

for the weekend. Beloved Aunt Claire, whose only flaw was that she lived two hours away from the Penderwicks' home in Cameron, Massachusetts. But she tried to make up for it by visiting often, and now she was arriving this evening. Rosalind had so many things to tell her, mostly about the family's summer vacation, three wonderful weeks at a place called Arundel in the Berkshires. There had been many adventures with a boy named Jeffrey, and for a while Rosalind had thought that she might be in love with another boy—an older one—named Cagney, but that had come to nothing. Now Rosalind was determined to stay away from love and its confusions for many years, but still she wanted to talk it all over with her aunt.

There was lots to get done before Aunt Claire arrived—clean sheets on the bed, clean towels in the bathroom, and Rosalind wanted to bake a cake—but first she had to pick up her little sister Batty at Goldie's Day Care. She did so every day on the walk home from school, and even that was part of her happiness. For this was the first year her father had given her the responsibility for her sisters after school and until he came home. Before now, there had always been a babysitter, one or another of the beautiful Bosna sisters, who lived down the street from the Penderwicks. And though the Bosnas had been good babysitters as well as beautiful, Rosalind considered herself much too old now—twelve years and eight months—for a babysitter.

The walk from Cameron Middle School to Goldie's took ten minutes, and Rosalind was on her last minute now. She could see on the corner ahead of her the gray clapboard house, with its wide porch full of toys. And now she could see—she picked up her pace—a small girl alone on the steps. She had dark curls and was wearing a red sweater, and Rosalind ran the last several yards, scolding as she went.

"Batty, you're supposed to stay inside until I get here," she said. "You know that's the rule."

Batty threw her arms around Rosalind. "It's okay, because Goldie's watching me through the window."

Rosalind looked up, and it was true. Goldie was at the window, waving and smiling. "Even so, I want you to stay inside from now on."

"All right. But—" Batty held up a finger swathed in Band-Aids. "I just was dying to show you this. I cut myself during crafts."

Rosalind caught up the finger and kissed it. "Did it hurt terribly?"

"Yes," said Batty proudly. "I bled all over the clay and the other kids screamed."

"That sounds exciting." Rosalind helped Batty into her little blue backpack. "Now let's go home and get ready for Aunt Claire."

Most days the two sisters would linger on their

walk home from Goldie's—at the sassafras tree, with leaves shaped like mittens, and at the storm drain that flooded just the right amount when it rained, so you could splash through without getting water in your boots. Then there was the spotted dog who barked furiously but only wanted to be petted, and the cracks in the sidewalk that Batty had to jump over, and the brown house with flower gardens all around, and the telephone poles that sometimes had posters about missing cats and dogs. Batty always studied these carefully, wondering why people didn't take better care of their pets.

But today, because of Aunt Claire's visit, they hurried along, stopping only for Batty to move to safety a worm that had unwisely strayed onto the sidewalk, and soon they were turning the corner onto Gardam Street, where they lived. It was a quiet street, with only five houses on each side, and a cul-de-sac at the end. The Penderwick sisters had always lived there, and they knew and loved every inch of it, from one end to the other. Even when Rosalind was in a hurry, like today, she noted with satisfaction the tall maples that marched along the street—one in every front yard—and the rambling houses that were not so young anymore, but still comfortable and well cared for. And there was always someone waving hello. Today it was Mr. Corkhill, mowing his lawn, and Mrs. Geiger, driving by with a car full of groceries—and then Rosalind stopped waving back, for Batty had broken into a run.

"Come on, Rosalind!" cried Batty over her shoulder. "I hear him!"

This, too, was part of their everyday routine. Hound, the Penderwicks' dog, always knew when Batty was almost home, and set up such a clamor he could be heard all up and down Gardam Street. So now both sisters were running, and in a moment Rosalind was unlocking their front door, and Hound was throwing himself at Batty as though she'd been away for centuries instead of just the day.

Rosalind dragged Hound back into the house, with Batty dancing alongside in an ecstasy of reunion. Down the hall they all went, through the living room and into the kitchen—where Rosalind opened the back door and shoved the joyful tangle of child and dog into the backyard. She shut the door behind them and leaned against it to catch her breath. Soon Batty would need her afternoon snack, but for now Rosalind had a moment to herself. She could start on the cake, which she'd decided should be a pineapple upside-down one.

Humming happily, she took the family cookbook from its shelf. It had been a wedding gift to her parents, and was full of her mother's penciled notes. Rosalind knew all the notes by heart, and even had her favorites, like the one next to candied sweet potatoes—

An insult to potatoes everywhere. There was no note next to pineapple upside-down cake. Maybe if it was a great success, Rosalind would add her own. She did that sometimes.

"Melt a quarter cup of butter," she read, then put a skillet on the stove, lit the burner under it, and dropped in a stick of butter. Almost right away the butter started to melt, crackling a little, and filling the kitchen with a delicious bakery-ish smell.

"Add a cup of brown sugar." She measured the sugar and dumped it into the skillet. "Stir butter and sugar mixture until dissolved."

The sugar all melted into the butter, Rosalind took the skillet off the stove, opened a can of pineapple slices, and arranged the slices atop the sugar mixture. She stood back and admired her handiwork. "Looks magnificent, Rosy. What a fabulous cook you are."

She went back to the cookbook, humming again, and then noticed a suspicious lack of noise in the backyard. With a glance out the door, she understood why. Batty and Hound were crouched in the forsythia border, peeping into the next-door neighbors' back-yard. And not the neighbors to the right, the Tuttles, who'd lived there forever and wouldn't have cared if Batty and Hound watched through the kitchen win-dow while they ate. No, they were spying on the neighbors to the left, the Aaronsons, who'd just moved in. There had been great hopes for these new neighbors. A large family would have been perfect, for there can never be too many children in a neighborhood. The Aaronsons, however, turned out to be a small family indeed—a mother and a little boy just learning to toddle around, but no father, for he'd died before the boy was born. Both the mother and boy had red hair, which was good, as there were no other redheads on the street, but an interesting hair color only goes so far. Mr. Penderwick already knew Ms. Aaronson slightly. They were both professors at Cameron University—he was a botanist and she an astrophysicist—but the rest of the family had not yet been introduced.

Rosalind didn't think that spying should come before introductions.

"Batty!" she called out the door. "Come here!"

Batty and Hound wriggled out of the forsythia and dragged themselves reluctantly to the house. "We're only playing secret agents."

"Play something else, then. The neighbors might not like to be spied on."

"They weren't in their backyard, so they wouldn't know. Anyway, we were actually looking for the cat."

"I didn't know the Aaronsons had a cat."

"Oh, yes, a large orange cat. He usually sits in the window, and Hound loves him already."

Though Hound thumped his tail in agreement, Rosalind had her doubts that love was what he had in mind. She'd never seen him with a cat, but she knew how he felt about squirrels, as did all the squirrels that tried to make their home on Gardam Street. There was, however, no point in arguing with Batty about Hound's innermost feelings, so she changed the subject.

"How about your afternoon snack?"

Batty was never one to turn down a snack, especially when it was cheese, pretzel sticks, and grape juice, and when, like today, Rosalind let her eat it under the kitchen table, which happened to make an excellent hideout for secret agents.

With Batty settled, Rosalind went back to her cooking. "Sift a cup of flour—" But once more she was interrupted, this time by her other two sisters arriving home from school and storming the kitchen.

"Something smells good." This was Skye, her blond hair crammed messily into a camouflage hat. She stuck her finger into the skillet and scooped out a blob of the sugar mixture.

Rosalind tried to wave her off, but Skye dodged around, laughing and licking her finger.

"Call Daddy," said Rosalind. "You're the last one in."

That was the rule after school. While Rosalind was picking up Batty at Goldie's, Skye and Jane were walking home together from Wildwood Elementary School, where they were in sixth and fifth grades, respectively. Whoever was the last to arrive at the

14

house called Mr. Penderwick at the university to let him know all was well.

"Jane, call Daddy," said Skye.

"I'm too distraught about English class," said Jane.

This was unlike Jane, who loved English class more than anything, even soccer, which she adored. Rosalind turned away from the cookbook and looked hard at the third Penderwick sister. She did look upset. There were even traces of tears.

"What happened?" asked Rosalind.

"Miss Bunda gave her a C on her essay," answered Skye, reaching under the table and swiping some of Batty's cheese.

"My humiliation is complete," said Jane. "I'll never be a real writer."

"I told you Miss Bunda wouldn't like it."

"Let me see the essay," said Rosalind.

Jane pulled several crumpled balls of paper out of her pocket and tossed them onto the kitchen table. "I have no profession now. I'll have to be a vagrant."

Rosalind smoothed out the pieces of paper, found page one, and read, "*Famous Women in Massachusetts History, by Jane Letitia Penderwick. Of all the women that come to mind when you think of Massachusetts, one stands out: Sabrina Starr.*" She stopped reading. "You put Sabrina Starr in your essay?"

"Yes, I did," said Jane.

Sabrina Starr was the heroine of five books, all of

them written by Jane. Each was about an amazing rescue. So far, Sabrina had saved a cricket, a baby sparrow, a turtle, a groundhog, and a boy. This last, *Sabrina Starr Rescues a Boy*, had been written during the summer vacation at Arundel. Jane considered it her best.

"But your assignment was to write about a Massachusetts woman who was actually once alive."

"Just what I told her. Ouch!" Skye jumped away from the table, for Batty had just pinched her ankle as revenge for the stolen cheese.

"I explained all that," said Jane. "Look at the last page."

Rosalind found the last page. *"Of course, Sabrina Starr is not a real Massachusetts woman, but I wrote about her because she's more fascinating than old Susan B. Anthony and Clara Barton,"* she read. "Oh, Jane, no wonder Miss Bunda gave you a C."

"I got a C because she has no imagination. Who cares about writing essays, anyway, when you can write stories?"

The phone rang and Skye raced for it. "Hi, Daddy, yes, we're all here and we were just about to call you. . . . We're fine, except Jane's upset because she got a C on her essay. . . . Really?" Skye turned to Jane. "Daddy says remember that Leo Tolstoy flunked out of college and went on to write *War and Peace*."

"Tell him I'll never even get into college at this rate."

Skye spoke into the phone again. "She said she'll never get into college. . . . What? Tell me again. . . . Okay, got it. Good-bye."

"What did he say?" said Jane.

"That you don't have to worry because you have *tantum amorem scribendi*." Skye said the last three words slowly and carefully, for they were Latin.

Jane looked hopefully at Rosalind. "Do you know *tantum am*—whatever it is?"

"Sorry, our class hasn't gotten much past *agricola, agricolae*," answered Rosalind. She had just that year started studying Latin in a desperate attempt to understand her father, who was always tossing out phrases in that ancient language. "So far, I'll only know if Daddy says something about being a farmer."

"Fat chance," said Skye. "Since he's a professor."

"How old do I have to be to read *War and Peace*?" asked Jane. "It would soothe my wounds to find a kindred spirit in Mr. Tolstoy."

"Older than ten, that's for sure," said Skye. Unwilling to be pinched in the ankle again, she headed back for the sugar mixture in the skillet, but this time Rosalind was ready with a body block.

"No more," she said. "I'm making a pineapple upside-down cake for Aunt Claire, and you're ruining it."

"Aunt Claire is visiting!" Jane's face lit up. "In my agony, I'd forgotten. *She* will soothe my wounds."

"And while I'm finishing the cake, you two can get the guest room ready for her."

"Homework . . . ," muttered Skye, drifting toward the door.

"You never do homework on Fridays," Rosalind said briskly. "Go."

Despite Skye's attempt to avoid helping, she was an excellent worker, and the next hour at the Penderwick house went smoothly. The clean sheets and towels were taken care of, the living room was straightened up, and, as a special touch, Batty and Hound were both brushed. Just as Rosalind pulled the finished cake out of the oven, Jane's joyful yell rang through the house.

"Aunt Claire's here!"

CHAPTER TWO
The Blue Letter

THIS VISIT OF AUNT CLAIRE'S started out like her visits always did. There was the usual tussle to see who could hug her first, and she had dog biscuits in one pocket for Hound—just like she always did—and in the other pocket, chocolate caramels for everyone else. And when Mr. Penderwick came home she sat on the kitchen counter, just like always, while he made dinner—eggplant parmigiana—getting in his way and teasing him every time he mislaid a cooking spoon, or his glasses, or the salt, which was every two minutes. All through dinner she continued to be the same old Aunt Claire—telling funny stories about her job and peppering the girls with questions about school. It wasn't until everyone had stuffed themselves with eggplant and the table had been cleared that the visit started to turn odd. Rosalind was just bringing out the pineapple upside-down cake when Aunt Claire abruptly pushed back her chair and stood up.

"I think—" She sat down again. "Maybe not."

"Maybe not what?" asked Jane.

Aunt Claire stood up again. "I mean, I guess this would be as good a time as any. Though, actually, later would be better."

She sat down yet again, and smiled at everyone. They would have smiled back if it hadn't been obvious that her smile was a guilty one, though the idea of Aunt Claire being guilty of anything was beyond imagination.

Mr. Penderwick frowned. "What's wrong with you?"

"I'm fine. Just ignore me," she said gaily. "The cake looks delicious, Rosalind. Aren't you going to cut it?"

Rosalind picked up the cake knife, but before she could make a cut, Aunt Claire was back on her feet.

"No, no, definitely best to get it over with. I'll go get the presents from my car." And she rushed out of the room.

"What presents?" Skye asked, but no one knew. It wasn't Christmas or a birthday.

"Is Aunt Claire going crazy?" This was Batty, and no one could answer her, either. If Aunt Claire wasn't going crazy, she was doing a good job of acting like she was.

Then she was back, pulling a shiny new red wagon full of interestingly shaped packages and talking very quickly. "The wagon is for Batty, of course. Sorry I couldn't wrap it, dear, but it's too big and bulky. The wrapped packages are for the other three girls."

"All right, Claire," said Mr. Penderwick. "What is all this about?"

"Can't I bring gifts without a reason?"

"You never have before," said Rosalind. Aunt Claire was making her nervous.

"You're hiding something, Claire," said Mr. Penderwick. "You know that never works. Remember my submarine?"

"What submarine?" asked Skye.

"Your aunt destroyed my favorite model submarine and blamed it on our dog, Ozzie. But I knew it was her."

"It's nothing like your submarine this time!" cried Aunt Claire.

"Then what is it?" Rosalind burst out—she couldn't stand it anymore.

"Are you sick, Aunt Claire?" asked Jane, looking suddenly pale and sickly herself.

"No, no, I'm not sick. It's—I mean, I should have started all this with your father later, in private. Not that it's anything so terrible. I just— Oh, Martin!"

Mr. Penderwick took off his glasses and cleaned them on his sleeve. "Girls, give me a few minutes alone with your aunt, will you?"

21

"Can't they open the presents first?" pleaded Aunt Claire. "Or at least take them with them?"

"They may take them."

It was a miserable group that filed into the living room, with Rosalind dragging the red wagon, and Skye dragging Hound, who would have preferred to stay in the vicinity of the pineapple upside-down cake. No one was in the mood for presents.

"It would be ungrateful not to open them," said Jane after a few moments of gloomy silence. She still wasn't in the mood for presents, but she'd noticed that the package with JANE on it was the right size and shape to be books.

So Rosalind handed out the packages. Jane's was indeed books, six of them by Eva Ibbotson, one of her favorite authors. Skye got an impressive pair of binoculars, army issue and with night vision. And Rosalind's gift was two sweaters, one white and one blue.

"Two!" she said. "Something is definitely wrong."

"And my books are all hardbound, and two of them I haven't read even once yet," added Jane. "These must be Aunt Claire's dying gifts."

"She said she wasn't sick. Besides, she looks perfectly healthy."

"People often look perfectly healthy right before they die."

"Then we could all die." Batty climbed into her new wagon. Perhaps it was safer in there.

"Nobody's going to die," said Rosalind.

"Shh," said Skye, and now everyone noticed that she was lurking near the door.

"You're eavesdropping!" said Jane.

"Eavesdropping isn't honorable. I just happen to be standing here, that's all," said Skye.

Her reasoning was so logical that her sisters decided to stand with her, and if they were quiet because there was nothing left to say, was that really the same as eavesdropping? Whether it was or not, it didn't do them any good, for all they heard were bits and pieces. Aunt Claire was talking quickly, and their father said "NO" once loudly, and then they went back and forth, and the girls heard their mother's name—Elizabeth—several times. Then there was silence, until without warning the door flew open, almost hitting Skye in the nose.

It was their father, his hair rumpled and his glasses sliding down his nose. He was holding a piece of blue notepaper, holding it gently as though it were delicate and precious. At the sight of it, Rosalind suddenly felt cold inside, so cold she shivered, though none of it made sense—the letter, the cold, or the shivering.

"It's all right, girls. Not a tragedy. More of a comedy, or perhaps a tragicomedy. Come back in."

They filed back into the kitchen, sat down, and thanked Aunt Claire for their gifts. The pineapple upside-down cake sat, ignored, in the middle of the table.

"You tell them, Claire," said Mr. Penderwick. "This is your doing."

"I explained to you, Martin, it's *not* my doing," she said.

"Tell them," he said.

"Well, girls—" She paused, then hurried on. "What would you think of your father beginning to date?"

There was a shocked silence. Whatever anyone had imagined, it wasn't this.

"Dates? You mean, like movies and dinner and romance?" asked Jane finally.

"Romance! Bah!" said Mr. Penderwick, his glasses falling off altogether and clattering to the floor.

Aunt Claire picked up the glasses and gave them back to him. "Movies and dinner, yes, but there's no rush for romance."

Again, no one could think of what to say. The only sound was Hound's snuffling search for crumbs on the floor.

"I don't think you're the type for dating, Daddy," said Skye after a while. "No offense."

"None taken," he said. "I agree with you."

Batty slipped off her chair and onto her father's lap. "Why would you, Daddy?"

"Your mother thought it best, honey," said Aunt Claire.

"Mommy?" This was Jane, whispering.

Rosalind was feeling dizzy. The kitchen now

seemed too warm and the lights too bright. "No, I don't believe it," she said. "There's been a mistake."

"It's true, Rosy. This was your mother's idea," said Mr. Penderwick, looking down at the blue paper he was still holding. "She was afraid I'd be lonely."

"But you have us," said Rosalind.

"Grown-ups sometimes need the company of other grown-ups," said Aunt Claire. "No matter how wonderful their children are."

"I don't understand why this is happening now," said Skye, picking up a fork and stabbing the table. "Is there someone you want to date, Daddy?"

"No, there is not." Mr. Penderwick looked like he wouldn't mind doing some stabbing himself.

"Your mother believed you girls would be old enough by now that Martin could expand his world a bit, and frankly, I don't think she was wrong," said Aunt Claire. "So he and I have agreed upon a plan. Your father will jump into the dating pool, shall we say, and stay there for the next several months. During that time he'll take out at least four different women."

"Four!" Stab, stab, stab, stab went Skye's fork.

"If, after that, he wants to go back to being a hermit, at least he will have tried, and I mean seriously tried. No pretending there aren't any available women in western Massachusetts." Ignoring her brother's groan, Aunt Claire soldiered on. "And, since I thought he might have trouble getting started, I called a friend of mine who has an unmarried friend here in Cameron."

Rosalind's dizziness was getting worse—her ears were ringing, and the refrigerator appeared to be tipping to one side.

"And?" Skye jammed the fork so hard it bent.

"And thus, tomorrow night I have a blind date with a certain Ms. Muntz," said Mr. Penderwick. "The die is cast. *Iacta alea est.*"

Rosalind stood up so abruptly that her chair fell over with a loud clatter. They were all asking her what was wrong, but she couldn't explain. She only knew that she couldn't breathe properly and she had to get outside. She stumbled toward the door, pushing away someone's hands, and heard Aunt Claire saying that they should let her be.

Yes, let me be, she thought, reaching the door.

"Rosy!" That was her father.

Answering him—even looking at him—was impossible. She escaped, slammed the door behind her, and took great, hungry gulps of the night air. Yes, now she could breathe.

"I'll walk for a while," she told herself. "I'll feel better if I walk."

She set off down Gardam Street.

CHAPTER THREE
Bedtime Stories

"—AND HE HUNG HIS NEW COAT on the hook for his coat, and his new handkerchief on the hook for his handkerchief, and his pants on the hook for his pants, and his new rope on the hook for his rope, and himself he put in his bunk," read Mr. Penderwick.

"You left out Scuppers's shoes." Batty was in her bed, listening intently.

"So you did," said Aunt Claire.

Mr. Penderwick went back a line or two. "His new shoes he put under his bunk, and then himself he put in his bunk."

"And here he is where he wants to be—a sailor sailing the deep green sea," finished up Batty. "Now for the song."

"It's late for songs. Time for sleep, Battikins."

"Rosalind always sings the song. Doesn't she, Hound?"

Hound barked nervously from his spot beside the bed. He liked to side with Batty, but after all, it was Mr. Penderwick who fed him.

"Traitor beast," said Mr. Penderwick.

"Come on, Martin," said Aunt Claire. "Let's raise our voices in—I guess 'celebration' wouldn't be quite the word for tonight. Let's just raise our voices."

"As usual, I am outnumbered and outmaneuvered. I will sing, but only once, mind you."

And together all three sang, with Hound barking along:

I am Scuppers the Sailor Dog—
I'm Scuppers the Sailor Dog
I can sail in a gale
right over a whale
under full sail
in a fog.

I am Scuppers the Sailor Dog—
I'm Scuppers the Sailor Dog
with a shake and a snort
I can sail into port
under full sail
in a fog.

When they finished, the two grown-ups tucked in Batty's unicorn blanket and kissed her good night. She snuggled into her pillow and closed her eyes, and stayed that way while they turned off the light and left the room, and then for another few moments, to give them enough time to go downstairs. Then she turned the light back on, slid out of bed, and tiptoed across the room to her new red wagon. It was the best wagon she'd ever seen, and she wondered how she could have lived without it until now.

"I'll sit in it and wait for Rosalind to come say good night," she told Hound.

This was such a good idea that she climbed right into the wagon. And there she sat, certain that Rosalind would be along any minute. True, Rosalind had left the house in a big hurry, even slamming the door—Rosalind, who never slammed doors—but she would be back soon to tell Batty a story like she did every night. Though Daddy and Aunt Claire had read about Scuppers very nicely, it just wasn't the same.

She sat and she sat, humming the Sailor Dog song to herself, and she sat so long that Hound fell asleep, and still she sat, but Rosalind didn't come. Finally she couldn't stand it anymore. She climbed out of the wagon and pulled it down the hall to the room Skye and Jane shared. She knocked, and the door opened and a pair of binoculars peered out.

"Oh, it's only you," said Skye from behind the

binoculars. "I thought you were Rosalind come home."

"I need another story."

"I don't know any stories. Go back to bed."

But Skye stepped aside and let Batty and her wagon into the room. It was a room divided dramatically in half. Skye's side was tidy, with white walls and a plain blue coverlet on the bed. The only decoration was a framed chart showing how to convert from U.S. to metric measurements. Jane's side was not at all tidy, and lavender, with a flowery coverlet that should have been on the bed but was instead in a heap on the floor. Scattered everywhere was stuff: books, piles of paper, old school projects, and more books. And then there were the dolls, for Jane had kept not only every doll she'd ever been given, but every doll ever given to Skye, too.

Batty pulled her wagon into Jane's half of the room. There was more space for it on Skye's side, but Skye would get upset if she knocked against anything, and Batty was still unsure about steering. And, in fact, one wagon wheel did get caught in a towel hanging from Jane's bureau—and down tumbled a pile of laundry, including a pair of red-and-yellow-striped kneesocks.

Sprawled on her bed, Jane looked up from the book she was reading, *The Island of the Aunts*. "So that's where my soccer socks have been. Batty, you don't happen to see the rest of my uniform anywhere, do you? We have a game tomorrow."

Batty was too sleepy to find a missing uniform in all that clutter. "Actually, I want you to tell me a story."

"I'm in the middle of a chapter. I could read the rest out loud to you."

"But I wouldn't understand it." Batty knew she was close to crying. She fought hard against it, but one tear managed to escape and roll down the side of her nose.

"She's going to cry," said Skye.

"I am not." A second tear joined the first.

Jane shut her book and patted the bed beside her. Batty gratefully clambered up.

"Let me think of a story," said Jane. "Oh, I know. Once upon a time—"

"No Sabrina Starr," interrupted Skye. "I couldn't stand it. Not tonight."

"Sabrina Starr happens to be excellent for times of stress. That was not, however, what I had in mind. Once upon a time—"

"And no Mick Hart, either." Mick Hart was Jane's soccer-playing alter ego, a rough-mouthed profes-sional from England. During soccer season, Skye heard more than enough about him, as she shared not only a bedroom but also a soccer team with Jane.

"I don't care who you tell about," said Batty.

"Thank you, Batty. Onceuponatime"—Jane paused and looked at Skye, who shrugged and pointed her binoculars out the window—"there lived a king and queen who had three daughters, all princesses and greatly beloved by the people of their country."

"What was the country called?"

"It was called Cameronlot. The oldest princess was beautiful and kind. The second princess was brilliant and fearless. And the third princess was a spinner of tales, a fountain of creativity, a paragon of discipline, and all of Cameronlot declared her the most fascinating and talented princess who had ever lived."

"Ahem," said Skye from the window.

Jane ignored her. "Still, the king and queen felt that something was missing from their lives. 'We need just one more princess,' said the queen. 'One who . . .'"

"One who what?" asked Batty, for Jane had stopped.

"Why, one who can do what the other three princesses can't."

"Like what?" This was Skye again, being not at all helpful.

"She could understand the animals," said Batty.

"Yes, of course!" exclaimed Jane. "The king and queen needed a princess who could understand the animals, and so they had a fourth princess."

The door opened and Rosalind wandered in,

looking as though she'd been staring into strange and unfamiliar places.

"You've come back!" cried Batty, running to her.

"And you've got leaves in your hair," said Skye.

Rosalind reached up and seemed surprised to find that, yes, she had leaves stuck to her curls. Nervously she plucked them out and let them drop to the floor.

"Where have you been?" asked Jane.

"I don't know. Walking. And lying down, too, I guess."

It didn't matter to Batty where Rosalind had been. What mattered was that now she was back. "Daddy read to me about Scuppers," she said. "But then I wanted another story, and Jane was telling me one about princesses, but I want you to tell me one."

"All right, honey." Rosalind sank down onto Skye's bed. "In a minute."

Skye and Jane were also relieved to see Rosalind come home, leaves and all. She was the eldest—the dependable—Penderwick, and dependable people should rally their troops in times of difficulty. They shouldn't run out of the house and slam the door. Right now, though, Rosalind didn't seem to have much rallying in her. Jane decided she needed encouragement.

"Your pineapple upside-down cake was delicious, Rosy." Jane reached under her bed and pulled out a sticky-looking lump of paper napkin. "I snuck a piece up here for you."

"No, I couldn't." She shook her head vehemently, releasing one last stray leaf, then lapsed back into silence.

Now Skye tried. "This is weird about Daddy, isn't it?"

"Weird?" snapped Rosalind. "That's what you think, that Daddy going on dates is *weird*?"

"You don't?" Skye backed away from her sister's ferocity.

"Oh, it's much worse than weird. What if he falls in love with one of these dates? We could end up with a . . ." Rosalind shuddered. She couldn't bring herself to finish the sentence.

"You mean a stepmother?"

"A stepmother!" Jane had never considered such a thing.

"Think of Anna," said Rosalind.

Rosalind's friend Anna had a perfectly fine mother, but her father was forever getting married and divorced, then falling in love and doing it over again. It had happened so many times that Anna no longer bothered to keep track of her stepmothers. She called them all Claudia, after the first one.

"Good grief," protested Skye. "Daddy's nothing like Anna's father."

"I know." Rosalind managed to look a bit ashamed.

"Yikes!" said Jane suddenly. "Think of poor Jeffrey and that disgusting Dexter."

Jeffrey was the boy the sisters had met that summer on vacation. And Dexter was the man who'd dated and then married Jeffrey's mother, the dreadful Mrs. Tifton. So disgusting—so truly awful—was Dexter that Jeffrey had chosen to go to boarding school in Boston rather than live with him.

"What's gotten into you two?" Skye was outraged, for her father's honor was being trampled in the mud. "Now you're comparing Daddy to Mrs. Tifton?"

Batty had been trying to follow the conversation, but though she adored Jeffrey and loathed Mrs. Tifton as much as her sisters did, she couldn't understand what either of them had to do with Daddy's dating. Indeed, she was so tired she couldn't understand much of anything. She felt like she could fall asleep right there, if only Rosalind would just tell her a story, even a little one. Maybe one about Mommy—that would be nice.

"Rosalind, please," she said.

But Jane was talking again. "Skye's right. Of course Daddy would never fall in love with anyone as horrible as Dexter, or, you know what I mean, Dexter if he was a woman."

"Much less horrible than Dexter can still be horrible," said Rosalind.

"Dexter, Schmexter," said Skye. "I trust Daddy.

And by the way, everyone seems to be forgetting that the dating was Mommy's idea."

"I didn't forget. Mommy was wrong."

"Rosalind!" Jane almost shrieked it. Their mother had never been wrong. They all knew that.

"Well, she was." Rosalind turned and stared out the window.

Batty didn't like any of this. She didn't like that Rosalind didn't seem to notice her, and she didn't like the leaves—messing up Skye's side of the room!—and she especially didn't like hearing about Mommy being wrong. All she wanted now was to get back to Hound and her bed, and if Rosalind wasn't going to go with her, she would have to go by herself. She tugged on her red wagon, but this time the wheel got caught on a pile of books, and when she tugged again, the whole wagon turned over and she couldn't seem to pick it back up and now there were so many tears that Skye would see and know she was a coward—

—and finally Rosalind had picked her up and hugged her and was murmuring sweet, loving apologies.

"I just wanted a story," sobbed Batty.

"I know." Waving good night to Skye and Jane, Rosalind carried Batty back to her bed and tucked her in. Hound opened one eye to check, then, satisfied that Batty was in no danger, rolled over and went back to sleep.

"My wagon," said Batty, snuggling in among her stuffed animals.

"I'll go get it, and then we'll have a story."

But by the time Rosalind returned with the wagon and parked it beside the bureau, her little sister was as fast asleep as Hound. "Sleep well, Battikins," she whispered, then watched over her for a long time, just in case she woke up again, still wanting a story.

CHAPTER FOUR
Tempers Lost

THE NEXT DAY, while the rest of the family was eating lunch, Skye was alone in her room. She and Jane had a soccer game in an hour, and while Jane believed that a big meal was essential for victory, Skye believed in a glass of milk, a few bananas, and solitary contemplation.

Their team was Antonio's Pizza, their uniforms red and yellow, with ANTONIO'S and a slice of pizza on the back. This season Skye had been elected captain, surprising her family and herself, for the year before she'd had a little trouble with her temper. Actually, a lot of trouble. There was the time she called the referee a kumquat and the time she stomped on a water bottle, which exploded, drenching several parents, and the time—well, all that was behind her now, she hoped. So far this season she hadn't lost her temper even once. The C on her jersey stood not just for *Captain* but for *Calm*, she'd decided, and she meant to keep it that way.

Her routine before each game went like this: ten leg stretches, ten neck rolls, ten push-ups, thirty sit-ups, reciting out loud the prime numbers up to 811—this was for concentration—then five minutes of picturing the other team bloody and repentant. After that came the most difficult part of the routine—five minutes of positive thoughts. Her father had suggested that she add this to the rest, particularly on those days when she'd done an extra-good job of picturing blood and repentance. Balance is always good, he'd said. Skye agreed with him about balance, but somehow it always seemed to take her at least fifteen minutes to get in five minutes' worth of positivity. Maybe today would be different.

The leg stretches, neck rolls, push-ups, sit-ups, and prime numbers went well. And the five minutes with the other team zipped by, for Antonio's Pizza was going to be playing their greatest rival, Cameron Hardware. And since the Cameron Hardware captain was the annoying Melissa Patenaude, who was in Skye's class at school, and always giggling at their teacher, Mr. Geballe, she had all the more motivation to overwhelm them with a glorious victory.

"Annihilation and humiliation for Cameron Hardware," she said when she was done, lingering happily on an image of Melissa vanquished.

Now it was positive-thought time. What should she think about? Before the last game, she'd been able to look forward to Aunt Claire's visit, and if it had turned out to be a normal visit, she would right now be having positive thoughts about it. But instead, there was all this baloney about dates—and Daddy's first one that very night!—which, while strange and confusing, shouldn't make people go wacko, especially if they are the oldest sister and—

"Stop!" Skye told herself. Positive thoughts!

She could think about school. Other than having to sit behind Melissa, school was great. Mr. Geballe was letting her spend math class in the library teaching herself geometry, since she already knew all the sixth-grade material so well she could have taught it herself. In English, he was letting them read whatever they wanted, and she'd picked *Swallows and Amazons*, which was all about adventures with boats. Of course, there was that problem with history class, for Mr. Geballe was making them each write a play about the Aztecs. Skye would have been happy to write an essay about the Aztecs' mathematical systems, or even their crops. But a play! With characters and drama and a plotline! She didn't have even a glimmer of interest in any of that, and that idiot Melissa was already bragging about how she was almost finished writing her play and how great it was.

"Stop!" Frustrated, Skye checked the clock. She had to come up with four more minutes of positivity.

Then she got it. This past summer at Arundel. Now, those would be positive thoughts. She leaned back against the bed, and away she went, into the Arundel woods and gardens—two-on-one slaughter with Jeffrey and Jane, shooting arrows at pictures of Dexter, climbing out of Jeffrey's window and into that huge tree, then getting rescued from the huge tree by Cagney, and on and on she thought, and was quite proud of herself, for the next time she looked at the clock, she'd managed to have the entire five minutes of positive thoughts, and so efficiently that there was time left before she had to suit up. She could give herself a treat, and knew exactly what treat she wanted—to try out her new binoculars by the light of day.

A moment later, with her binoculars slung around her neck, Skye climbed out through her bedroom window and onto the garage roof. This was her special place. It was also sort of a secret place, meaning that though all her sisters knew she came out here, her father didn't. Neither did Aunt Claire or any of the babysitters who'd taken care of the Penderwicks over the years. Skye knew that adults wouldn't approve of sitting on roofs, even roofs only one story up, so she hadn't told any of them. And her sisters hadn't told on her. Penderwicks didn't do that to each other.

She settled on the shingles, raised the binoculars, and focused them. Wow. They were truly great binoculars. With them she could see details all up and down Gardam Street. There at one end of the street were the ivy leaves painted on the Corkhills' mailbox, and there at the other end a license plate—NTRPRS—on a green car parked in the cul-de-sac.

"Double wow. Triple wow," she said, and pointed the binoculars directly across the street at the Geigers' house.

The Geigers—Mr. and Mrs. Geiger, Nick, and Tommy—had lived in that house for as long as the Penderwicks had lived in theirs, and Skye had looked at it a million times, but she'd never seen it through binoculars before. There, suddenly so close Skye almost reached out to touch it, was the scar on the garage door where Tommy had crashed his bike three years ago. And the soccer ball Jane had kicked onto the roof—she could read J. L. PENDERWICK THIS IS MY BALL—was still resting precariously in the gutter. And there was the rhododendron Nick had backed the car over when he was first learning to drive last year. Mrs. Geiger had been doing her best to nurse that bush back to health, but it didn't look like it was going to make it.

Now here came someone rounding the corner of

the house at top speed—Tommy, wearing shoulder pads and his football helmet. Skye tried to focus the binoculars on him, but he was gone around the house again before she could, his long legs and arms flailing at top speed. Training. He was always in training. Running. Lifting weights. Doing drills. Rosalind said that if he had as much discipline with his schoolwork as he did with football, he'd be at the top of the seventh grade. Here he came again.

"Skye, five minutes until we have to suit up for the game." It was Jane, leaning out the window. "Annihilation and humiliation for Cameron Hardware. How did your positive thoughts go?"

"Good. Now go away, I'm still being alone."

Skye looked across the street again. Tommy was nowhere in sight, and though she waited for a few minutes, he didn't reappear. He was probably doing squat thrusts somewhere. Tommy loved squat thrusts.

She pointed her binoculars up into the sky, for she'd heard a flock of Canada geese honking their way across Cameron. There they were—she focused—

"Hey."

What was the good of a special secret place if everyone kept visiting her there? This time it was Tommy, not doing squat thrusts after all, but instead perched in the tree that grew behind the garage. He was still wearing his helmet. It looked pretty goofy in a tree.

"Go away," she said.

"Do you want to do some football drills?"

"No, I've got a soccer game."

"What about Rosalind?"

"She'll be watching the game. The whole family's going, because Aunt Claire's here."

"Do you think she'll want to later? Rosalind, I mean, not Aunt Claire. I mean, I'm sure Aunt Claire could do football drills if she wanted to, but I'd rather have Ros—I mean . . ."

Tommy had trailed off into an embarrassed silence. Skye aimed the binoculars at him. All she got was a gigantic blurry nose inside a football helmet. "What's wrong with you?"

"Nothing." But the blurry nose was turning red.

"Hail ye, god of the goalposts." It was Jane again. "How's the Russian going?"

Tommy was studying Russian in school. It was the first of many languages he planned to learn, for he was going to be a pilot when he grew up, and thought he should be able to speak properly with people everywhere he flew.

"Not bad. *Neplokho*," said Tommy.

"Oh, that's lovely," said Jane. "Skye, it's time."

"Right." Skye slithered along the roof and dropped back into the bedroom.

"What was Tommy doing in the tree?"

"Being peculiar," said Skye. "Let's suit up."

For the first half of the game nothing could bother Skye, not even Melissa's phoney "Good luck" during the captains' handshake. It was a warm, bright September afternoon, gorgeous with color—green grass, blue sky, and red-and-yellow uniforms (and purple-and-white, for anyone who cared about Cameron Hardware)—like a crayon box come to life. The teams were evenly matched enough to make it interesting, but not so much that Antonio's Pizza couldn't pull ahead, and did, mostly because of Jane. Always a quick and wily striker, today she was on fire. By halftime, she'd scored two of their team's three goals. Cameron Hardware had scored none. Antonio's Pizza spent the whole halftime doing a wild war dance of joy, sort of a hip-hop version of the hula, with a touch of the cancan thrown in. Skye was delighted with herself, her sister, her team, and life. They were winning, and she hadn't felt even the least little bit of temper.

Unfortunately, Melissa and her team spent a more productive break, for they started off the second half playing like champs. And maybe Melissa even knew about Skye's weakness, because as soon as Jane got control of the ball, she was roughly knocked over by Cameron Hardware's hulking midfielder.

"Whoops!" Melissa chortled, almost in Skye's face.

In times past, that would have driven Skye into an

insane rage. This was the new Skye, though, and if she had to pinch her own arm—hard—to keep herself from lunging at Melissa, no one knew that but her. Besides, now she had bigger worries than Melissa, since when Jane got hit too hard, bad things happened. Sometimes she started to cry, and sometimes she forgot how to play. And sometimes—and this was Skye's least favorite possibility—she became Mick Hart and shouted odd things in an English accent.

Jane was given a penalty kick for being fouled. She scored calmly and easily, and Skye relaxed. Maybe the midfielder wasn't as hulking as she looked and the hit hadn't been that bad, and Jane was fine. The ball was passed to Skye and she made a run upfield, stumbling only a little when a shout rang out behind her.

"CAMERON'S HARDWARE ARE GORMLESS DUFFS!"

Rats, thought Skye, she isn't fine and now she's Mick, and who knows what "gormless duffs" means, but it sounds terrible. She passed the ball up to Jane, hoping that actual play would straighten her out. That was all Skye could do—she certainly couldn't stop playing to scold. Just keep going, she told herself, maybe Jane will run it out of her system. She always did, eventually, if no one bothered her too much.

Jane was running all right, charging toward the goal with the ball. But long before she'd run far enough to get anything out of her system, there went

Melissa after her, and by the look on her face, she also thought that being a gormless duff sounded terrible. She dove at Jane, trying to steal the ball.

Jane easily dribbled around her. "HA! MAD COW! YOU'RE ALL MAD COWS!"

"AND YOU'RE A"—shouted Melissa furiously— "YOU'RE A MADDER COW!"

This was so pathetic an insult that even Melissa's own teammates laughed at her. If being called a gormless duff and a mad cow was unpleasant, being laughed at was horrible, and it wasn't long before Melissa took revenge by tripping Jane just as she was about to score another goal. Skye, still proudly holding on to her composure, waited for the referee to give Jane another penalty kick, but somehow the referee had missed the trip, and worse, as soon as Jane got to her feet and took another few steps, Melissa tripped her again, and this time—she later *said* it was an accident—kneed Jane in the ribs as she fell.

Just like that, Skye's temper was gone, and she didn't care. For what good was a temper if you couldn't throw it away when your sister was being kneed in the ribs? She stopped thinking and started running, firecrackers of anger going off in her brain. Like the wind, she ran, and then faster even than that, her feet pounding the earth, her fists clenched, ready to smash in Melissa's face. Which she would have done if Melissa's midfielder hadn't jumped her from behind. And then of course the Antonio's Pizza forwards leapt on the midfielder to avenge Skye, and then Melissa started screaming "MURDER!" and her forwards attacked the other forwards, and then all of the midfielders, the defenders, and even the goalkeepers had joined the battle, and referees' whistles were blowing, and coaches and parents were shouting and running onto the field, and then—

The game was officially declared over, and everyone was sent away in disgrace.

The Penderwicks' ride home was an unhappy one.

"The referee told me this league has never had a brawl of that magnitude," said Mr. Penderwick after a long, painful silence. "Of course, at the time I was pretending to be a casual passerby and not a father at all."

"I'm sorry, Daddy." Skye was more than sorry—she was miserably unhappy with herself. After working so hard to stay calm, she'd thrown her temper to the winds and, in doing so, ruined the game. What would have been a glorious win for Antonio's Pizza was now nothing, null, a forfeit. She'd let down her team, her coach, and the entire Penderwick family. "Aunt Claire, I apologize to you, too, since you probably had to pretend you weren't my aunt."

"Apology accepted." Aunt Claire smiled, which did much to lighten Skye's heart. "I must say your mad charge at Melissa was impressive. Perhaps you should switch to ice hockey or professional wrestling."

"Claire, please be serious," said Mr. Penderwick.

"I am being serious."

"Skye was only defending me, Daddy. For all she knew, Melissa had dealt me a mortal blow," said Jane, who hadn't been hurt at all. "And it was my fault for being Mick Hart."

"Yes, Jane, about Mick Hart. His charm is wearing thin. Can't you send him back to Manchester or wherever he came from?"

"I suppose so. It's just that being Mick Hart keeps me from crying. Maybe I should have cried instead."

"If crying was truly your only other choice, yes, you should have."

Jane bid a wistful farewell to Mick Hart. "But, Daddy, in defending me, Skye was also defending the family honor, you know."

"Of course I know. The point is that perhaps the family honor need not be defended so vigorously."

"I think Skye was wonderful," said Batty.

"No, I wasn't, you nincompoop," said Skye. "I'm the captain and I wrecked the game. But for the rest of the season I'll be well behaved if it kills me."

"Try not to take it that far." Mr. Penderwick sighed. "How I came to be surrounded by such war-like women is beyond me. Rosalind, give me the Latin for 'war.'"

"I know that," said Rosalind, pleased with the change of subject. *"Bellum, belli."*

"Correct. And from *bellum* came *bellatrix,* which means 'female warrior.' "

"Bellatrix Penderwick!" Jane put up her fists, longing for the chance to show the world a true female warrior. Batty, unwilling to be any less of one, put up her fists in challenge.

The ensuing boxing hilarity lasted the rest of the way home, which gave Skye time to ponder the mysteries of temper. For as much as she wished she'd kept hers that day, the ensuing battle between teams had been glorious. And then, too, there was the sweet memory of Melissa being scolded by her furious coach. Should that have felt so good? It was all quite confusing, and Skye needed to sort it out. As soon as she could, she'd go up to her roof and think.

But when they pulled into the driveway, the new next-door neighbor was pulling into her driveway, too, and Mr. Penderwick said that this was an excellent time to formally introduce themselves. So rather than escaping to her roof, Skye found herself reluctantly following her family next door. She wasn't in the mood to be introduced to anyone, but especially not to the new neighbor, not now. For she knew that this woman taught astrophysics at her father's university. Having a great deal of respect for astrophysicists—and a dream of being one herself someday—Skye didn't want to meet one without some intelligent questions prepared. A soccer free-for-all isn't the best thing for making you feel intelligent.

The woman was tugging the baby out of the car seat when they reached her. Up close, her red hair turned out to be a pretty auburn, with lots of wave, and her eyes were a golden hazel, large behind glasses. Large and shy. Like a deer's eyes, Jane said later.

If Mr. Penderwick noticed that she was shy, he gave no indication of it. "We've come over to say hello. Ms. Aaronson, this is my sister, Claire, who's visiting for the weekend. And here are my daughters: Rosalind, the eldest, then Skye, and then Jane. My youngest . . ."

He paused and looked around doubtfully, as though expecting Batty to be gone, which is what usually happened around strangers.

But she was beside him, tugging at his sleeve. "I'm right here," she whispered.

"How interesting. Yes, you are." He put his hand on her head. "My youngest, Batty."

"Daddy, ask her what the baby's name is."

Though Batty was still whispering, the woman had heard. "His name is Ben," she said. "Ben, say hello to the Penderwicks."

"Duck," said Ben. His red hair was a shade brighter than his mother's.

" 'Duck' is his only word," she said apologetically. "And, please, everyone, call me Iantha."

"Iantha, astrophysicist," Skye blurted out before she could stop herself. Humiliated, she edged over until she was hidden behind Rosalind. That was the end of impressing the new neighbor. Skye told herself that she didn't really care, anyway. After all, that Ben would be around all the time. She had no use for babies.

Jane was making faces at her, but their father hadn't seemed to notice the gaffe.

"Iantha," he said. "A lovely name that means 'purple flower.' The base is Greek, but then there's the Latin adjective *ianthinus*, too, which means 'violet-colored.' "

"Oh?" Iantha was clearly puzzled, though not unpleasantly.

"Don't mind him," said Aunt Claire. "It was nice to meet you, and I hope none of us drive you crazy."

The grown-ups shook hands, and Rosalind did, too, as the oldest sister, then they all drifted back toward their own house.

"Just a tip, Martin," said Aunt Claire when they were far enough away from Iantha. "Don't blather on about Greek and Latin to your blind date tonight."

"Curses rain down on my blind date!" said Mr. Penderwick vehemently.

"Daddy!" Rosalind was shocked, for their father never showed temper.

But Skye laughed and squeezed his arm, and together everyone went inside.

CHAPTER FIVE
The First Date

Aᴄᴛᴇʀ ᴄʜᴀɴɢɪɴɢ ᴏᴜᴛ of her soccer uniform, Jane
gathered some supplies—an apple, a pen, and a blue
notebook—and headed up Gardam Street. She was
going to Quigley Woods, her favorite place in the
whole world.

Quigley Woods was forty acres of glorious wilder-
ness carved out of the middle of Cameron. No one remembered who the Quigleys were, or what they'd
done when they lived there. The only traces of them
were low stone walls that wandered here and there
through the woods—so maybe the Quigleys had been
farmers, or herders, or as Jane liked to pretend, aris-
tocracy escaping the French Revolution, though she
hadn't come up with a good reason why French dukes

and duchesses would have been named Quigley. Anyway, now the land was owned by Massachusetts, but since the major entrance was off the Gardam Street cul-de-sac, the children of Gardam Street considered it their private domain.

It was an unwritten rule of the neighborhood that you didn't go into Quigley Woods alone until you were ten, and even then, you didn't go deep in without at least a teenager, if not an actual grown-up. Everyone knew what "deep in" meant—past the wide burbling creek that cut across the main path about a quarter of a mile from the entrance. This still left what felt like a vast natural kingdom to play in, and Jane and her sisters knew every tree and rock and dip of land.

That day she headed to what she called her Enchanted Rock. Though she was ten, all certainty of magic had not yet been squashed out of her, and she believed that if there was any at all in Massachusetts, it would be stored in that rock. Her sisters could know none of this—Rosalind was too old for magic adventures, Batty too young, and Skye had given up on magic the day she discovered long division.

"Hello," she said when she reached her destination. "It's me, Jane."

She was in a round clearing in the woods, filled with wild asters and ancient rambling roses planted long ago by the mysterious Quigleys. But the asters and roses, however lovely, were overshadowed by Jane's Enchanted Rock, in the center of the clearing. It was big—taller even than Jane, and just as wide as it was tall—and with lots of smaller rocks piled up around it. Jane was sure that such a large rock would have a fabulous history. Maybe it was even a meteorite, tossed out of the heavens to land here in Quigley Woods. The smaller rocks she wasn't so sure about. Maybe they'd been dragged to that spot by some fantastical magnetic force in the big one, doomed for eternity to serve as its worshipful underlings.

"And I have an offering."

She hoisted herself up onto the smaller rocks, then knelt and reached way down, feeling along the surface of the big rock. Years ago she'd discovered a natural crevice down there, just wide enough for her hand and just deep enough to make it the perfect hiding space. She used it for only certain of her treasures, those most likely to be happy in magical surroundings. Like the shells she'd collected on Cape Cod the last summer her mother was alive; the poor doll named Anjulee, whose head Skye had knocked off; the pen with which she'd written her first Sabrina Starr book; and a Bruins ice hockey puck that Tommy had left in the Penderwicks' driveway last winter. Many times she'd imagined him wondering aloud what had ever happened to his Bruins puck, and she would be able to say, Why, Tommy, I've kept it safe for you all this time.

There was the crevice—she'd found it. And now for her offering. She pulled several sheets of paper out of her sweatshirt pocket and stuffed them deep into the rock.

"As you protect my treasures, Enchanted Rock, please accept in addition this awful thing, and purify it, and take away its power."

Jane's offering that day was the Famous Women in Massachusetts History essay, the one that had gotten her a C. Despite what her father had said about Mr. Tolstoy and *War and Peace*, Jane felt that the essay with its big red C was a curse, a blight on her life. She had still more essays to write for Miss Bunda—how could she even begin another with this hanging over her? But if anything could lift a curse, the Enchanted Rock could. It had before. Like the time her friend Emily was so sick, and Jane had given the rock a photograph of her, and by the next day she was already getting better.

Still, sometimes the rock was a bit unpredictable. Just recently, when Jeffrey had visited Cameron on his way to boarding school in Boston, Jane had brought him here. Together they'd drawn a picture of Dexter on a piece of paper and given it to the rock. They'd hoped that the rock could get rid of Dexter's badness, or better, simply make him disappear. But a week later,

Jeffrey was calling from Boston with the news that his mother and Dexter had just gotten married and were about to leave on an extended honeymoon in Europe.

Jane hadn't blamed the rock, since she and Jeffrey hadn't mentioned marriage one way or the other, and they also hadn't told the rock when Dexter should lose his badness. For all she knew, he could become a better person ten years from now, when it hardly mattered anymore. So she'd decided that she needed to be as specific as possible when asking for a favor.

"And, please, dear Rock, don't let me ever get another C on anything I write. Thank you. Oh! And, please, no D's or E's, either. Thank you again. Your friend, Jane."

Now she was done, but there was still a ceremony to perform, the same one she performed every time she came here alone. She hadn't even once gotten results, but that was no reason to stop trying. So up to the top of the big rock she climbed, there to sit cross-legged and raise her arms in what she thought was a come-hither-to-me kind of prayerful salutation.

"O Aslan," she said, "I await you."

She looked this way and that, and when no golden lion from Narnia appeared, raised her arms again. "O Psammead, I await you."

Likewise, when no bad-tempered sand-pit creature out of E. Nesbit's books scurried into view, Jane tried once more. "O Turtle, I await you."

She always gave Edward Eager's wish-granting turtle extra time to arrive—he *was* a turtle—by counting to one hundred. "One–one thousand, two–one thousand, three–one thousand—"

"Hi, Jane."

Her arms dropped and she almost fell over with shock. Was it true, after all, what Mr. Eager had written? But it wasn't a wish-granting turtle who had spoken but only Tommy Geiger, in his helmet and shoulder pads, and carrying a football.

"Hail ye, hero of the ten-yard line," said Jane when she realized she wasn't so disappointed after all.

"I'm not. You've got to stop saying that stuff."

"But you are."

"Stop saying it anyway." He tossed his football straight up, then leapt high to grab it out of the air.

"Speak some Russian, then."

"*Odin, dva, tri, chetyre.*"

"The language of tsars, Tommy! What did you say?"

"I counted to four. Is Rosalind around?"

"Only me," said Jane. "That is, I. I mean, only I, Jane, am here."

"Because I'm going to do some rough-terrain drills in the woods, and I thought she'd like to do them with me."

"I'll do them with you."

"You're too young. Maybe Rosalind will want to

later." Again he tossed the football straight up, even higher this time.

"She's busy later," said Jane tartly. But she regretted her tone when Tommy missed his catch and the football crashed down on his head, which must have hurt, even with his helmet on. To make up for it, she told him why Rosalind would be busy—which meant explaining about Aunt Claire's visit and how the blind date with Ms. Muntz was happening that very evening.

"Wow, Mr. Pen on a date," he said when she'd finished. "Poor Rosalind."

"Poor all of us." Jane felt herself getting tart again.

Tommy didn't seem to notice her tone. The rough-terrain drills were calling, and with a casual good-bye, he was gone.

Now the glade was once again empty except for Jane. She considered going back to summoning magical creatures but, after all, she thought, ten is quite grown-up, whatever some people might think, and therefore too old to believe in such things. So instead she ate her apple, then picked up her notebook and pen, intending to start on her next essay for Miss Bunda. Twenty minutes later, she was still just sitting there on the rock, staring off into the trees. The problem was that the topic was How Science Has Changed Our Lives, which had to be even more tedious than Famous Women in Massachusetts History.

If she had to write about science, why couldn't she write about Sabrina Starr inventing a device that could neutralize nuclear warheads from afar? Now, *that* would be fascinating. But unfortunately, dopey old Miss Bunda would give her another C, or worse.

Jane stretched out on the rock and closed her eyes. Maybe if she just lay here on her Enchanted Rock, the perfect idea for an essay would come to her. But the sun was so warm and comforting, and she was a little worn-out from the soccer game—being Mick Hart always took extra energy—that soon she was drowsily drifting away to a marvelous world where people looked for her instead of her older sisters. The next thing she knew, she was being shaken awake by Skye.

"Jane! What the heck are you doing on top of this rock?"

She retrieved her pen, which had rolled away while she slept. "Working on my essay."

"Yeah, right. Daddy's getting ready for his date, and he won't leave until I manage to produce you. Thank goodness Tommy said he'd seen you here, because I was getting tired of looking." Skye slid off the big rock to one of the small rocks, then leapt to the ground.

"What else did Tommy say?" asked Jane, following her.

"I don't know. Who cares? Hurry!"

They sped through Quigley Woods, burst out onto the cul-de-sac, and finished up with a race down Gardam Street. When they reached their own front steps, Skye issued a warning.

"Listen to me," she said. "Daddy's a wreck and Aunt Claire wants us to be helpful."

"I'm always helpful," protested Jane, but when she and Skye walked into the living room, she understood. Her father hadn't looked this anxious since he'd gone to the dentist to have two teeth pulled. It didn't seem to be helping that Aunt Claire and Batty were attacking him with lint brushes, trying to remove all traces of Hound.

"Jane, thank goodness," he said. "I thought I'd lost one of you. It did, however, occur to me that if you stayed lost for too long, I would have the perfect excuse to cancel this blasted date."

"Sorry, Daddy," she said. "Is there another lint brush I can use?"

"No, we're done with the brushing." He flapped his hands at Aunt Claire and Batty. "Now, can anyone locate my glasses?"

"I can," said Rosalind, who'd been hovering on the outskirts. She took them off the mantelpiece and set them gently on her father's nose. Jane thought Rosalind looked even more anxious than he did.

"Now at least I'll be able to see the dinner menu," he said, reaching up to adjust them.

Aunt Claire came back at him with her brush.

"There's at least another pound of dog hair on your sweater."

"Too bad. If Ms. Muntz cares about dog hair, she's clearly not the woman for me."

"And you're sure you won't wear a suit?"

"He hates suits," said Skye.

"Thank you, Skye Blue, and I'm not fond of blind dates, either."

The red clock on the mantelpiece chimed five. Mr. Penderwick was due to pick up his date at quarter after. It was time to go. He kissed each of his daughters, and Hound—he never kissed Hound—and came last to Aunt Claire.

"Don't you think we could put this off another year or so?" he asked.

"That's a good idea," said Rosalind.

"Have a good time, Martin," said Aunt Claire.

"What about—?"

"We'll be fine." Aunt Claire put her arm around Rosalind. "Won't we, girls?"

"I will," said Batty. "We're having macaroni and cheese for dinner."

"And the rest of you?" asked Mr. Penderwick.

"We'll all be fine," said Skye firmly, and Jane nodded, managing to look enthusiastic. Rosalind nodded, not looking enthusiastic at all.

"Then I guess I'm ready. I who am about to die salute you."

"Good," said Aunt Claire. She pushed her brother

out the front door, then leaned against it as though he might try to shove his way back in. "Okay, girls, now let's have some fun."

Unfortunately, fun on such a night was in short supply. The macaroni and cheese was excellent—made from scratch with celery and onions and three kinds of cheese—and afterward Aunt Claire took the sisters into town for ice cream sundaes, but it was impossible not to notice all the while that their father wasn't there. Back home again, they pulled out a pile of movies, but when no one could agree on which one to watch, and Skye and Batty almost came to blows over it, Aunt Claire lost patience and sent everyone to bed with Batty at seven-thirty.

"Are you asleep?" Jane asked into the darkness.

"No," answered Skye. "I keep listening."

"Me too."

"I know."

Now they listened harder, but the only thing to be heard was the creak of a door opening down the hall.

"That's Rosalind," said Skye.

"I know."

They both slid out of bed and crept quietly out of their bedroom. And there was Rosalind, wrapped in a quilt. She opened the quilt, and now there were three girls huddled together at the top of the steps. Only a few minutes later came the sound they'd all been waiting for—their father's car pulling into the driveway.

The sisters leaned back into the shadows as Aunt Claire appeared in the hallway below them—she must have been listening for the car, too. The front door opened and Mr. Penderwick came inside.

"Well, Martin?" asked Aunt Claire.

He laughed, but his laugh was part groan. "*Cruciatus.*"

"In English, please."

Then the adults went into the living room. If a translation was given, it wasn't heard by the three upstairs. Skye and Jane looked hopefully at Rosalind.

She shrugged. "I don't know *cruciatus* yet."

"You need to hurry up and learn more Latin," said Jane. "Or we'll never know what's going on."

"Though maybe that would be for the best," said Skye, yawning.

"No, it absolutely, positively would not be!" Rosalind stood, jerking the quilt off her sisters. "Now go back to bed and get plenty of rest. Tomorrow we have a lot of thinking to do."

Skye and Jane watched her stalk back to her room.

"Thinking about what?" asked Jane.

"Who knows?" Skye shook her head. "But I bet I'm not going to like it."

CHAPTER SIX
The Save-Daddy Plan

"I'M SURE I BROUGHT a pair of slippers with me," said Aunt Claire. It was Sunday afternoon, and Rosalind was helping her pack to go home.

"Are they red?" asked Rosalind from the floor. She pulled a pair of fluffy red slippers from under the bed. They were damp in patches, and one had a ragged hole where the toe used to be.

"Hound?"

"I hope they weren't your favorites."

"Only my second favorites," said Aunt Claire, dropping them into the wastebasket. "I figured Hound was annoyed with me about the blind date, but I didn't think he was annoyed enough to eat my slippers."

Rosalind knew her aunt was trying to make her

laugh, but she wasn't ready to laugh about the blind date, or the dating scheme, or anything about her father and dates. Too obviously not speaking, she folded a bathrobe and placed it neatly into the suitcase on the bed.

"And, sweet niece, you're annoyed with me about the blind date, too. Here, chew on these." Aunt Claire pulled a pair of socks out of the bureau and handed them to Rosalind.

"I'm not annoyed with you."

"Liar."

"Well, just a little, I suppose."

"That's better," said Aunt Claire. "Honey, I know that your dad's dating is odd and maybe a little scary for you. Your mother was worried that it would be, but she was also so worried about him being lonely."

"He's never said he was lonely." Rosalind tossed the socks into the suitcase and slammed it shut.

"I know he hasn't, but still it could be nice for him to meet new people—women, I mean—every once in a while. You can understand that, can't you?"

No. Besides, so far, meeting new women had been anything but nice. Rosalind had looked up *cruciatus* in her Latin dictionary, and it meant "torture." Her poor father, being tortured over dinner and a movie. Still, she was glad he'd hated his date, for he definitely would not be marrying Ms. Muntz.

But she couldn't tell Aunt Claire any of that. "I'll

take your suitcase out to the car" is what she did say, giving Aunt Claire a hug to soften her abruptness.

After she'd put the suitcase into the car, Rosalind sat down in the grass and went back to what she'd been doing for the last day and a half—trying to figure out how to stop this terrible dating. So far she'd come up with nothing but a name: The Save-Daddy Plan. She knew in her deepest heart that a more honest title would be the Save-Rosalind-and-Her-Sisters Plan, but she was not ready to admit that even to herself. And besides, she wasn't the one using words like *cruciatus*.

A football flew from out of nowhere and bounced in front of her.

"Tommy!" yelped Rosalind, for there was only one person in the neighborhood annoying enough to throw a football at her.

And it *was* him, loping across the street after his ball, in his helmet and shoulder pads. "I thought you might want to do some drills."

"No." She grabbed the ball and tossed it neatly back to him.

He caught the ball and flopped down beside her. "Maybe later, then."

"No." She went back to the Save-Daddy Plan. Having Tommy there didn't distract her. He was as much a part of Gardam Street as the maple trees and the cul-de-sac.

"Jane told me about Mr. Pen's blind date," said

Tommy after tossing the football in the air several times. "How did it go?"

"It was fine, I guess."

"Fine like he liked her?"

"No, fine like he didn't, thank goodness. Tommy, I can't help thinking about Anna's father, and about that boy we met this summer—"

Tommy interrupted. "Cagney."

"What?" Rosalind hadn't meant Cagney. And now she realized that she'd never gotten around to telling Aunt Claire about him—and love—and heartache. All of that seemed so long ago now.

"Cagney the gardener, who was older than you and so cute, blah, blah, blah."

"What do you mean, blah, blah, blah? I've barely mentioned him to you. Besides, I meant Jeffrey, who's Skye's age."

"Sorry. Of course you did."

Rosalind shook her head. Sometimes Tommy didn't make any sense at all. "Well, anyway, Jeffrey's mother—"

"But you have to admit you've told me plenty about Cagney. I'll prove it. He's a Red Sox fan. He played basketball in high school. He wants to be a high school history teacher. He's obsessed with the Civil War. He gave you a rosebush as a good-bye gift and you planted it beneath your bedroom window. He dated some girl named Kath—"

Rosalind cut Tommy off with an impatient wave of

her hand. "All right, fine, I won't ever bring up Cagney again when you're around. I wasn't talking about him, anyway. I was talking about Jeffrey's mother dating this Dexter creep—"

"Of course, I don't care that you liked Cagney."

"You know what, Tommy? I don't know why I bother to talk to you at all."

"I don't, either." He stood up. "I'm going to run some drills by myself."

"Fine. And by the way, you look goofy wearing that helmet all the time."

"Fine, and—and—and . . ." He spluttered to a stop, then stomped away.

Spluttering and stomping were not usual for Tommy, and for a while Rosalind wondered what had set him off. But her father's dating was the greater problem, and by the time the family was gathering to say good-bye to Aunt Claire, she'd forgotten all about Tommy and his nonsense. Blah, blah, blah, indeed.

No one ever liked seeing Aunt Claire go away, but the sisters were relieved that this particular weekend was almost over. The First Awful Blind Date Weekend, it would be called for the rest of their lives.

"Thank you for all of our gifts," said Rosalind, who was first in line for hugging.

"But don't bring any next time," added Skye, second in line.

Aunt Claire laughed. She knew what Skye meant.

So did Jane. When she hugged Aunt Claire, she whispered, "I don't mind getting books even when there isn't strange and disturbing news."

Batty proudly stood tall in the red wagon for her hug. Hound tried to do the same, but managed instead to knock both Batty and the wagon over. After picking Batty up and inspecting her for damage—none—Mr. Penderwick helped Aunt Claire into the car. "When can we expect you again?"

"I'll check with you in a few weeks. Maybe you'll have managed to go on another date by then."

He closed the car door with a bit of a bang. "I don't know where you think I'm going to find all these dates."

"You can at least try. And if you can't, I'll find you some more." Aunt Claire waved cheerfully, then drove off.

"Maybe she'll develop selective amnesia before she comes back," said Mr. Penderwick, "and I will be spared the rest of the dates."

"Maybe," said Skye doubtfully.

"*We* would still remember, Daddy," said Jane. "And you did promise. Besides, our serene and happy family life has already been irretrievably altered by your first date—a few more won't make much of a difference."

"Terrific." He looked pleadingly at Rosalind, but she had no comfort for him, only the Save-Daddy Plan, and she couldn't have told him about that even if she actually knew how it was going to work. "Well, I'd better go grade some papers, unless anyone needs to have a talk first. Like about your lives being irretrievably altered, for example."

"No, thank you," said Rosalind, speaking for all of them.

He wandered alone back into the house, his shoulders drooping. Rosalind was more determined than ever to save him—and yes, all of them—from this burden of dating.

"Time for a MOPS," she said.

A MOPS—a Meeting Of Penderwick Sisters—could be held anywhere, but unless the weather was too cold or wet, the girls preferred a certain fallen oak tree in Quigley Woods. It had crashed to the ground years earlier in a great storm, its huge gnarled roots torn out of the ground. These roots had in the past given the Penderwicks protection from invading armies, imaginary or real, real meaning mostly Tommy and his brother, Nick. But as Rosalind, Skye, and Jane were too grown-up now for war games, and Batty wasn't allowed in Quigley Woods alone, the oak had become less of a fort and more of the perfect private meeting place.

When the sisters arrived, Rosalind chose her root first—her right as the caller of the MOPS—and the other three sat on lower roots on either side of her. Hound settled down beside Batty, facing back along the path, just in case anyone threatening should come by. When everyone was in place, Rosalind officially opened up the meeting.

"MOPS come to order."

"Second the motion," said Skye.

"Third it," said Jane.

"Fourth it," said Batty. "And fifth it for Hound."

"For the millionth time," scolded Skye. "Hound does not have to fifth it."

"He wants to, don't you, Hound?"

"Woof."

"Order. You, too, Hound," said Rosalind before he could woof again. Then she made her right hand into a fist and held it out toward her sisters. "All swear to keep secret what is said here, even—actually, this time, especially—from Daddy, unless you think someone might do something truly bad."

The others piled their fists on top of hers, and together they all chanted, "This I swear, by the Penderwick Family Honor," then broke their fists apart.

"We know why we're here," said Rosalind.

"No, we don't," said the others.

"Because of Daddy and the dating. Honestly, aren't any of you paying attention to what's happening in our family?"

"I am." Batty dug a ginger cookie out of her pocket, ate half, then gave the rest to Hound.

"Thank you, Batty. So I've been trying to come up with a way to stop this dating nonsense. And don't anyone say that it was Mommy's idea. I know it was,

73

and I don't care." Rosalind glared defiantly at the others, daring them to protest.

Skye wasn't cowed. "None of us like the dating idea, but Daddy agreed to it, and he's honor-bound to keep going."

"Besides, men have needs," added Jane. "I read that in a magazine."

"What needs?" asked Batty.

"What magazine?" asked Skye.

"Order." Rosalind thumped on her root. "Skye's right about Daddy agreeing to the dates. But we all know that he hates it as much as I—we—do. I looked up that word he used last night, *cruciatus*. It means 'torture.' "

"Ms. Muntz tortured Daddy?" Jane was horrified. For her, torture meant being stretched on racks and beaten with chains.

"Of course not. He just meant he was miserable," said Rosalind. "We need some way to rescue him without compromising his honor. I'd hoped to have a plan before we got here, and I've tried and tried, but I haven't come up with anything except a name: the Save-Daddy Plan."

"Good name," said Skye. "All in favor of it, say 'aye.' Aye."

"Aye-aye, Captain," said Jane, realizing that her favorite heroine had not yet had a nautical adventure. "Why, Sabrina Starr could rescue a whale next!"

"Jane, please!" Rosalind clutched her head. Suddenly a headache was coming on. "Am I the only one who understands how serious this is?"

"Sorry, Rosalind. I do understand," said Jane. Batty passed her a cookie as a mark of camaraderie.

"So we have a name for a plan, but no plan," said Skye. "How about murder? As quickly as Aunt Claire comes up with blind dates, we kill them off."

Batty looked fascinated. "How would we do it?"

"Please, please stick to the point, everyone. We have to help Daddy. And we have to make sure we don't end up with a—" Rosalind, still unable to say that word, clutched her head harder.

"—stepmother," finished Skye. "And I *am* sticking to the point. But if you don't like murder, how about this? We can't actually stop the dating altogether— promises, honor, et cetera, et cetera—so why don't we find three more dates for Daddy that he'll hate as much as Ms. Muntz? He won't date any of them more than once, and the whole experience will be so horrible that he'll never date again, and we'll never end up with a stepmother. Brilliant, yes?"

Rosalind let go of her head and stared at her younger sister. "It might be brilliant."

"Really?" Skye wasn't used to people calling her plans brilliant. Ridiculous, crazy, dangerous even— these were words she heard more often than brilliant.

"Wait a minute," said Jane, still puzzling it out.

"We're going to choose awful dates for Daddy? Isn't that mean and dishonorable? Wouldn't Daddy hate it if he knew?"

"He won't know unless we tell him." Rosalind's head all at once felt better. "And remember that it's for his own good."

"I guess so, for though it is a mean and dishonorable plan, still, it is ultimately kinder."

"I don't know," said Skye, who didn't want to go down in family history as the one who came up with a mean and dishonorable plan. "You never use my ideas. Why this one?"

"Because there are no better ideas," said Rosalind. "Are there?"

Skye frantically ran through several more possibilities, all of them wilder even than murder. "No," she admitted finally.

"As I thought. Let's take a vote. Batty, what say you?"

They all looked at Batty, who had finished the ginger cookies and was now digging crumbs out of her pocket and feeding them to Hound.

"I say Daddy should date the lady next door, and then I could play with her baby."

"Iantha?" Rosalind was incredulous. "Honey, we don't want Daddy going out with anyone from Gardam Street. Besides, that's not what we're talking about."

"On top of that, we don't know that Iantha's not married," said Jane. "Her husband could be—well, lost in the Bermuda Triangle and she sits, weeping, at an upstairs window every night, peering out into the darkness, hoping and praying he'll someday come back to her. Or he could be in prison, falsely accused—"

Rosalind interrupted her. "Iantha's husband died, remember? Daddy told us. But we're supposed to be voting on Skye's Save-Daddy Plan, which would rule out Iantha anyway, because she's not awful. Now, Batty, how do you vote, yes or no?"

"This won't be an official vote," said Skye, still hoping for an escape. "Since Batty clearly doesn't understand what we're voting about."

"I do, too, understand. Rosalind wants to find creepy ladies for Daddy so we don't have to worry about stepmothers." Batty popped the last of the crumbs into her own mouth. "I vote yes."

"And I vote yes," said Rosalind. "That's two for Skye's plan."

"And I make three votes," said Jane. "Sorry, Skye."

Skye groaned loudly, but Rosalind thumped for order until she stopped.

"So speak I, Rosalind," she said. "It's a majority. The Save-Daddy Plan is official and in place."

Now they had to find an awful date, which turned out to be not so easy. Everyone they could think of was too young or too old, or already married, or not awful enough. And the few who seemed just right could cause problems afterward. For example, the librarian at Cameron Library who never let them check out more than five books at a time. What if she got mad at them after a bad date and lowered their limit to four books, or even three? That would be a disaster. Or Jane's teacher, Miss Bunda, who Jane figured would make the most awful date ever. For if Jane was getting bad marks on her essays before a bad date with their father, what would it be like afterward?

Defeated, they decided they needed outside help. But who could be trusted on such a private and sensitive matter? After much racking of brains, Rosalind suggested Anna.

"Great." Skye wasn't any closer to liking the Save-Daddy Plan. "Maybe she can lend us her father's former wives."

"At least we'd know how awful they are," retorted Rosalind, whose headache was coming back. "MOPS dismissed."

CHAPTER SEVEN
A Skating Coach and an Orange Cat

AFTER SCHOOL THE NEXT DAY, Rosalind asked Anna to come home with her. "For advice," she explained, and Anna accepted happily. She always jumped at the opportunity to give advice, as she was the youngest in her family—her two older brothers were away at college—and she had no one to tell what to do, not even a pet.

They picked up Batty at Goldie's and walked home. When Skye and Jane arrived, too, everyone gathered in the kitchen for snacks and to lay out the Save-Daddy Plan for Anna.

"So you're looking for a date Mr. Pen won't like," said Anna when they were done. "Interesting concept. I should have tried it with my father years ago."

"You don't think it's diabolical?" asked Skye.

"I prefer the term 'Machiavellian.' When you're older, Batty, I'll explain Machiavellian to you."

"I already know. It's a kind of nut."

"A nut!" said Skye scornfully.

"Never mind that," said Rosalind. "Anna, we came up with the plan, but we can't come up with any actual women. Do you know any awful ones who don't already have husbands?"

"Though not totally awful," said Jane. "Poor Daddy."

"I'll try. Let me think."

While Anna ate pretzels and thought, she let Batty play with her long, honey-colored hair, twisting it into fantastic shapes. Batty adored Anna's hair, just as she adored Anna's pointy nose and pixie smile. For Batty, Anna was indeed gorgeous, though not, of course, as gorgeous as Rosalind.

"I got one," Anna said suddenly. "Valaria, who works with my mother. Her house is full of crystals for meditating and she's always talking about who people were in their previous lives. She divorced her husband because she decided he was a cannibal five lifetimes ago."

"No," said Skye. "No, no, no, and no."

"Skye's right, Anna," said Rosalind. "We want Daddy to have a bad date, but we don't want to put him through agony."

Jane agreed about no agony. Still, reincarnation intrigued her. She'd sometimes wondered if she might have been a famous author—Shakespeare or Beatrix Potter, maybe—in a previous life. "Anna, who was she before? Valaria, I mean."

"Anne Boleyn, Madame Curie," said Anna, ticking them off on her fingers. "Mary Magdelene, Mary Queen of Scots, Mary Lincoln—there were a bunch of different Marys—"

Skye clapped her hands over her ears. "Stop!"

Anna popped another pretzel into her mouth and went back to thinking.

"How about my ice-skating coach?" she asked after a few moments. "Her name is Laurie Jones, but she calls herself Lara Jonisovich so that parents will think she's European and pay more for lessons."

"Daddy hates dishonesty," said Skye, though making up a new last name was certainly better than crystals and reincarnation.

"Is she pretty?" asked Rosalind.

Anna shrugged. "If you like that half-starved look. Oh, and she never reads. She believes that reading channels your mental energy away from skating."

"Never reads!" Jane couldn't imagine a life without reading.

"Does she like dogs?" asked Batty.

"I don't know about dogs," said Anna. "But she wears a coat made out of rabbit fur."

Batty went so pale and dizzy with shock that Rosalind and Anna had to dangle her upside down to get the blood flowing again.

"Okay, so we definitely don't like this Lara, and neither will Daddy," said Rosalind when Batty had revived. "How do we do it? I mean, how can we set up a date?"

"I'll figure something out." Anna's face was alight with the thrill of conspiracy. "I have a lesson tonight after dinner. Can you convince Mr. Pen to pick me up at the rink afterward?"

"I think so. Call me at the end of your lesson, and I'll tell him your mom is working late."

There was the sound of the front door opening.

"Everyone act normal!" whispered Rosalind fiercely.

By the time Mr. Penderwick came into the kitchen, they were all chewing pretzels and trying to remember what they normally acted like, which meant that they all looked a bit odd.

"Hello, daughters of mine," he said, lifting up Batty for a hug. "Hello, Anna."

"Hello, Mr. Pen. Isn't it a lovely day?"

Mr. Penderwick looked out the window at the dreary clouds hanging over Cameron. "What are you up to, Anna?"

"Nothing, that is, *nihil*." Anna was in Rosalind's Latin class.

"Rosalind!"

"Yes, Daddy."

"Tell Anna that she's not fooling me."

"Yes, Daddy."

Anna took a last handful of pretzels, then stood. "I have to go home and do homework before my skating lesson. Good-bye, everyone."

She left with Mr. Penderwick shaking his head. "Either a saint or a master criminal. But how are my girls? How was school? How was Goldie's? Tell me everything while I fix dinner."

After dinner, Rosalind told her sisters she'd do their kitchen cleanup chores. She wanted them out of the way before Anna called, since it was going to be hard enough to carry on a sham conversation without everyone watching. Batty gladly retreated to the living room with Hound to play King of the Mountain on the red wagon. Skye and Jane not so gladly went upstairs to their room, for though it was great to skip cleanup, that only meant starting homework sooner.

They settled down at their desks. Skye flew through a book report on *Swallows and Amazons*, filed it neatly in her notebook, then pulled out a fresh piece of paper and wrote *The Stupid Aztecs* across the top. Her play was due at the end of the week, and she had to buckle down and write it, whether she wanted to or not.

The phone rang downstairs.

"That's Anna," said Skye. She had a sudden urge to warn her father before there was no going back.

Jane looked as cold feet–ish as Skye felt. "We're about to be caught in a web of lies and deceit, and lose our honor and integrity forever."

"I know."

A minute later, Rosalind stuck her head in the door. "Daddy and I are going to the rink, and Batty and Hound are coming with us. Wish us luck."

"Luck," said Jane as Rosalind withdrew.

Pondering the meaning of luck, Skye tipped her chair back and to the side until it rested on one leg. In mathematics, she thought, luck doesn't exist, only random chance. If there were such a thing as luck, fathers would never go on dates, and Melissa Patenaude would never have been born or would at least live in another state, and it would be possible to balance on one leg of the chair with both feet off the ground. She lifted one foot, then both. Crash!

"If you keep doing that, you'll crack your head open and only I will be here to listen to your dying confession," said Jane.

"I don't have anything to confess." Skye picked herself and her chair up off the floor. "Except that I wish I'd never had the idea about finding awful dates for Daddy, and the Aztecs bore me, and writing a play about them bores me so much I can hardly stand it."

"You're supposed to write a play about the Aztecs? Lucky you."

There it was, luck again, thought Skye. What would she really want, if she was to be lucky? To visit Jeffrey in Boston. To have someone else write her Aztec play. She looked over at Jane, who was bent over her desk, scribbling on a piece of paper. Maybe she'd finally settled on a science essay topic. Skye picked up her binoculars and found that by standing on her chair and focusing on Jane's desk, she could read the scribbling.

I hate science essays. I hate science essays. I hate science essays. I hate . . .

"Jane," she said, climbing down from the chair. "Remember last year when I built that model wind tower for you and you wrote those poems for me?"

"And you said you'd never switch homework assignments with me again."

"For good reason. My teacher had a hard time believing I wrote *Tra-la the joy of tulips blooming, Ha-ha the thrill of bumblebees zooming. I'm alive and I dance, I'm alive though death is always looming.* When I finally convinced her that I had, she asked me if I needed to talk to the school counselor."

"Humph." Jane couldn't stand anything that sounded like criticism of her writing.

"Anyway, maybe I shouldn't have said I'd never switch with you again."

Jane didn't answer, and Skye went back to trying

to balance on one leg of her chair without any feet on the floor. She figured that if she did crack her head open, at least she'd get out of writing the play.

"I'm truly interested in the Aztecs," said Jane after a while.

Skye let her chair bang down. "And I'm truly interested in writing a science essay about—what's it supposed to be about?"

"How Science Has Changed Our Lives."

"I could write one of those. I could write a dozen of them without blinking. But can you write a play without any tra-las or ha-has?"

"Of course."

"Then, have at it." Skye dumped her Aztec books on Jane's desk. "Oh, and no Sabrina Starr."

"Of course not." Jane opened the first book, eyes shining.

A half hour later, Skye tossed aside her pen triumphantly. Her essay—*Antibiotics as the Ultimate Warriors*—was a winner, well written, with just the right amount of science thrown in. She was dying to show it off, but Jane was still writing feverishly, happily lost in Aztec land. Skye would leave her to it. She grabbed her binoculars and slipped out onto the roof.

Lights were shining in the houses up and down Gardam Street. It took great strength of will not to point the binoculars at one of the lit windows, and Skye actually did—but just for a second—point them at the Geigers' house, but Nick happened at that very moment to be looking out his window, and she knew if he caught her spying he'd kill her, so that was the end of that. Instead, she looked up into the sky, clear now, for the earlier clouds had blown away, and searched for geometrical patterns formed by the stars. She particularly wanted to find a rhombus, which was her latest favorite shape. A square askew. What could be more interesting than that?

Then there was a thump, and Skye was no longer alone on the roof. She lowered her binoculars and saw a large orange cat several feet away. He must have come up the tree just like Tommy had.

"Go away," said Skye, sick of interlopers.

The cat turned his head slowly toward her. He had large yellow eyes and a look almost intelligent, if you believed that cats could be. Skye didn't. She had as much use for cats as she did for babies.

"You can't stay here," said Skye. "Go away or I'll make you."

The cat, without taking his eyes off her, calmly sat down and began to wash his left paw. So make me, he was saying. Skye couldn't ignore such a clear challenge, especially from a cat. Carefully she slid along the roof—closer—closer—but just as she was about to grab the intruder, he jumped lightly into her lap.

"Idiot," she said, but she put her arms around him and was surprised at how nice he felt there.

Now she saw that he was wearing a collar with a tag that read MY NAME IS ASIMOV AARONSON. So Iantha did have a cat, after all. Batty had said so, but she was always making up stuff. Well, thought Skye, Asimov was going to have to get off her roof, even if he did belong to an astrophysicist. But before she could decide how much force was needed to move such a big cat, he'd settled in her lap as though he meant to stay awhile. And when he started purring, Skye went back to looking for rhombuses through her binoculars, and time passed pleasantly until the lights of the stars were outshone by the lights of her father's car returning home.

"Now you really do have to leave, Asimov," said Skye.

Asimov, who seemed determined to impress Skye with his brain power, obediently climbed off her lap, lightly leapt from the roof to the tree, and disappeared into the night.

"And don't come back!" Skye called after him, just as determined not to be impressed, then crawled back through the window into her bedroom. Jane, surrounded by piles of crumpled paper, was still scribbling furiously.

"They're home from the rink," said Skye.

"I've got the first few pages of the play already. The title is *Sisters and Sacrifice*, and here's how it starts: *Long ago in the land of the Aztecs, there was great* worry. *The rain had not come for many months, and without the rain, the maize didn't grow, and without the maize, the people starved.*"

"That's nice. We should go downstairs now."

"Nice? That's all you can say? Nice? It's a brilliant setup to the drama of what is to come! Two sisters are in love with the same man, and then one of the sisters is chosen to be a sacrifice for the gods, and the other one—"

"Jane, I don't care about the play! Daddy's home from the rink!"

This time Jane heard her. She pulled herself away from the Aztecs and ran out of the room with Skye. They got to the bottom of the steps just as the others were coming in the front door. They all looked disgruntled, Batty especially. Skye and Jane learned later that not only had the skating coach been wearing a rabbit coat, she'd had rabbit fur around the tops of her boots.

"Hello, everyone," said Skye, not knowing how to find out what had happened. "Did you have fun?"

"Fun? No." Mr. Penderwick took off his jacket and threw it onto a chair—just what he was always telling his daughters not to do. "It seems that I have another date."

"So you liked her, Daddy?" asked Jane.

He looked at her with suspicion. "Liked whom?"

"Whoever—*whom*ever you have the date with, of

course," said Skye, stepping hard on Jane's foot. "Which is who, by the way?"

"Anna's skating coach," said Rosalind. "Named Lara."

"My goodness!" Skye tried to look amazed. "Who would have thought of her?"

Mr. Penderwick took his jacket from the chair, then threw it down again. "Yes, who would have thought of the skating coach? Certainly not I. We were casually chatting as I was waiting for Anna, who was heaven knows where, when this Lara mentioned how much she liked classical music, and I agreed. Then she told me she had tickets for Bach this Thursday, and I politely said that she was lucky to have them, and then she asked me to go with her, and I, pathetic soul that I am, couldn't figure out how to refuse."

"But you truly do like classical music," said Rosalind.

"Yes, but I truly don't understand how this woman knew enough about me even to ask. Anna couldn't have said anything—no, no, no, never mind. What a distrustful old father I've become."

"No, Daddy, you're not," said Skye.

"Old or distrustful?" He managed a smile.

If guilt had a color—say, purple—the Penderwick sisters would have turned so purple that it dripped off them and spread its way through the house, turning everything purple, upstairs and down. It was a terrible moment, and when everyone gathered in Rosalind's room a little later, they agreed that they had never loved their father more.

"And yet we torment him," said Skye.

"Should we stop?" asked Jane, for whom "torment" was almost as bad a word as "torture."

"We must have the courage to follow the Save-Daddy Plan," insisted Rosalind. "It's for his own good. It really is."

"I have courage, Rosalind," said Batty. "But I hate that lady with the rabbit coat and boots."

Batty started to cry, for she did love rabbits so, and some of her sisters felt like crying, too, because they felt like low, unworthy daughters, and then they all slunk away, each to be alone with her misery.

CHAPTER EIGHT
Funty and the Bug Man

BATTY HAD FINALLY DISCOVERED how to fit all her stuffed animals into the red wagon. Sedgewick the horse had to be upside down, and Funty the blue elephant had to sit on Ursula the bear's lap, but Batty figured they didn't mind—a trip to the backyard in a wagon is always better than being stuck inside on the bed, even if you aren't comfortable.

Of course, getting the wagon and all the animals to the backyard meant many trips up and down the steps, for everyone had to go back up to Batty's room again each evening—none of them would have gotten a good night's sleep without Batty nearby—and since Hound had to go up and down the steps with her each time, naturally there was a lot of noise made in the process, especially when Hound let go of his side of the wagon, and it clattered down the last six steps.

And, of course, lots of noise can make it difficult for people to do their Latin homework. But still, why would people frown and call other people the noisiest little sister who had ever lived and hurt their feelings very much?

Batty didn't know why. Her Rosalind, that most patient of older sisters, had never done it before. Even after Batty settled the animals in the wagon and pulled it to the other side of the yard, away from the kitchen window—Rosalind was working on her homework in the kitchen—and wiped away some tears, she still couldn't figure it out. Maybe it had something to do with Daddy's date with the horrible skating lady.

"That date is tonight," she told Hound. "But I'm not mad at you about it. Promise you'll never be mad at me because of dates, okay?"

As Hound never got angry at Batty for any reason, this was an easy promise to make. But he went further than that, licking away the last of her tears and butting her stomach with his big head until she laughed. When she'd laughed, she felt better and looked around for something to do. While she was looking around, she heard a voice coming from beyond the forsythia hedge.

"Duck," said the voice. It was that baby Ben, and he was in his backyard.

"Say 'Mommy.' " And Iantha was with him.

"Duck!"

"Say 'I am a bubba bubba boy.' "

"Duck!"

Batty was pleased. All the spying she'd done on the new neighbors' yard, and they'd never actually been there. Here was a chance to spy on real people rather than grass and trees.

She whispered to Hound, "We're secret agents now."

They tiptoed to the forsythia border and lowered themselves quietly to the ground. Through the bottom branches of the bushes they could see the feet of the neighbors: little baby feet in red sneakers, zigzagging tipsily around the yard, and grown-up lady feet in white sneakers, following behind.

"Duck, duck, duck!" Ben was calling happily, his feet zigging and zagging even faster.

"Oh, Mr. Silliness," laughed his mother, and kept on chasing.

Batty thought that Iantha had a nice voice and an even nicer laugh. It was hard to tell about Ben's voice, since he only kept saying "duck."

Now the little red sneakers stumbled, and suddenly there was an entire Ben in view. Batty pulled herself and Hound back a bit, but before the baby could notice them his mother had scooped him off the ground.

"Oh, dear, are you hurt, my Ben, my pumpkin, my lumpkin, darling Ben?"

Batty caught her breath. Yes, it was a truly extra-nice voice.

"My pumpkin, my lumpkin, darling Batty," she whispered to herself.

Ben, not hurt at all, was soon wriggling out of his mother's arms, and then all the feet disappeared and the voices stopped, and Batty knew that they'd gone back into their house.

"My pumpkin, my lumpkin, *darling* Batty." This time she made her voice lower, so that it would sound more like Iantha's voice. She must have done it well, because Hound nuzzled her joyfully, and then she pounced on him, and they wrestled around the yard until they knocked the red wagon over and all the animals tumbled out. And then there was putting them back in, which was fun, and altogether, it was turning out to be an okay afternoon, even if Rosalind had scolded her for being noisy.

Then the afternoon got even better, for Jane arrived.

She told Batty, "I need your help."

Batty slipped the last animal—Mona the turtle—into the wagon and stood straight and tall. No one ever asked her for help. "I can help you."

"I'm writing—I mean, actually, Skye is writing—a play called *Sisters and Sacrifice,* and I thought you could act out the parts with me. Just so I can see how it reads, so that we can tell Skye."

Batty knew about plays. Rosalind and Tommy had been in one about a man who became evil when he drank a magic potion—Batty remembered this because she'd refused to drink anything but water for a week afterward. But she was much older now, and knew the difference between plays and real life. She liked the idea of being in one. "Can I wear a costume?"

"You don't need a costume. It's just a read-through."

But Batty had been impressed with the fake black beard Tommy had worn in his play, and refused to go any further without a costume, and she was sure that Hound wanted one, too. So Jane went back into the house and came out again with towels she'd taken from the bathroom.

Jane draped towels on her own and Batty's heads—saying they were ceremonial wigs—and plopped a third onto Hound's head. Hound, not in the mood for a ceremonial wig, dashed around the yard until the towel fell off and he could rip it to shreds. By then Jane had started reading from the script.

"*Long ago in the land of the Aztecs, there was great*

worry. The rain had not come for many months, and without the rain, the maize didn't grow, and without the maize, the people starved. Okay, Batty, you're one of the chorus now. Say: *Alas, alas, alas, my people are starving.*"

"*Alas, alas, alas, my people are starving.*"

"Too many 'alas'es." Jane made a note in her notebook, then read on. "*So the powerful priests knew that the gods must be angry with the people.* Now you say: *Alas, alas, the gods are angry.*"

"*Alas, alas, the gods are angry.*"

"*There was only one thing that would soothe the gods' anger.*" Jane struck a dramatic pose. "*Blood.*"

"*Blood,*" said Batty, striking the same pose. This was even better than secret agents.

"*Innocent blood!*"

"*Innocent blood!*"

"Good!" said Jane. "Now you're going to be a different character, named Rainbow. Your sister, Grass Flower, has been chosen to be sacrificed to the gods, but you're too nice to let that happen, and besides, the man you love happens to love Grass Flower instead, which breaks your heart, and you don't want to live anymore. So you say: *Sister, because Coyote loves you more, I will take your place in the ceremony.*"

"*Sister, because Coyote*—I forget the rest."

"*Loves you more, I will take your place in the ceremony.*"

"What ceremony?"

"The ceremony where the maidens' hearts get cut out." Jane put down her notebook. "I wish you could read."

"I can read. I read *Little Brown Bear Won't Take a Nap!* to Rosalind last night."

"You memorized that. It's not the same thing. How about if I just read both parts and you tell me if you like it. Rainbow speaks first." Jane folded her arms across her chest and looked noble. *"Sister, because Coyote loves you more, I will take your place in the ceremony."*

Hound bounded up, the last shreds of towel dangling from his mouth.

"Look, Hound," said Batty. "Jane is acting."

Jane turned to face in the opposite direction. "Okay, now I'm Grass Flower. *Rainbow, I cannot let you give your life for me.* Now I'm Rainbow again, shedding a quiet tear."

"You mean you're crying?"

"Yes, quietly. And I say: *What good is my life, now that I know Coyote loves you, Grass Flower?*"

Hound barked. Apparently he didn't approve of Coyote letting two sisters fall in love with him at once.

"There's lots more," said Jane. "But how do you like it so far?"

"It's good."

98

"I've been thinking about the sacrifice scene. Of course I can't have the priest carve out any maidens' hearts for real, but I thought I could have them behind a sheet so that all the audience can see are scary-looking shadows, then afterward the priest could jump out from behind the sheet holding the heart dripping with blood while he did a ritual dance."

Jane picked a leaf off the oak tree to represent a dripping heart, and did a convincing ritual dance full of writhing and stomping. Batty and Hound joined in and added much to the terror of the scene.

"The priests will cut out the hearts of only the unimportant maidens," said Jane when she had to take a rest from stomping. "I can't—I mean, Skye can't let Rainbow get sacrificed, since she's the heroine of the play. I'm sure that Coyote will try to rescue her, but Grass Flower will cling to his arm, begging him not to risk his own life. So I thought of lightning. Maybe a big bolt of it could break the altar in half right before Rainbow's heart is cut out."

"Lightning!" Batty gave one last writhe, then fell dead to the ground, struck by lightning.

"Yes, of course! The priests could be killed by the lightning, too. Brilliant!" Jane started scribbling on the script and soon had a gone-away look on her face that Batty had seen a hundred times before. She leapt up and stomped a few more times, but halfheartedly, for Jane didn't notice and indeed was soon wandering back toward the house, muttering about lightning.

Batty turned to Hound. "I wish we could be in a play, don't you?"

Hound dragged the towel from her head and chewed a big hole in one corner. He was willing to be in a play only if he didn't have to wear a costume.

"Well, then, what do you want to do now?" Batty peeked through the forsythia, but Iantha and Ben had not reappeared, so being secret agents again was out. She thought, then turned back to Hound. "We could go on a date."

Going on a date was a new game for Batty and Hound, and Batty threw herself into the preparations. She tucked in her shirt and wiped the dirt from her knees, for she was to be her father, and he wouldn't go on a date looking like a slob. Then she tried to wrap the towel around Hound's shoulders, for he was to be the awful skating coach in her rabbit coat. But Hound would rather eat the towel than wear it, so Batty decided that Funty would be the awful skating coach.

"And you can drive the car," she told Hound.

The red wagon would be the car. Batty took out all the animals but Funty and lined them up carefully along the forsythia hedge. Using the remains of one of the towels, she tied Hound's collar to the wagon handle, climbed into the wagon next to Funty, and made loud and enthusiastic engine noises, which Hound rightly interpreted to mean that he should start pulling the wagon.

He discovered that pulling the wagon was more fun than standing still. Then he discovered that pulling it faster was even more fun, and that the faster he pulled, the more fun he had, until he was dashing wildly around the backyard, the wagon careening behind him, with Batty screeching for him to stop and Funty hanging on for dear life.

Soon Hound was going so fast that the backyard was too small for him, and—"STOP, HOUND, PLEASE STOP!"—there they all went, flying around the garage and toward Gardam Street, and Batty in her panic saw that a green car was coming. When at the last moment Hound screeched to a halt, the wagon turned over and Batty tumbled safely onto the grass. But in a flash she was up and running, for poor Funty had tumbled out, too, and had kept rolling, and there he went, rolling into the street, and Batty was screaming, and Hound was barking—

Then there came the sound of squealing tires, and Batty saw—oh, what joy!—the green car stopping inches from Funty. She raced out to scoop him up and tell him he was her dearest and that she promised to take better care of him for ever and ever, and when she was sure that Funty was over his terrible shock, she knew that she had to thank the driver of the car.

If anything was scarier than Funty almost getting

run over, it was having to thank a stranger. However, motherhood gave Batty courage, and she marched bravely around to the driver's window. But when she got there, her courage deserted her, for the driver was not just a stranger. He was an extra-strange stranger, and Batty ran back into the house without speaking to him. She didn't stop running until she was upstairs and telling Jane all about it.

"Extra-strange how?" asked Jane.

"He wore a hat pulled way down and also these big black sunglasses."

Jane made circles with her fingers and held them up to her eyes. "Big like this?"

"No, much bigger." The man's glasses had reminded Batty of something. Then she remembered—it was a drawing of a giant fly she'd seen in one of Rosalind's schoolbooks. "Big like a bug's eyes. Jane, maybe they weren't glasses at all! Maybe he was a Bug Man!"

"I'm pretty sure there's no such thing."

"I saw him!"

"How did he talk?" Jane made a buzzing noise and flapped her arms. "Like this?"

"I don't know. He didn't say anything."

"Then you have no proof."

"But, Jane—"

"The important thing is that Funty's not hurt." Jane picked up her pen, for Batty had interrupted work on *Sisters and Sacrifice*.

So Batty wandered off, and no matter what anyone else said, she did know one thing: That stranger had not been a nice man, even if he had stopped his car in time. Batty knew another thing, too. It was good that she and Hound had practice being secret agents. Just in case Bug Man ever came back to Gardam Street.

CHAPTER NINE
Passes and Pizzas

THE FOUR SISTERS STOOD in a cluster outside their father's bedroom door. He was due to pick up Lara the Skating Coach in fifteen minutes.

"Knock again," said Jane.

Rosalind rapped on the door. There was no answer.

"Do you think he's sick?" Batty was anxiously clutching Funty. She hadn't put him down since his adventure with the green car.

"Of course he isn't sick. He's just getting ready for his date," said Rosalind, knocking once again. "Daddy, do you want help picking out a tie?"

The door swung open. Mr. Penderwick was wearing a suit and had three ties hung around his neck. "I won't be fussed and brushed over like last time, and I'm capable of selecting my own tie."

"But none of those match your suit," said Jane.

"I don't care." He closed the door in their faces.

"He's upset," said Rosalind. "He never acts like this."

"The strain is getting to him," said Skye. "Too many more awful dates and he'll go bonkers and we'll be virtual orphans and get stuck living who knows where."

"We could be separated and starved and put into cold garrets until we're rescued by rich old gentlemen with Indian manservants." Jane had read *A Little Princess* so many times she'd lost count.

Batty, not liking the sound of starvation and cold garrets, hugged Funty even tighter.

Rosalind raised her hand to knock, then didn't. Maybe all the knocking was bothering him. "Daddy, we'll just wait out here for you."

The door opened again, and he came out with just one tie this time. It wasn't any of the three he'd had a minute ago, but somehow he'd gone further astray. The new one not only didn't match his suit, it absolutely clashed.

"That tie—" said Jane.

"—looks great," said Rosalind, elbowing Jane into silence.

"*Mendax, mendax, bracae tuae conflagrant,*" said Mr.

Penderwick. "That's *mendax*, Rosy. M-e-n-d-a-x. Look it up after I leave."

He led the way downstairs, his daughters straggling along behind and exchanging guilty glances. Hound was at the bottom of the steps, looking woozy—he'd spent the last hour throwing up pieces of towel.

"Woof," he said sadly.

"Poor Hound," said Batty.

"Poor Hound, indeed." Mr. Penderwick was not sympathetic. "Even he should know not to eat towels. Now, as for dinner, I've ordered pizzas, which should arrive in about forty-five minutes. I've already told the babysitter that I'm leaving the money for the delivery-man on the kitchen counter."

"Babysitter!" exclaimed all the sisters at once. This was a terrible shock. Now that Rosalind was in charge in the afternoons, surely she could handle evenings, too.

"Yes, babysitter," said Mr. Penderwick cheerfully, just as the front doorbell rang. "Here he is now."

Jane opened the front door. There stood Tommy, with a football tucked under his arm.

"Why, Tommy, what a pleasant surprise," said Jane. "But where's your helmet tonight?"

"I decided it looked, you know, goofy," he answered, looking past her. "Hi, Rosalind."

"You're the babysitter? *You?*" The blow to Rosalind's dignity was too great.

"No, I am." An older version of Tommy—with the

same long arms and legs, the same unruly hair and big smile—stepped out from behind him, holding yet another football.

"Nick," said Rosalind bitterly. Tommy's older brother as a babysitter wasn't as humiliating as Tommy himself, but still she wasn't happy.

"Coach Geiger, if you please." Nick picked up Batty and hoisted her, squealing happily, high above his head.

"Daddy, if Nick's in charge, he'll make us do football drills," said Skye. Nick wanted to be a coach when he grew up and was always practicing on anyone he could get hold of.

"If I can go on a date with Anna's skating coach, you can do a few football drills."

"More than a few, I think," said Tommy.

"I'm working on a new passing pattern that I want to test out," said Nick. "You told me I could push the girls hard, Mr. Pen."

"So I did. Push them hard and promise me you'll never get suckered into a date."

"Absolutely."

"But, Daddy!" Rosalind had planned a quiet evening of baking almond cookies and talking to Anna on the phone. The Geiger brothers and their footballs would ruin all that.

"I have spoken," said Mr. Penderwick. He made a quick round of his daughters for good-bye hugs, then left.

" 'I have spoken'?" Jane appealed to the others. "Since when does Daddy say things like that?"

"He's not himself," said Skye. "I tell you he's being pushed too close to the edge."

"Oh, Skye, *stop*!" said Rosalind.

Nick put Batty down and ruffled her curls. "Time for the drills. Outside, everyone. Assistant Coach Geiger, you know what to do."

Tommy pulled a whistle out from under his shirt and blew a sudden, sharp blast on it. Rosalind clapped her hands over her ears, giving Tommy so withering a look it was astonishing he didn't perish right there on the spot.

"You—you—oaf!"

"Rosalind!" Jane was astonished that Rosalind would say such a thing. Penderwicks never called a friend an oaf, especially when the friend was Tommy Geiger, who in Jane's opinion could never be close to oafish.

But Rosalind wasn't done. She stomped her foot angrily, and when even that wasn't enough to express the depth of her annoyance, she ran upstairs.

"What did I do?" asked Tommy, staring woefully after her.

"You didn't do anything. She's fine," said Jane. "Let's start the drills."

Skye wasn't so sure that Rosalind was fine. She never called people names and stomped her foot.

Losing tempers was Skye's job—Rosalind was supposed to be the imperturbable Penderwick. Someone needed to check on her, and though Jane was the best one for talking about emotions, she and Batty had already followed the Geiger brothers outside. The only one left was Hound, still too sick for football drills. Skye prodded him with her foot, but he just sighed and looked pathetic. He was no help. Skye was on her own.

She marched resolutely upstairs and found Rosalind in her room, leafing through a Latin-English dictionary.

"What did Daddy say in Latin, Skye? *Mendax, mendax—*?"

Skye was relieved. Latin was easier than feelings. "*Mendax, mendax, bracae tuae con*—something."

"*Conflagrant,* I think," said Rosalind, flipping pages. "I'll start with *mendax. M-e-n-d-a-x.* It means liar. Daddy called me a liar!"

"You'd just told him his tie looked great."

"Oh, right. Let me look up the rest of it. Okay, *bracae* is next. It means 'trousers' or 'breeches.' *Tuae* I already know—it means 'your.' And *conflagrant* is a verb form, I'm pretty sure. Yes, here it is. *Conflagrare.* 'To burn.'" Rosalind shook the dictionary as if it were malfunctioning. "That couldn't be right. 'Liar, liar, your trousers are burning'? What does that mean?"

It means Daddy's going wacko and it's our fault,

Skye almost said, but she stopped herself. She was here to make sure Rosalind was all right, not get her more upset. There must be something soothing to say. Skye started out tentatively. "Maybe it doesn't mean anything. Maybe we got the Latin wrong. Or"—she had a sudden inspiration—"maybe the stuff Daddy's been saying all these years never made any sense, and we just didn't know it. Just forget about the *mendax* thing."

"You really think I should?"

"Yes," answered Skye firmly, and proudly, too, for it wasn't often that Rosalind asked her for advice.

Rosalind flopped onto her bed and stared mournfully at the ceiling. "I guess I shouldn't have called Tommy an oaf."

"Well, it's just Tommy."

"I know."

Rosalind sank into a reverie, and Skye wandered around the room, vaguely aware that something was different. Had Rosalind moved furniture around? No. And she still had the same plaid curtains and bedspread she'd always had. Then Skye realized that it wasn't that something had changed. It was that something was missing—a framed photograph of their mother holding Rosalind when she was still a tiny baby.

"Rosy, where's Mommy's picture?" It was always by Rosalind's bed. She'd even taken it with her to Arundel that summer.

Rosalind flushed. "It's in my drawer."

"Why?"

"I didn't want to look at it right now."

Skye stopped herself from asking why again. She'd done all right with the emotional stuff so far, and she didn't want to ruin it now. Besides, there was a lot of shouting in the backyard, which meant the football drills were under way. Skye poked gently at her older sister.

"I'm hungry, and you know Nick won't let us eat until we throw around his football."

"Right." Rosalind reluctantly got off the bed. "Let's get this over with."

No matter how much any of the sisters complained about Nick and his football drills, somehow every fall they ended up doing them, even without the pizza incentive. And it wasn't just football. In the winter, he put them through basketball drills—and they complained about that just as much. And one summer it had been the Gardam Street Softball Camp— he'd even managed to make them pay for that with quarters skimmed off their allowances, though they protested the whole time that they hated softball drills even more than football and basketball drills.

Maybe they put up with it all because Rosalind had turned into one of the best girls' basketball players in her school, and could outshoot most of the boys, too, when it came to that. And Skye was a decent softball pitcher and a much more than decent

hitter. And when Skye and Jane had first started playing soccer, Nick taught himself the skills he needed to
help them with that, too, though he'd never cared
about soccer before and had even been known to call
it ice hockey without the ice or the excitement. And
all the Penderwicks knew what good soccer players
Skye and Jane were now.

Only Batty had not yet shown any marked im-
provement from being trained by Nick, but Nick
wasn't giving up on her. Though no one else could see
it, he insisted that she had the makings of a great
athlete.

"Batty, don't duck and cover your head when Jane
throws the ball to you!" he was shouting when Rosalind and Skye ran outside. "Stretch up and try to
catch it!"

"Okay," she said, and did manage to stretch up
this time, though long seconds after the ball had
flown over her head. "Rosalind, look! I'm playing
football!"

Without turning around, Nick barked, "Rosalind,
Skye, five laps around the house for being late!"

"I'm too hungry for laps," protested Skye.

"Make that six laps. Assistant Coach Geiger, you
know what to do!"

When Tommy blew his whistle—softly this time,
and pointed away from Rosalind—the girls took off
around the yard. Skye got hungrier and more annoyed

with each lap, but the exercise seemed to cheer up Rosalind. She cheered up more when the laps were over and she joined the drills, especially after tackling Tommy and knocking him down. She didn't even lose her good mood when Tommy tackled her back and knocked her down, though Nick made them each do ten squat thrusts for it, since they were supposed to be doing drills for passing, not tackling.

He'd worked them through some standard pass patterns, and had just moved on to his own personal creation—the do-si-do, with lots of weaving, spinning, and fake hand-offs—when a new player suddenly appeared, a streak of orange flying after the ball that Jane had just fumbled. Tommy blew the whistle, and everyone stopped to watch as Asimov the cat dove onto the ball, bringing it to a stop.

"Interference," said Jane, not pleased that a cat was a better ball handler than she was.

"Who's this?" asked Nick.

"He lives next door," said Batty, crouching down to stare curiously at Asimov, who stared just as curiously back.

"I'll take him home before Hound realizes he's here," said Skye. She was by now hungry enough to do anything to get out of the drills, even pick up Asimov.

"Hound's in the house," said Nick.

"He could bust out through a window if he smells

cat," she improvised. "Really, Nick, this is an emergency."

Before Nick could come up with another argument, Skye scooped up Asimov and crashed through the forsythia. Her first instinct was to dump him there in his own yard and leave, for she still wasn't feeling intelligent enough to talk to Iantha, especially one on one. On the other hand, the longer she spent on this side of the bushes, the fewer drills she'd have to do.

"What should I do?" she asked Asimov.

"Mrroww," he said. Skye got the uncomfortable sense that not only was he judging her, she was falling short.

"All right, you win," she said. "I'll take you to your house."

"Mrroww," he said again, less sternly this time.

"Stupid cat." But Skye scratched him under the chin while she carried him to Iantha's front door.

She rang the doorbell, and a moment later the mail-slot flap flew open. Skye leaned down—for it was set in the door at knee level—and saw Ben peering out at her.

"Duck," he said.

"Duck yourself," said Skye. "Where's your mother?"

He swung up out of sight, and now the door opened, and there was Iantha. She was holding Ben and smiling in a way that made Skye forget to worry so much about feeling intelligent.

"Why, it's Skye, the second Penderwick sister. And you've brought Asimov back—how nice of you. Ben keeps letting him out. Don't you, Ben?"

Ben had been intently studying Skye. "Pretty," he said.

Iantha almost dropped him. "What did he say? Did he say you were pretty?"

"I'm sure he didn't," said Skye, making ghastly faces at him to prove that she wasn't.

"No, no, he said 'pretty'! How wonderful! Say it again, Ben."

"Duck."

"Well, he did say it once. You must be a good influence, Skye."

The last thing Skye wanted was to be a good influence on a baby. She put Asimov down. As he stalked—ungratefully, Skye thought—into the house, there was a sudden increase in the clamor coming from the Penderwicks' backyard. It sounded as though everyone was shouting and blowing whistles at once.

"Football drills," she said, just now realizing how loud they'd been. "I hope we haven't been bothering you."

"No, I like it," said Iantha. "Your father was a football player?"

"Daddy? Good grief, no. He played squash and chess."

The clamor next door increased even more, with cries of "PIZZA, PIZZA, PIZZA!" added in. Which meant that dinner must have arrived, and the football drills were finally over.

"I have to go," said Skye.

"Yes, of course you do. Thanks again for bringing Asimov home."

Skye started to leave, then impulsively turned back, for she'd seen a look—of what, loneliness? She wished Jane were there to help—flit across Iantha's face.

"Would you like to come home with me?" she asked. "We're having pizza. Ben can come, too, if babies can eat pizza."

"Ben loves pizza. I mean, if your—" Iantha suddenly looked as shy as she had the first time Skye met her. "Well, your father might mind."

"He's not there. And he wouldn't mind, anyway." Skye wasn't sure how she knew this, but she did. "Please come."

It wasn't the best time to introduce new neighbors to the Penderwick home. The kitchen floor was wet, for Hound had knocked over his water bowl during a game of Chase the Tennis Ball. Jane was loudly describing the big fight in the last soccer game to Tommy at the same time that Rosalind was scolding him for starting on the pizza before the table was even set. And Nick was on his hands and knees, with Batty being a broncobuster on his back and Hound trying to knock them over. Still, Iantha didn't seem to mind the chaos, not even when Hound jumped up and licked her face—she said she loved dogs—and Ben clearly adored it, especially when Tommy got down on the floor and let him be a broncobuster, too. By the time the floor was mopped, the table set, and the pizza served—and instantly devoured—the kitchen was so full of happy noise that no one heard Mr. Penderwick's car pulling into the driveway. Which was why it was a shock to hear the front door slam, followed by an impassioned burst of Latin.

"*Nam multum loquaces*—how does it go? Blast the woman! She sucked my brain dry. *Merito* something. Oh, yes—*merito omnes habemur, nec mutam profecto repertam ullam esse aut hodie dicunt mulierem aut ullo in saeclo*. And I mean it! Except for my Elizabeth, who never talked over an orchestra. Never!"

Mr. Penderwick reached the kitchen and went silent at the same instant. His hair was sticking straight up, his tie was stuffed into his pocket, and he was gaping at Iantha.

"I do apologize," he said after a moment. "I didn't realize we had company."

"Sure you did, Mr. Pen," said Tommy. "Remember

you asked Nick to babysit and you said I could come along?"

"He doesn't mean you and Nick," said Jane.

Blushing, Tommy shoved a stray bit of pizza crust into his mouth.

"Daddy, I invited Iantha and Ben over for supper," said Skye into the silence.

Mr. Penderwick ran his hand through his hair, apparently trying to flatten it but only making it stick up more. "You're always welcome, Iantha, though pizza . . ."

But Iantha was also talking. "Maybe I shouldn't have come without your—but Skye was so friendly . . ."

They both trailed off at the same time, and once more silence filled the room.

"How was your date, Mr. Pen?" asked Nick finally.

"Ghastly." He surveyed the kitchen, checking even under the table, where Hound was gnawing on a pizza box. "Anna's not here, is she?"

"No, Daddy," said Rosalind.

"Well, tell her that Lara the Skating Coach talked through Bach's first five concertos." He turned back to Iantha. "The Brandenburgs."

She nodded. "How about the sixth?"

"We left before the sixth," he answered grimly.

Ben, impelled by no one knew what sympathetic urge—though they were all certain he knew nothing of Bach—staggered over to Mr. Penderwick and tugged on his pants. Mr. Penderwick crouched down until they were eye to eye.

"Duck?" asked Ben.

"Indeed, one should always duck out of misbegotten dates," said Mr. Penderwick. "I might add, Ben, that the state of datelessness is not to be lightly discarded."

"Amen," said Nick, who didn't believe in romance during football season.

Rosalind, who thought she'd scream if another silence descended on the room, suggested dessert, but Iantha said that it was already long past Ben's bedtime, and soon the impromptu party was over. The Geiger brothers left for their home, and Iantha and Ben for theirs, with Mr. Penderwick insisting on carrying Ben.

Now it was just the four sisters.

"Poor Daddy," said Rosalind, for his "Ghastly" had stabbed her heart, though it was exactly what she'd hoped for.

"I—" began Skye.

Rosalind stopped her. "Do *not* say I told you so."

"I wasn't! I was just going to say that I'll have dessert if nobody else will." Skye took an ice cream bar from the freezer and bit into it.

"Rosy, what was that Latin Daddy was shouting?" asked Jane.

"I don't know. I won't know that much for years and years, but I think he was complaining about Lara."

"Anyway, two awful ladies down. Now we just need to find two more."

"How?" asked Batty from under the table, where she'd curled up with Hound and his pizza box.

"I don't know that, either." Rosalind wearily prepared herself to re-embark on the bad-date quest. "We'll talk about it tomorrow."

CHAPTER TEN
Reversals

AFTER SCHOOL THE NEXT DAY the sisters tried to come up with a new awful woman, but with so little enthusiasm, they decided to put off the vile discussion until the morrow. The morrow was a soccer-game Saturday, and Antonio's Pizza won, with Skye never losing her temper once, and no one wanted to spoil the celebratory mood with a depressing topic. Then that night there was an early frost, and by Sunday morning, autumn had truly arrived. The sky was a rich cloudless blue, the air still and dry, the maple trees glowing with glorious reds and oranges and yellows, and everywhere on Gardam Street squirrels bustled about with self-importance, burying their nuts in the most unlikely places. The Penderwicks agreed it would be sacrilege to conduct a serious MOPS in the midst of all that splendor, so instead they organized a dam-building in Quigley Woods, and Batty fell into a deep part of the creek and was pulled out by Tommy, though only Jane remembered to thank him—Rosalind was too busy wrapping her own sweater around Batty and racing her home to a hot bath.

Then it was the school week again. Batty took it upon herself to teach Ben more words, though after several afternoons at Iantha's, she still hadn't got him past "duck" and the occasional "pretty." Jane finished writing *Sisters and Sacrifice* and took it to her Enchanted Rock for luck before giving it to Skye. Skye handed it in without reading even a page, then forgot all about it. Rosalind aced two pop Latin quizzes, and for a science project, she and Anna built a catapult that turned out to be the perfect thing for tossing dog treats to Hound. With so much going on, nearly the whole week went by without anyone mentioning dates or stepmothers. Rosalind's fears drifted into the background. After all, she told herself, no one can worry constantly, and anyway, maybe she should learn to trust fate a little more.

Humming cheerfully, Rosalind plucked ingredients from the kitchen shelves, measured them, mixed them, then dropped bars of dark chocolate into a saucepan for melting. She was making brownies, and she knew the recipe by heart.

"By *heart*," she said.

It was because of her heart that she'd memorized the recipe. Cagney the gardener had professed a great fondness for brownies, and so that summer she'd baked brownies for him again and again and again, until she figured she could whip up a batch in her sleep. These brownies weren't for Cagney, of course, as he was far away in Arundel. No, these were to be snacks for the eighth graders' dance—the Autumn Extravaganza—coming up that weekend. It was traditional for the seventh graders to organize the Extravaganza, just as in the spring, the eighth graders would organize the Spring Spree for the seventh graders, and Anna and Rosalind had volunteered to be snack providers. Anna, after much deliberation, had decided on potato chips, since, as she said, Rosalind's brownies would be luscious enough to cover for both of them.

Stirring the chocolate, Rosalind wondered what the Spring Spree would be like. She pictured herself— in the blue sweater Aunt Claire had given her— walking into the decorated gym with Anna. And then they would dance, she supposed, though probably not with boys, since she couldn't think of any seventh-grade boys she'd like to dance with. Briefly, she tried to imagine dancing with Cagney there in the gym, but the thought made her shudder. How juvenile it would all seem to him.

Now the chocolate was melted and ready to be poured, but just as Rosalind lifted the saucepan, the phone rang. She plunked the pan back down and answered the phone.

"Rosy, dear, it's Aunt Claire."

Never in her life had she imagined that Aunt Claire's voice on the phone would make her frown. But that's what happened before she could stop herself. And by the time the conversation was over and she'd hung up the phone, she knew she'd been right to frown. Her week of rest—her week of insane denial!—was over, and danger was once again imminent.

Hands shaking, Rosalind turned off the stove. The brownies would have to wait. There was work to do, and quickly, before Daddy got home. She looked at the clock. They had forty-five minutes. That was more than usual, because it was Parents' Night at Wildwood Elementary, and her father was stopping there after work to meet with Mr. Geballe and Miss Bunda. But would even forty-five minutes be enough?

Gather the troops, Rosalind told herself. She picked up the phone again, called Anna, and told her to come over as quickly as she could. And now her sisters. Skye and Jane were in the backyard doing soccer drills, and Batty—where was Batty? For a moment

Rosalind panicked. And then—of course she knew where Batty was!

Rosalind ran next door to Iantha's. Loyal Hound, stretched out on the front step, did his best imitation of a neglected dog, but Rosalind knew he was perfectly happy waiting there for Batty. Besides, she saw Asimov sitting in a nearby window, positioned just right for keeping a wary eye on Hound, and vice versa, and she knew that Hound was beyond happiness and into ecstasy. For Batty had been right about that, at least—Hound did seem to love that cat. Now Rosalind noticed watchers at another window, too—Batty, wearing a pair of Jane's old sunglasses, and Ben, wearing Batty's old swimming goggles. She rang the doorbell, and the two heads disappeared from view.

Iantha opened the door with what Jane called her among-the-stars look on her face, which meant she'd been wrenched away from her research by the doorbell. How she could concentrate on astrophysics with both Batty and Ben in the house was beyond understanding, but each time Rosalind asked her, she said the same thing—Batty makes Ben happy, and that's what's important.

"I'm sorry to bother you, Iantha, but I need Batty right away."

Before Iantha could answer, Batty popped up beside her, with Ben in tow.

"I can't leave, Rosalind. Ben and I saw Bug Man drive by, and we have to stay on watch."

Batty had been reporting Bug Man sightings all week, and Rosalind was sick of him. She, Skye, and Jane had all had imaginary friends in their younger lives—Batty was the first to have an imaginary half-man-half-insect stalking Gardam Street.

"Bug Man will do fine without you," she said. "Come home now."

"But—"

"Batty!" Rosalind rolled her eyes at Iantha, who smiled.

"Batty believes that Gardam Street needs continual surveillance," she said.

"So does Ben," said Batty, who had no idea what "surveillance" meant.

"Well, it doesn't," Rosalind said in her end-of-discussion voice. "Now tell Iantha thank you for letting you visit."

"Thank you, Iantha." Batty, defeated, kissed Ben good-bye and whispered something to him before she went quietly with Rosalind. Hound, after one last yearning look at Asimov, followed them.

"What did you tell Ben?" Rosalind asked as they crossed over into their own yard.

"I told him to keep his goggles on."

"Because—?"

"Because if I wear sunglasses and he wears goggles,

Bug Man will think we're more like him and won't try to hurt us."

Rosalind briefly considered a lecture about putting fears in small children's heads. But then, Skye and Jane had played lots of Hide the Baby from the Monster when Batty was too little to defend herself, and Batty had turned out all right. Rosalind decided she'd worry about lectures later. Right now she had to get Skye and Jane in from the backyard, for in a minute or so Anna would arrive.

Soon all five girls were settled in the kitchen.

"Aunt Claire called," Rosalind began. "She's coming to visit tomorrow."

"Goody," said Jane.

"She's going to check on the progress of Daddy's dating, and if there's been no progress, she has another possible blind date for him."

"Not goody," said Skye.

"Maybe this one will be as bad as the first blind date," said Anna.

"Except that Aunt Claire says she's intelligent and funny and likes children. And"—Rosalind took a deep breath—"she's a high school Latin teacher."

Groans went round the table.

"What about dogs?" asked Batty.

"She probably raises them," said Skye bitterly.

"Threatened by the specter of stepmother-dom,

the sisters paled with horror." And Jane did look a little pale.

"Wait a minute," said Anna. "You're all giving up too soon. *Possible* blind date, Aunt Claire said, right? So it's not set up yet. We'll just have to find another awful date before she gets here. Your dad can't go on two dates in one weekend, so you'll be safe for a while."

"But where can we find another date?" cried Rosalind. "We thought and thought before, and all we came up with was your skating coach."

"Then we'll think and think again." Anna took a bag of pretzels from the cupboard and put it on the table. "Can't think on empty stomachs."

So they thought and ate pretzels, and ate pretzels and thought, and no one came up with even one new idea for an awful date. Rosalind started to wonder if she should just give in. How terrible could it be, really, to have her father dating a nice woman he could talk Latin to? And he'd have her over for dinner, and then she'd be cooking dinner, and then rearranging the kitchen, and then giving him advice on raising girls, and then—

"Are you desperate enough to try my mother's friend Valaria?" asked Anna finally. "You know, the one who used to be Mary Magdalene?"

"Maybe," sighed Rosalind.

"No, we're not," said Skye.

"It might be fun to meet Valaria," said Jane. "She could tell us lots about history."

Skye looked pleadingly at Batty, but before Batty could vote for or against the much-lived Valaria, a sound came that froze everyone.

"I'm home!" It was Mr. Penderwick, back too soon from Wildwood and the teachers' conferences. He strolled into the kitchen. "A summit meeting?"

"Not a meeting at all," said Rosalind. "I mean, we were just talking."

"But not about you, Mr. Pen," said Anna.

"It never occurred to me that you were talking about me, Anna."

"Good." Anna looked like she wished she could sink into the floor.

He sat down between his two middle daughters. "Anyone interested in reports from their teachers?"

Now Jane looked like she wished she could sink into the floor, for it was close to impossible that Miss Bunda would have said anything good about her. But no, her father reported that Miss Bunda was happy with Jane's progress in math and even happier with the science essay that she'd written.

"About antibiotics, I believe," he finished up.

"I think so," said Jane. "I mean, of course, yes, it was about antibiotics."

"Skye, I saw Mr. Geballe, too. He's quite impressed with a play you wrote about the Aztecs."

"What did he say about it?" Jane asked excitedly before Skye could stomp on her foot.

"Apparently the play shows a great deal of imagination and flair, not what Mr. Geballe normally expects from you. He was particularly pleased because you'd resisted the project so strenuously. He's so pleased, in fact, that he's chosen it to be the play in this year's Sixth Grade Performance Night."

"What?" Skye was appalled.

"Wow!" Jane was thrilled. The Sixth Grade Performance Night was Wildwood's gala event of the autumn. Usually they picked some moldy old play from a teachers' guide. But this year it would be her play! Though, alas, no one would ever know it was hers.

"They've never used a student's play before," said Skye. "Why this year of all years?"

"Mr. Geballe thought you'd be pleased," answered her father. "Aren't you?"

"It puts a lot of pressure on me." So much pressure that Skye felt like blurting out that she hadn't written the play at all. But if she admitted to this, she'd never again be able to swap homework with Jane, and then who would write her fiction assignments all the way through twelfth grade? After that, they could give up the charade and become honorable again, because in college Skye wouldn't need any fiction written—she was going to stick to math and science. "But I can take it, I guess."

"Well, all right, then." Mr. Penderwick pulled Batty onto his lap. "Why are you wearing sunglasses, sweetheart?"

"For spying on Bug Man. Daddy, Iantha tried to make pudding for me and Ben, but she ruined it. She says she's a terrible cook."

"Then it was particularly nice of her to try anyway, wasn't it? How was your day, Rosy?"

"Fine." She gripped the table and looked to Anna for courage. "Daddy, Aunt Claire called. She's coming to visit tomorrow."

"She called me, too. Did she mention the Latin teacher blind date? I told her not to bother."

"Not to bother?" echoed Rosalind, thinking she must have heard him wrong.

"Because I already have a date this weekend."

"You—" Rosalind choked and could go no further.

"—already have a date, yes. Tomorrow night, in fact."

His daughters would have been less shocked if he'd said he was going to become a circus clown. Anna asked what none of them could. "Who is she, Mr. Pen?"

"A woman I met recently. I thought she was interesting and decided I'd like to spend some time with her. Nothing very dramatic. Now everybody go away and let me cook dinner."

No one went away. They couldn't move. They

could only sit there, unhappy and confused, wondering who or what had taken over their father.

"What's her name?" asked Jane finally.

"Her name?"

"Her name, Daddy." This was Skye.

"*Nomen, nominis,*" burst out Rosalind, close to tears.

Mr. Penderwick looked round the circle of stunned faces. "Her name is Marianne."

CHAPTER ELEVEN
Clues

ALTHOUGH AUNT CLAIRE ARRIVED later than usual the next day—it was almost dinnertime—she found no freshly baked dessert, no flowers by her bed, no fresh towels. She didn't even find Rosalind.

"She's at Anna's," said Skye, after all the hugging and distribution of dog biscuits and chocolate caramels. "She couldn't stand the strain."

"What strain?" asked Aunt Claire.

"The dreadful strain of the date with Marianne," said Jane. "Even Rainbow fears that her courage may not be enough."

"Rainbow?"

"My sister raves," said Skye. Ever since the announcement that *Sisters and Sacrifice* was going to be staged, Jane had been blabbing about Rainbow as if she owned her, which of course she did, but no one could know that.

"I might rave about some things," said Jane. "But not about the strain, Aunt Claire. We're all feeling it. And Daddy won't tell us anything about this Marianne."

"He told me on the phone that he met her in a bookstore, but nothing else."

"Rosalind, Skye, and Jane are afraid Daddy's going to marry her," said Batty. "Did you bring any presents?"

"Marry her! That's a little premature." Aunt Claire laughed at them. "And no, my pirate, I didn't bring you presents this time."

"Truly, though, Daddy's acting weird, and it would make anyone anxious." Skye took Aunt Claire's suitcase out of the car trunk. "See for yourself. He's upstairs getting ready."

They all trooped inside and up the steps. When Aunt Claire knocked on her brother's door, he came out into the hall. He was dressed in a very un-datelike manner.

"You're wearing that ancient sweater on your first date with this woman? What about that nice blue shirt I gave you last Christmas?" asked Aunt Claire.

"Hello to you, too, Claire, and the shirt you gave me is flannel. Marianne doesn't like flannel."

"Doesn't like flannel." Aunt Claire looked sideways at Skye, who made a we-told-you-he-was-acting-weird face. "So you do know something about her."

"Certainly I do."

"What's her last name?"

"Dashwood. Marianne Dashwood."

"An unusual name."

"Perhaps, but it suits her." He headed down the steps, the flock of female Penderwicks trailing along behind him. Halfway down, he turned, pushed past everyone to get back to his room, then came out again, wearing a sports jacket.

"Why are you taking that along?" Aunt Claire pointed to the orange book peeking out of the jacket's pocket. "Are you going to read to her?"

"No, of course not."

Skye was almost sure he blushed, but before she could look closely enough to be positive, he was running out of the house, calling over his shoulder about the soup and sandwiches he'd left for their dinner. His three daughters, who couldn't remember the last time he'd gone away without hugs, stared forlornly at the door after it shut behind him.

Aunt Claire stared a little forlornly, too, then shook herself and said brightly, "Come on, let's do something fun while we eat. I know—it's been a long time since we've played Clue. How about it?"

Clue was a general favorite. While Jane helped Aunt Claire serve up the dinner, Skye dug the Clue box out of the hallway closet, where all the games were kept, and set up the board amidst the sandwiches. Then everyone had to switch chairs so they could be near their favorite characters. Jane chose Miss Scarlet because she secretly longed to wear a long, slinky gown like hers someday. Skye claimed Professor Plum, noticed that he had red hair, and decided he was a professor of astrophysics. Batty would be no one other than Mrs. Peacock, as only Mrs. Peacock was named for an animal. That left Aunt Claire, and since no one ever wanted to be Colonel Mustard because of his whip, and since Mrs. White was now represented by the top from a vitamin bottle—Hound had eaten the original long ago—she went for Mr. Green.

"Highest throw starts," said Skye when they were all settled. She picked up the dice—and the front doorbell rang.

Jane ran to open the door. Was it Daddy home again already, so confused by love and romance that he'd lost his keys along with his heart? But it was Tommy.

"Is Rosalind home?" he asked. "I need to talk to her."

"She's fled her troubled abode, but come in anyway. Aunt Claire's here and we're playing Clue." When he hesitated, Jane added, "And we have plenty of sandwiches."

The sandwiches pulled Tommy in, and soon he was Colonel Mustard—they all decided that a whip wasn't so bad if it was just for show—with a stack of sandwiches in front of him. Everyone rolled the dice. Batty had the highest roll with ten, and Clue could begin.

They played six games that night. Not one of the games was played according to the rule book, what with Batty using secret passages where there weren't any on the board, and Tommy and Skye throwing the tiny weapons at each other, and Jane forgetting her strategy because the mansion on the board reminded her of Arundel Hall—though Arundel Hall didn't have a conservatory, and it certainly didn't have a billiard room—and Aunt Claire guessing everything wrong on purpose so that she wouldn't win. But, as Jane said, rules aren't the most fun thing in life, and everyone enjoyed themselves immensely until Aunt Claire dragged a reluctant Batty up to bed for story time and sleep.

"What now?" Skye asked the other two.

"We could watch a movie," said Jane, looking at Tommy. It was always more fun to watch a movie with Tommy around.

"Sure," he said. "At least until Rosalind comes home."

"Thanks for the ride home, Mrs. Cardasis. Good night, Anna," said Rosalind, yet she made no effort to get out of their car and go into the house. The first thing she'd noticed when they drove up was that her father's car wasn't in the driveway. He was still out with Marianne.

"Come back with us," said Anna. "You can spend the night, can't she, Mom?"

"Of course."

"Thanks, but I shouldn't." The evening at Anna's house had been so much fun—they'd played basketball, listened to music, and made caramel popcorn—that Rosalind had almost forgotten to worry about her father. But she couldn't stay away from home for a whole night, not with Aunt Claire visiting. It would be heartless and selfish.

"Everything will work out fine with your father, Rosy," said Anna's mother. "You'll see."

"I guess so," said Rosalind, finally getting out of the car. She hated it when people said that everything will work out fine. How could they know?

As Anna and her mother drove away, Rosalind started up the front walk, wondering if she could sneak up to her bedroom without talking to anyone. She didn't want to hear about how Daddy had acted when he left, and she didn't want to wait up for him to come home. Just this once it would be lovely to go to bed without new things to fret over.

Quietly she let herself into the house, then peeked into the living room. Aunt Claire was on the couch, watching a movie—one of those old-fashioned English dramas, it looked like—and Jane and Skye were stretched out on the floor, both sound asleep. Aunt Claire spotted her and blew her a kiss. Rosalind waved back and tiptoed away. So far, so good. She would just go upstairs, look in on Batty—but as she passed the kitchen, she heard the refrigerator door being shut. Who could that be? Surely Batty wasn't awake and rummaging around in the refrigerator on her own.

It was Tommy, eating ice cream right out of the container. He hadn't seen her, and she thought about slipping away before he did, but suddenly ice cream seemed like a good idea.

"People with manners use bowls, you know," she said.

Tommy looked around helplessly. Taking pity on him, Rosalind got two bowls out of the cupboard and spooned a huge helping of ice cream into one bowl for him and about half as much into the other for herself.

"Thanks," he said. "That movie they're watching made me hungry."

"Everything makes you hungry."

"True." Tommy's bowl slipped from his hands and fell upside down onto the table. The ice cream splattered widely, though it seemed most attracted to Tommy's shirt.

What was wrong with him? He certainly couldn't be nervous, thought Rosalind, not around her. She dabbed at his shirt with a damp towel, then gave him another bowl of ice cream. "Are you all right?"

"Of course I am." To prove it, he got this new bowl safely to the table. "Rosy, do you know Trilby Ramirez?"

"I know who she is." An eighth grader, Trilby had straight black hair that fell to her waist, and she was in gymnastics club. Rosalind had seen her do perfect splits on the balance beam.

"She asked me to go to that Autumn Extravaganza thing with her tomorrow night."

"Are you sure?" That was rude, so she tried again. "I mean, why?"

"I don't know." Tommy sounded almost as surprised as she was. "I guess she likes me."

Rosalind stopped herself from asking why again. After all, there wasn't any reason for anyone not to like Tommy. "Well, of course she likes you. I only meant . . ." The one time Rosalind had tried a split on the balance beam, she'd fallen off and bruised her elbow. But what was the balance beam next to brains, anyway? "That is, I don't know what I meant. Are you going?"

"I don't know. Do you think I should?"

"Why not?" Suddenly Rosalind was tired. She wished Tommy would leave. Him and his Trilby Ramirez and her long hair.

"I just thought maybe that you—" Tommy rapped

his spoon against his head, then flinched. He'd forgotten he was helmet-less.

"That I what?"

"Nothing. I mean, it would be more comfortable if you were going, too."

"Comfortable." Rosalind stood up and put her bowl in the sink. "Well, I didn't get invited to the eighth-grade dance."

"I know that. Don't be mad at me."

"Why would I be mad? I've just had a long day."

He stood up, too, and said, "I'll go home, then. Thanks for the ice cream."

"You're welcome."

"Good night, Rosy."

Out of patience with men and their confusions, Rosalind didn't answer, waiting with her back turned until he left. Really, she was dreadfully tired.

But before she could rest, there was a littlest sister to check on. Rosalind crept upstairs and into Batty's room, hoping that she wasn't awake and expecting more stories. Yes, all was well. Batty was very much asleep, though she'd managed to kick her covers and most of her stuffed animals to the floor. But someone else was awake. Hound, sprawled across the bottom of the bed, was now blinking sleepily—and guiltily—at Rosalind.

"Off," she whispered.

He dropped to the floor, taking the rest of the

stuffed animals with him, and slunk into the corner where he was supposed to sleep.

"And stay there." Rosalind said it firmly, though she and he both knew he wouldn't.

She managed to get all of the covers and animals back to where they should be without disturbing Batty, then gave Hound one last stern—just for form's sake—look. As she slipped back into the hallway, she heard the front door open downstairs. Daddy was home. Really, truly, Rosalind didn't want to hear about the date, but some horrid fascination kept her rooted in the shadows at the top of the steps.

Aunt Claire was out of the living room now, speaking quietly, so as not to wake Skye and Jane. "How was your date?"

"Fine," he answered, just as quietly.

Rosalind, despite herself, leaned closer to listen.

"Fine great? Fine okay? Fine like you'll see her again?"

"Perhaps." He yawned. "She's a charming woman. She likes taking walks."

"You took a walk with her, Martin? That was your date? That's not much more exciting than reading a book to her."

"I know what I'm doing, Claire. Everything will work out fine."

Rosalind stumbled off to her room, badly needing someone or something to punish. And—perfect!— there on her desk were the brownies she'd baked for the Autumn Extravaganza, hidden away from hungry sisters.

BAM! BAM! BAM! She smashed the brownies into a million little pieces, then threw open her window and tossed the whole mess out into the night.

"The eighth graders," she said, brushing crumbs from her hands, "are not good enough for my brownies."

Before closing the window again, Rosalind stuck out her tongue in the general direction of the Geigers' house. Why had she bothered? She didn't know or care. Some things, she thought, were too unimportant to fuss over.

CHAPTER TWELVE
Jane's Grand Gesture

SKYE BURST OUT THROUGH the big front doors of Wildwood Elementary School, looking around frantically. She was searching for Jane. There were dozens of people swarming around, but no Jane. Where was she? Where? Where? Skye had to find her immediately and kill her.

"See you tomorrow, Skye!" That was her friend Geneviève, waving from the school bus as it pulled away. Skye waved back, but without enthusiasm. She wondered if she would ever be enthusiastic again.

"Hey, Penderwick. Race you to the end of the parking lot." Pearson, who sat across from her in Mr. Geballe's class, punched her on the arm.

"No," she said, punching him back. She'd never

turned down a race before, but she wanted nothing more to do with Pearson today.

Now here came Melissa Patenaude. Skye looked through her as though she were invisible—maybe if she was invisible, she wouldn't be able to talk. But no such luck.

"Congratulations, Skye," said Melissa. "I'm sure you'll do well."

"Thanks," muttered Skye. After she murdered Jane, she would murder Melissa. A person could only be sent to prison once, and prison might not be as bad as what she was facing now.

Finally! Here came Jane, strolling out of the school with a group of her friends. Skye was beside her in a flash, taking her firmly by the arm and steering her away from the others.

"Ouch," said Jane. "Unhand me, you minion."

"Minion yourself," said Skye. "We have to talk."

Jane went white and dropped her backpack. "What's wrong? Is Daddy okay? Batty?"

"Everyone's fine except me. I'm not at all fine. My teacher assigned parts in your play today. Guess who's going to be Rainbow."

"Kelsey."

"No."

"Isabelle? Maya?"

"No, Jane, think awful. Really awful."

"Don't tell me Melissa got the starring part!"

"No, she's going to be Grass Flower."

"That's okay, I guess, since Grass Flower is kind of a jerk, though I'd rather Melissa never utter any words of mine, even for jerky characters." Jane thought. "Well, who then?"

"Me."

Now all was horrifyingly clear to Jane. Skye, as courageous as anyone when it came to physical deeds of derring-do, was terrified of being on a stage. A scarring experience in first grade—a hula skirt that fell down during a skit about Hawaii—had set her against performing for the rest of her life. "Did you explain to Mr. Geballe?"

"I tried, but he thought I was just shy about being in a play I wrote. I couldn't explain to him that I didn't care about that, since you wrote it. And by the way—" Skye turned ferociously on her younger sister. "Guess who's going to be Coyote—Pearson!"

"Oh, he'll be good."

"Jane, who cares how good he'll be? Remember all those speeches about undying love and romance? I'll have to say them to *him*! What the heck were you thinking?"

"I wasn't thinking that you were going to have to say them to Pearson. I wasn't thinking you'd have to say them at all. You're the last person I'd choose for the part," Jane said. The truth was that when she wrote *Sisters and Sacrifice,* she'd imagined herself as Rainbow. It was a glorious role.

"What am I going to do? I don't know if I can memorize all that stuff about maize and self-denial. If it were primary numbers. Or geometry! I've memorized lots of geometry. Listen: If two lines are cut by a transversal, and—and what? It's gone! This stress has ruined my brain!"

"Calm down. The bus line is staring." By the bus line, Jane meant Melissa, who was not only staring at them, but trying to listen, too.

"I could break my leg. That's the solution, Jane. I'll accidentally-on-purpose fall off the garage roof and break my leg. They can't force me to be in a play with a broken leg, can they?"

"No, but you can't play soccer with a broken leg, either."

"Then how about pneumonia or malaria or tuberculosis?"

"Same problem." It wrung Jane's heart to see her brave sister brought so low. "It won't be that bad, Skye. I'll help you memorize the lines. Come on, let's go home."

Skye allowed herself to be led home, all the while calculating how many people would be in the audience for the Sixth Grade Performance Night. Since all of the sixth graders would be involved in one way or another, all of their families would come, which meant, well, twenty-six students in each of the four sixth-grade classes, and if at least two—no, probably three—family members came for each student, plus all the teachers, plus various fifth graders . . .

"Four hundred people," she said in sepulchral tones. "At least four hundred people will watch me make a fool out of myself."

"Four hundred," Jane repeated, but her tone was not sepulchral, for not until then had she realized how many people would see her play performed. It was intoxicating.

"It's nauseating." And Skye did look a little sick at the idea, and when they got home, she went right in through the front door and upstairs.

"Four hundred," said Jane again, following her sister into the house, lost in the vision of the Wildwood Elementary School auditorium, with its real stage, with wings and flies and a huge billowing curtain. The four hundred people in the audience were applauding wildly, and there was Jane, herself, on the stage, taking the author's bow and holding a huge bouquet of roses, no, being pelted with roses from the audience— maybe first graders could do the pelting—while humbly—

"Rats," she said, stopping herself. She wouldn't be taking the author's bow. Skye would be doing it, and worse, not even enjoying it. Oh, well. There would be other plays and other triumphs, and as for now, she was hungry. She went into the kitchen, where Rosalind and Anna were doing their Latin homework.

"*Qui, quae, quod,*" said Rosalind. "*Cuius, cuius, cuius.*"

"*Cui, cui, cui,*" said Anna. "*Quem, quam, quad.*"

"Not *quad*—*quod*. Jane, you're last in. Call Daddy."

"Are you sure?" Anna looked down at her textbook. "You're right. *Quod.* Let me start over."

Jane took a box of raisins from the counter for a snack, then called her father at the university. He didn't answer his phone, but she left a message that all his daughters were home safe, which she doubted he could hear with all the Latin chanting in the background. She hung up and had started to wander off, when the Latin stopped and a familiar name caught her ear.

"What did you say?" she asked Anna.

"That Trilby Ramirez is all whacked out over Tommy." Anna saw the confused look on Jane's face and explained. "They were together at the Autumn Extravaganza on Saturday night. Rumor has it that Tommy even danced with her. We didn't know that Tommy *could* dance."

"Plural," said Rosalind. "*Qui, quae, quae, quorum, quarum, quorum*—"

"I don't understand," interrupted Jane. "Rosalind,

it's you he adores and wants for a girlfriend, not some-
body named Trilby."

"He doesn't want me for a girlfriend, and if he did,
he couldn't anyway." Rosalind sniffed at the idea. "No
one can for years and years, and even then, it won't be
Tommy."

"Still, why Trilby?" asked Anna. "She's about as
smart as concrete, and she's a wimp, too. There was a
spider in the girls' locker room and she practically
passed out."

"I heard it was a large spider," said Rosalind
calmly. "*Quibus, quibus, quibus.*"

"Don't you care?" asked Jane. She was shocked at
this display of indifference. Why, if she were old
enough and Tommy looked at her the way he looked
at Rosalind, she would never let him date someone
named Trilby.

"Why should I? *Quos, quas, quae, quibus, quibus,
quibus.* Anna, let's go again. *Qui, quae, quod, cuius—*"

Jane went upstairs, thinking that there certainly
was a lot of trouble with dating in the Penderwick
house. When she got to her room and found Skye's
copy of *Sisters and Sacrifice* dumped on the floor—and
no Skye—she sighed. There was a lot of trouble, pe-
riod, in the house. She looked out the window, and
yes, there was Skye on the roof, staring glumly at the
clouds through her binoculars.

"May I come out?"

Skye nodded, and Jane climbed out gingerly and settled herself. Next door, two faces in odd glasses were staring at her from an upstairs window. She waved, and Ben waved back, but Batty disappeared, and then Ben disappeared, as though Batty had yanked him out of sight, too. Ah, to be young and feckless again, thought Jane. "Feckless" was one of her favorite words lately. She'd even managed to work it into *Sisters and Sacrifice.*

"Did you get to the place where Rainbow calls Grass Flower feckless?" she asked Skye. "That's a good line, right?"

Skye put down her binoculars. "It doesn't matter whether the lines are good. I can't memorize them, and even if I could, I can't act at all. We read the first few scenes out loud, and I was terrible."

"Maybe I could coach you." Suddenly Jane saw herself as a director. She could wear a slouchy hat and have her own chair and a script scribbled all over with notes. Maybe she could even skip her science class to do it, if the schedule worked out right. "Please let me, Skye. It'll be fun."

"Fun like in 'fungus,'" said Skye, but after much pleading from Jane, she consented to climb back into the bedroom and pick up the script. After all, she figured, Jane couldn't possibly make her worse than she already was.

The next half hour was painful for both sisters. So

flat—so without feeling or expression—was Skye's reading that Jane began to doubt her own writing. She tried some rewriting, hoping to find the words that would bring a spark to Skye's delivery. But that just frustrated Skye more—she swore she'd *never* be able to learn the lines if Jane kept changing them. Desperate now, Jane drew Aztec-ish lines on Skye's face with wet colored pencils, thinking stage makeup would help her. After that, she did manage to put feeling into one line.

"You forget, sister, how good I am with the bow and the knife."

"That's too much feeling," said Jane. "You sound violent."

"I'm feeling violent!"

"But, Skye, in this scene—"

"I hate this play! Hate it! Hate it!" Skye threw her script to the floor and would probably have stomped on it, too, if just then their father hadn't called for them to come downstairs. He was home from work and had some news.

The girls felt that there'd been enough news lately, and agreed that if it was more dating news, they didn't want to hear it. However, as the play rehearsal was clearly over, they wiped the Aztec marks off Skye's face and went down to the kitchen. Anna had gone, and Rosalind had fetched Batty from next door, so it was the four sisters who gathered around the table while their father took off his jacket and sat down with them.

"Churchie called me at the office this afternoon."

It definitely wasn't about dating, for Churchie was Mrs. Churchill, who, as housekeeper at Arundel, had practically brought Jeffrey up. The Penderwicks had gotten to know and love her that past summer, and now everyone started firing off questions. Was there trouble? Was Jeffrey all right? Was Churchie all right? How about Cagney?

Mr. Penderwick held his hand up for quiet. "Everyone's fine. Churchie called because she's going to Boston this weekend to visit Jeffrey. She'll be staying overnight at her daughter's house, and as there's room there for an extra person, she's invited one of you to go along."

A clamor broke out once more, as all the sisters loudly asked which one of them was going. Mr. Penderwick put his hands over his ears. When the kitchen was again quiet, he said, "Churchie is letting us decide who goes. Now, Batty, I'm not going to insist that you're too young—"

"I'm not!"

"—but I will mention that Hound is not allowed to go along."

"Oh," said Batty.

"One down," said Skye.

"Anyone else not interested?" asked Mr. Pender-wick. "Rosalind, how is your homework situation?"

She winced. "I would love to go, but I have a lot of assignments due next week."

"Two down," said Jane breathlessly. "Skye, I'll duel you for it."

"There's no need for dueling," said Mr. Pender-wick. "Churchie said that there will be more visits like this, and you'll all get a turn eventually."

"Eventually!" Skye thought that a terrible word. "Well, if not dueling, then what?"

"Hound Draw for Order," said Mr. Penderwick. "First pick goes to Boston."

"But he never picks me first!" Skye leaned down to look under the table at Hound, who looked back with a guilty expression on his face.

"Sure he does," said Rosalind, and started the preparations.

"No, he never does," Skye insisted to Jane. "It's a statistical anomaly."

Jane didn't know anything about statistical anom-alies, but she agreed that Hound seemed never to go first to the piece of paper marked SKYE. She wished she could assure Skye that this time would be differ-ent, but she wanted too much that it wouldn't be dif-ferent, because then she would be the one visiting Boston.

In a moment, all was ready. There were two pieces

of paper—each with one name on it, and folded so that no one could read it—and several chunks of dog biscuit, all mixed together in a bowl. Rosalind dumped the whole mess on the floor, Batty gave Hound an encouraging push, and when he headed for the biscuits, everyone watched closely, until his big nose bumped into one of the slips of paper.

"The winner!" cried Jane, scooping it up from the floor and waving it exuberantly. "The goer to Boston, the boon companion of Jeffrey and Churchie, the luckiest, most fabulous—"

"READ IT!" shouted Skye.

"Ah, yes." Jane flourished the slip of paper once more, doing imaginary spells over it, then slowly unfolded it, read it, and smiled. The right name was on the paper, and she would not have to wait for eventually.

But before she read the name out loud, she looked up and the first thing she saw was Skye's face, so anxious, so hopeful, with a faint trace of green Aztec makeup across her cheek. At the sight of that bit of green—only a smidgeon, really—one of Rainbow's lines came to Jane, all unbidden. *I will spill my blood to bring the rain to grow the maize to feed our people.* What a tragically beautiful line that is, she thought, and before she knew what she was doing—

"Skye," she said. "Hound picked Skye."

Immediately Skye was aglow with joy, hugging

everyone, even Hound, even Batty. In all the hugging, no one noticed when Jane left the kitchen. Especially Skye didn't notice, for she had to call Jeffrey to tell him the good news, then call Churchie to thank her for the invitation, then call her soccer coach, for this meant she'd be missing the game on Saturday.

"And no dodging homework," said her father after all the calls had been made. "Perhaps you should start getting ahead now."

Even the idea of getting ahead in homework couldn't dampen her spirits. She ran upstairs two steps at a time, burst into her room, and pulled up short. Jane was cleaning. Already she'd made her bed, and now she was dusting her desk. This was bad. For Jane, cleaning was worse even than crying. Skye could have kicked herself. She'd been so happy that she hadn't given a thought to Jane's disappointment.

"I'm sorry it's me and not you going," she said.

"I don't mind," answered Jane, dusting vigorously. "I'll get to visit Jeffrey eventually."

"Eventually" truly was a terrible word. Poor Jane—Skye wanted to make it up to her. "And I'm sorry I said those things about your play earlier. I didn't mean them."

"Really?" The dust rag slowed down a bit.

"All of your comments have been helpful. So I was thinking. . . ." Skye summoned as much enthusiasm as she could manage. "I'd like to have my lines memorized before I go to Boston. That gives us five days to get in a lot of practice—that is, if you don't mind."

"I don't mind. Sabrina Starr never shirks her duty."

"Because it really is a good play. It's just me that's bad."

"I know," said Jane, letting the dust rag fall unheeded to the floor. "Let's get to work."

CHAPTER THIRTEEN
Nyet!

ROSALIND HAD FOUND her favorite place in Quigley Woods long ago. She'd been taking a walk there with her mother, just the two of them. Skye and Jane had been—Rosalind couldn't remember where they'd been. She could only remember how wonderful it was to have her mother all to herself. They'd followed the stream, talking and laughing, until they came upon a low stone wall. It had been autumn then, just like now, and her mother had brushed the fallen leaves from the stones so that they could sit and watch the stream burble along. Next spring, you and I will have a picnic here, Rosy, her mother had promised. But by the next spring—

Rosalind pulled herself up. She hadn't come to her

favorite place in Quigley Woods to feel sorry for herself. She'd been doing too much of that lately. No, she'd come here with Batty and Ben to get away from the house, for Jane and Skye were back there practicing *Sisters and Sacrifice*—and arguing about it—just as they'd been doing all week. It would be a great relief when Skye went to Boston tomorrow, because there'd be no talk of Aztecs for two whole days.

"Blood! Innocent blood! You try it, Ben."

"Batty, don't teach him that!" Rosalind crunched through the leaves to where Batty and Ben were trying to stuff Hound into the red wagon.

"But he needs a new word."

"Not that word." Rosalind picked up Ben and kissed his fat cheek. "Say 'dog,' Ben. Say 'Hound.' Say 'Batty.' But please don't say 'blood.' "

Ben said nothing at all.

"How about 'Rainbow'? Say 'Rainbow,' Ben," tried Batty.

"Not that, either." Rosalind shook her head at Ben to discourage thoughts of Aztecs. He patted her face cheerfully, then pointed to the ground.

"He wants to get down," said Batty.

So Rosalind put Ben down, went back to the stone wall, and opened a book of Shakespeare's sonnets. She had to memorize a poem to recite in English class, and she'd signed up for Shakespeare without realizing that most of his poems were about love. Like "Say that thou didst forsake me for some fault," and "That thou hast her, it is not all my grief." As Rosalind had no intention of talking about love in public, she was looking for a sonnet that was confusing enough that no one would pick up on the love part. Rosalind flipped through the book. Here was a possibility: "Why didst thou promise such a beauteous day, And make me travel forth without my cloak—"

She was yanked away from Shakespeare by Hound. He'd knocked over the wagon, and was crouched low in combat position, his nose pointed deep into Quigley Woods, away from Gardam Street. And he was growling.

"What is it, Batty?" she asked, for Batty and Ben were flat on the ground beside Hound, their noses pointed in the same direction.

"We hear someone coming. It's probably Bug Man."

Rosalind couldn't hear anything. "Why don't you and Ben worry about someone else for a while? Aliens from outer space, for example."

"Because there aren't any aliens from outer space on Gardam Street," answered Batty patiently.

"And there's no Bug—" Rosalind stopped, for now she did hear something. A pounding noise, the kind made by a lot of running feet. If that was Bug Man coming out of the deep Quigley Woods, he had to be at least a centipede. Unless he had a lot of other Bug Men with him.

Now she could hear chanting along with the pounding. She strained to pick out the words. *See something something. See eight something?*

Hound had gone from growling to barking, and Batty and Ben had hidden behind the stone wall. Rosalind, though, wasn't going to hide. She stood, hands on hips, next to Hound, ready to confront whoever was pounding past her favorite place. The chanters were coming closer now, and their words becoming more clear, and then Rosalind realized that they weren't words at all—they were letters.

"C-H-S," she said. "Cameron High School."

Now a long line of tall boys in football uniforms came into view, running through the woods, *pound, pound, pound, pound.* Rosalind stepped away from the path, pulling Hound with her, for she had no need or desire to confront thirty or so high school boys in the middle of a training run. In fact, she wished now that she was behind the wall with Batty and Ben, just in case one of these giants in helmets was Nick Geiger and he was in the mood to humiliate her.

"ROSY!"

She groaned. Not only was Nick there, he was the first in line, and when he stopped in front of her, all the other football players stopped, too.

"Hi, Nick," she said, blushing and hating it.

"Men! Take a breather!" Nick shouted. "And say hello to ROSALIND!"

Grunted greetings came from dozens of manly

161

throats. Rosalind hoped a tree would fall on Nick's head.

"What are you doing?" she hissed at him.

"Rough-terrain training. I've been trying out my theories about it on Tommy, and Coach was interested enough to let me use the whole team for research. As long as nobody breaks any limbs, he said." Nick turned and shouted at the other players again. "Anything broken yet?"

More grunts, this time negative ones.

"Nick." She spoke slowly and carefully, as if to a person who didn't understand English. "I meant, why did you—and your team—stop here?"

"Because there you were, and I remembered that I need to talk to you in private."

"Private!"

"Don't worry about the boys," Nick said blithely, taking off his helmet. "You're in seventh grade. They barely realize you're here."

He was right. Not one of Nick's teammates was paying the least attention to her, though several were playing with Hound. She relaxed a little. "What do you need to talk about?"

"The Tommy and Trilby situation."

She knew what he meant, for Anna had been keeping her updated. Tommy and Trilby together in the cafeteria, in the library, in the gym. Tommy and Trilby sharing a lunch tray, exchanging romantic looks, holding hands. All nauseating behavior, in Rosalind's opinion. "It's none of my business, Nick."

"But he needs help, Rosy. This Trilby's telling everyone he's her boyfriend. She calls him every night, sometimes two or three times, and here's the worst—she goes to all of his football practices and cheers for him." Nick pitched his voice high. "Go, Tommy, go! You're the best!"

"I agree it's disgusting, but what can I do about it?"

"Talk to him. I've tried, but he doesn't listen to me."

"He doesn't listen to me, either, Nick. Besides, if I could stop people from going on dates just by talking to them, I'd start with Daddy."

"Poor Mr. Pen. Has he had a second date with Marianne?"

"Not yet." Rosalind put the emphasis on yet. Her father had said nothing about his plans for the weekend, and she feared the worst.

"Impending doom, huh? Sorry." Nick did look sorry, for which Rosalind was grateful, but being sorry didn't make him give up about Tommy. "Rosy, listen to me. Trilby wants Tommy to celebrate their anniversary. Their *one-week* anniversary. This is truly a sad comedown for a man and a Geiger. Please say you'll talk some sense into him."

"I can't." For what if Tommy got the idea that she cared one way or the other? Which she didn't, of course.

"That's your final answer?"

"Yes."

"All right, then. I didn't want to do this, but you've forced my hand," he said, then called to the football players hanging around Hound. "Jorge, come here!"

One of the largest of the group lumbered over. "What's up?"

"Tell Rosalind she must talk to Tommy about the Trilby situation."

"You must talk to Tommy about the Trilby situation," said Jorge from his great height.

"Thanks." Nick sent Jorge away, then called over another colossus. "Lachlan, you're next!"

Rosalind put up her hands in surrender. "Okay, Nick, you've won." She knew he was capable of parading every one of the football players in front of her until she broke down.

"Excellent," said Nick, waving off Lachlan. "Now, Rosy, promise that you'll talk to Tommy about Trilby."

"Under duress, I promise"—she said, glaring—"that I'll talk to Tommy about Trilby. Happy now?"

"Delighted. I'm counting on your famous Penderwick Family Honor to make you put forth your best effort." He jammed his helmet back on. "Say something in Russian to him. He likes that."

"The only Russian I know is *nyet,* for 'no.' "

"That'll do. Just talk to him." Nick turned and faced his team. "Break over! Forward, men!"

The line of football players took up their chanting again—"C-H-S! C-H-S!"—and pounded off down the path. When the last of them was gone and their noise had faded into the distance, Rosalind and Hound looked over the stone wall, and found Batty and Ben contentedly curled up together on a pile of leaves.

"It was only Nick and his friends," Rosalind told them. "Nothing to be afraid of."

"We weren't, were we, Ben?"

Ben yawned and beat his fists together.

"That means he agrees with me."

"I think it means he's hungry." Rosalind picked Ben up and nestled him in her arms. What a comfort he was. "Let's take him home."

Batty climbed into the wagon, and the little group set off down the path. It was more trampled than when they'd come, for the football players had not gone through gently. The leaves were smashed, their lovely rustle flattened out of them, and here and there tree branches had been snapped off by linebackers with extra-wide shoulders. Quigley Woods had not been improved by rough-terrain training, and Rosalind had to wonder if the football team would be, either. Nick's coaching theories were often like that— possibly brilliant and also possibly half-baked. What about his other theory, that Rosalind should discuss Trilby with Tommy? Definitely half-baked. Tommy hated being told what to do, a natural result of living with bossy Nick all his life. This talking-to was not going to be pleasant.

When they reached Iantha's house, Rosalind brushed off the leaves and dirt that Ben had accumulated in Quigley Woods. This was the first time she'd had Ben on her own, and she wanted to bring him back in good condition. For extra measure, she brushed off Batty, too, and then Hound, and then herself, and only then did she ring the doorbell.

When Iantha opened the door, she was holding a red pen and had several more stuck behind her ears and in the pocket of her shirt.

"Are we interrupting?" asked Rosalind. She'd taken the little ones away to give Iantha a break, and to make up for all the afternoons Batty spent at her house, causing who knew how much chaos. "Did we come back too soon?"

"No, your timing is just right. I keep getting annoying phone calls from a disgruntled ex-colleague, and when I haven't been arguing with him, I've been going insane reading my students' papers. Apparently several of them think the Hubble Space Telescope is used to search the universe for hubbles. Come in, come in."

Hound settled on the step beside the red wagon, hoping for a glimpse of his friend Asimov, and the rest of them went inside. It still felt strange for Rosalind to do so, as the previous owners had been unsociable people, especially when it came to children. Her few memories of the house were of a gray, dusty place with the blinds always drawn. It was nothing like that now that it was Iantha's. All the walls were pale green or ivory, and there were no blinds at all, just gauzy curtains pulled back to let in the light. And it smelled nice, like—Rosalind sniffed—oranges, maybe?

While Iantha took Ben and Batty into the kitchen to get snacks, Rosalind wandered across the living room to look at a display of family photographs. There were several of Ben—as a chubby infant with just a dusting of red hair, as a chubby six-month-old with his funny grin already in full force, as a not quite so chubby one-year-old—and then there was one of Iantha holding hands with a tall blond man. Rosalind leaned closer to see it better.

"My husband, Dan." Iantha was back with Batty and Ben and a plate of oatmeal cookies and—oh—orange slices.

"I'm sorry," said Rosalind. "I didn't mean to snoop."

"You didn't. Here, eat something."

"He was handsome."

"Yes, and even smarter than he was handsome. Do you know how he died? A drunk driver crashed into his car. It was six months before Ben was born," said Iantha. "That's the part I mind the most, that he never met Ben."

"Do you—" Rosalind wasn't quite sure how to ask. "Do you get used to it?"

"Yes." Iantha smiled. "After a while."

Ben and Batty drifted across the room to the window, where they whispered together while Asimov wove through their legs. Rosalind feared another Bug Man sighting, but when Batty did spot someone a few moments later, it turned out to be worse than Bug Man.

"It's Tommy! Tommy's home!" she called out. "Rosalind!"

"I heard you, Batty," she answered, glad that the window was closed, or Tommy would have heard her, too, even from all the way across the street.

"Nice boy, Tommy. Good-looking, too," said Iantha. "I think both the Geiger boys are. I do remember from my younger days, though, that adults never seemed to get that stuff right. What do you think?"

"They're okay, I guess." Rosalind had never paid much attention to the Geigers' looks. "Mostly they're just annoying, especially today. Nick made me promise to talk to Tommy about something that I don't want to talk to him about, and Tommy won't want to talk to me about it, either. It's going to be a disaster. How do you even start a conversation like that?"

"Do you want to practice? Pretend I'm Tommy."

Rosalind squinted at Iantha, trying to make her look like Tommy, but it was impossible. No one had that much imagination. "I don't know."

"Does this help?" Iantha took a lampshade from a nearby lamp and put it on her head. "Now I'm Tommy in a football helmet. Say 'Hello, Tommy' and go from there."

"Hello, Tommy. I want—" Rosalind couldn't get any further without laughing.

"Rosy, you're not concentrating."

"I am!" she protested, laughing harder.

Attracted by the laughter, Batty and Ben left their window and came over to watch their elders. Having an audience didn't help Rosalind gather her thoughts, and when Asimov made a flying leap from a chair to knock the lampshade off Iantha's head, Rosalind gave up altogether and surrendered to hysteria.

"Maybe I should just go see Tommy now and get it over with," she said when she could catch her breath.

"Are you sure?" asked Iantha. "We could practice more."

"Please, no more practicing."

"Good luck, then. You'll be great."

"And I'll go with you, Rosalind," said Batty. "Tommy is my good friend."

Discussing Trilby was going to be difficult enough without Batty chiming in. "Not this time, Battikins."

"Why not?"

"Batty, dear, stay here with me and Ben while Rosalind visits Tommy," said Iantha.

"But why?"

"Because sometimes older sisters want to be alone with people, without younger sisters around."

This set off a series of additional questions from Batty, which Iantha gracefully took on, giving Rosalind the chance to slip away unnoticed. She crossed the street to the Geigers' house, headed round to the back, and knocked on the kitchen door, just as she'd done a thousand times before. This time, though, it wasn't a Geiger who opened the door, but Brendan, one of Tommy's football buddies. Rosalind had already had her fill of football players that afternoon, and then it got worse, for when she stepped inside, she saw that Tommy hadn't brought home just Brendan. The kitchen was crammed full of boys—Simon, Josh, Kalim, Hong, Byron, and Jack—and the food they were consuming. Every horizontal surface was covered with milk cartons, blocks of cheese, cold pizza, fruit or its remains, jars of who knew what, and loaf upon loaf of bread.

"Hey, Rosy, you want a sandwich?" Tommy flapped a peanut butter sandwich at her from the other side of the room.

"No, thanks. Actually, I need to talk to you."

"Okay." He finished his sandwich and grabbed another.

"I mean, without them."

Brendan hooted obnoxiously, but Rosalind withered him with regal disregard. The rest of the boys, not wanting to be similarly withered, cleared a path to

170

Tommy and let her push him and his sandwich out into the hall.

"Hello, Tommy. I—" Now what? She realized, too late, that she had needed practice, after all. Stalling, she looked him over, one old friend surveying another. "You've grown a few inches."

"I know."

"Still too skinny, though."

"I know that, too." He shoved the rest of the sandwich into his mouth. "Sure you don't want anything to eat?"

"Yes, I'm sure, thank you."

"Then what do you want?" Tommy asked, most reasonably.

For a fleeting second or two, she considered asking him to put a lampshade on his head. Oh, just plunge in! "I want—"

Somewhere upstairs the phone rang. Tommy strode across the hall and shouted up the steps, "Mom, don't answer it!"

But Mrs. Geiger must not have heard him, for a moment later she came down holding the receiver. "Why, Rosy, how nice to see you with your bright cheeks. I swear you just keep getting prettier all the time."

"Mom?" Tommy pointed to the phone.

"Oh, yes, honey, it's Trilby again." Mrs. Geiger handed over the phone, and with a wave for Rosalind, went back upstairs.

171

Rosalind stared at the ceiling while Tommy was on the phone, doing her best not to listen, though since Trilby seemed to be doing all the talking, there wasn't much to hear. After a dozen or so nonspecific grunts, Tommy hung up and turned sheepishly to Rosalind. Now she knew how to begin.

"So that was Trilby. Does she call often?"

"I guess so."

"That must be annoying."

"Not necessarily," he answered, suddenly as stone-faced as Mount Rushmore, as Rosalind later told Anna.

"Oh, sure it is," she said, rushing on despite Tommy's lack of encouragement. "That and the cheering at football practice, the whole one-week-anniversary thing, and, well, et cetera. It must be driving you crazy."

"Et cetera?"

"You know, blah, blah, blah."

He folded his arms, and looked even more Mount Rushmore–ish. "Are you jealous?"

"Jealous of Trilby?" She was astonished at his stupidity. "*Nyet! Nyet, nyet, nyet, nyet.*"

"Then what business is it of yours?"

"None. You're right, absolutely none. Why should I care about what you do? That's what I told Nick, but he—"

"Nick? You and Nick have been talking about me?

172

The great and perfect Rosalind and my great and perfect big brother have been deciding what's best for me?" Tommy stomped around in a circle and came back to glower at her. "Now *that* drives me crazy!"

When pushed—and Rosalind was definitely feeling pushed—she could glower as well as anyone, and the glowering bouncing around that afternoon was truly frightening. As neither combatant had any intention of backing down, they could have been there for hours if Simon hadn't wandered out into the hall.

"Geiger, you're out of peanut butter," he said, then ducked, for all the glowering was suddenly turned onto him. "Never mind."

Simon disappeared, and Rosalind found that she was out of glowers and out of words, too. She'd been an idiot to start this, an idiot to promise Nick, an idiot all around.

"I'm sorry, Tommy," she said.

"Fine." He, at least, had plenty of glowering left in him.

"I'll leave now."

"Also fine."

Going back through that kitchen full of boys was impossible, so this time Rosalind took the front door. Despite good intentions, she slammed it on the way out.

CHAPTER FOURTEEN
Grilled Cheese Sandwiches

J ANE DIDN'T BELIEVE in having tragic days. She'd never made Sabrina Starr have a tragic day, or Rainbow, either, except for the day when the priest almost cut out her heart. But the priest *didn't* cut out her heart, and the rest of Rainbow's day after that was just perfect, with everyone treating her like a great hero and Coyote finally realizing it was her that he adored.

So why was Jane having a tragic day? She'd been trying with all her might not to, but first there'd been watching Skye leave for Boston with Churchie, when it should have been Skye watching Jane leave for Boston, and it would have been if it hadn't been for Rainbow and her noble attitude toward sacrifice. Jane believed now, though she hadn't when she was writing the play, that Rainbow's attitude might be too noble. She'd decided that she preferred Sabrina Starr's slightly less noble outlook on life—and promised herself that the next time there was a Hound Draw for Order, she would listen to Sabrina Starr, not Rainbow.

Then after the dreaded leave-taking, there'd been the soccer game against the worst team in the league. What should have been an easy victory—even without Skye—had been a 1–0 loss. And who had missed two easy goals for Antonio's Pizza? The same girl who'd felt so sorry for herself that she'd declined going out for pizza with the rest of the team after the game. Who was this sad soul?

"Jane Letitia Penderwick," said Jane to her bedroom ceiling. "Now lying alone on her bed and wallowing in misery."

She wondered what Skye was doing right at that moment. She and Churchie would already have arrived in Boston. Maybe they were eating lunch with Jeffrey at a glamorous restaurant. Maybe—Jane couldn't help but hope—Jeffrey had been the littlest bit disappointed that it was Skye who had come to visit. She reached under her bed and pulled out a blue notebook and pen, and wrote:

"Jeffrey, Jeffrey, I'm so happy to be with you at last," *said Skye.*

"Thank you." Jeffrey turned away to hide his sorrow.

"But what is this? Aren't you glad to see me?"

"Of course I am, dear Skye." He turned back to her, his face ablaze with honesty. "But it is your beautiful and talented sister, Jane, whom I prefer."

"Ha," said Jane, scribbling violently over what she'd written. "Like anyone would say that about me."

What should she do? She couldn't just lie here all day. Was she desperate enough to clean? Even to her jaded eyes, her half of the room looked dreadful. Reluctantly, she got off her bed and wandered around, pushing stuff hither and yon. Each time she pushed, she found herself closer to her desk, where the book she'd been reading, *The Exiles in Love*, just happened to be lying open. I won't look at it until I've straightened up, she told herself, but somehow, she looked at it anyway, and soon she was sinking to her bed, lost in the story, which all too quickly came to an end. Jane closed the book and put it back on her bookshelf. She hated finishing one of her favorite books, because she knew she'd have to wait at least a few months before she could read it again. It was a rule she'd imposed on herself after reading *The Various* twice in one week— a disaster, like eating three large slices of chocolate cake at one sitting.

So what to read now? Certainly not the book she'd been assigned for school, a novel about George Washington's winter at Valley Forge. A history lesson disguised as a story, Jane sniffed. She ran her fingers lightly along the books on the shelves, and the books in piles, and the books on the floor, but for once none of them seemed just right. She drifted over to the window. It was bright and beautiful outside, with fluffy clouds cruising across the sky and a crazy quilt of fallen leaves covering the ground.

Soon it will be Halloween, thought Jane. Maybe she should spend the rest of the day working on a costume to wear. Last year she'd been Sabrina Starr, in a dark cape covered with silver stars. That had been delightful. This year she could be . . . but she couldn't think of anything.

"Even my imagination has deserted me," she said, squashing her nose against the window.

She stood there until at last she grew tired of being pathetic and lonely, and left her room in search of a sister to talk to, any sister at all. The only person she could find was her father, in his study grading papers.

"Where is everyone?" she asked.

"Rosalind is at Anna's house, and Batty is next door with Ben and Iantha," he answered. "I, however, am right here. What can I do for you?"

"I'm not sure."

"You think about it and let me know."

While her father went back to his grading, Jane leaned against the desk and poked around among his books. Most of them were about botany, with names like *Magnoliophyta: Caryophyllidae, Part 1*. Jane shuddered. If she was ever stuck on a desert island with only these books to read, she'd have to give up reading altogether. At the bottom of the pile, she found one that wasn't about botany. It had an orange spine, and on the cover were two young women in old-fashioned clothes.

"*Sense and Sensibility.* Are you reading this, Daddy?"

He looked up, startled, then took the book from her and slipped it into a drawer. "Here and there, yes. It was one of your mother's favorites."

Sense and Sensibility wasn't as bad as *Magnoliophyta: Caryophyllidae, Part 1,* but it was still a boring title. In Jane's opinion, this was true of the titles of most grown-up books. None of them were ever as fascinating as, say, *Emily of New Moon* or *The Phantom Tollbooth*—a good reason not to grow up quickly. But she was too polite to criticize her father's book, especially if her mother had liked it.

She turned now to a stack of her father's mail. It was sure to be as dull as the books—only bills and scientific bulletins. But there was something different. An elegant invitation to a gala event at Cameron University, to celebrate the opening of a new science wing.

"Why, here's Iantha's name," she said. "She's giving a speech."

"She's representing the astrophysics department. If you read farther down the list, you'll see that I'm representing the botany department."

There it was: *Dr. Martin Penderwick*. "How exciting, Daddy. If you want help writing your speech, just let me know. And look, the invitation is for you and one other person. Have you decided who you'll take with you?"

"It's weeks away still."

"Marianne, maybe?"

Her father took the invitation and put it into the drawer with the book. "Jane, love, have you put any thought into going outside and getting some fresh air?"

"No." She glanced out the window, though. It wasn't any less bright and beautiful than before.

"You could rake some leaves. That's always fun."

"Not doing it alone, it's not."

"Then go find someone to do it with. Maybe Tommy or Nick."

"Nick!"

"Well, Tommy, then. Go now," he said. "*Nunc, celeriter.* Quickly."

So Jane wandered out of the house and across the street, where she found Mrs. Geiger in her garden, gazing mournfully at a squashed plant.

"Hello, Mrs. Geiger," said Jane. "It's a pretty day, isn't it?"

"It would be a prettier day if someone hadn't stomped on my chrysanthemums." She poked at the plant, looking for some life. "Some advice, Jane? If you want your flowers to bloom, don't let your sons play football."

"I'm not going to have any sons. Great writers need their privacy."

"As do chrysanthemums."

"Yes." Jane didn't think it was the same thing at all. "Do you know where Tommy is?"

"In the garage, dear."

Jane went in through the side door of the garage, or, as Nick liked to call it, Geigers' Gym. That past summer he and Tommy had pooled their grass-cutting money to buy training equipment, and set it all up in here. She found Tommy lifting a bar loaded with what seemed to Jane a great deal of weight.

"You're getting really strong," she said, wondering if in her next Sabrina Starr book, she should have Sabrina lift weights to build up her already impressive strength.

Tommy did one last lift, then put the bar back onto its rest. "Only one guy on the team can press more than I do, and he's a defensive lineman with a *D* average. Hold the bag for me, will you?"

He meant the punching bag—a large gray one, almost as big as Jane herself—hanging from a hook in the ceiling. As Tommy strapped himself into boxing gloves, Jane wrapped her arms around the bag and braced herself. Still, she wasn't prepared for how she was rocked around when he started pounding at it. Tommy really was quite strong, she thought. He would make a good hero in a book. Or a play.

"Maybe I'll be a boxer for Halloween this year," she said admiringly when he stopped and she could breathe again.

"Boxers wear shorts. You'd be cold."

Jane didn't like being cold. Then she had a better idea. "I could be a football player! Oh, Tommy! Will you lend me one of your old uniforms?"

"Sure." He hit the body bag several more times. "What's Rosy gonna be?"

"I don't know," said Jane, busily picturing herself in shoulder pads, doing that do-si-do thing that Nick had taught them. Side step, side step, forward run, turn around, side step, side step. "What about you?"

"Trilby's got it all worked out." He hit the bag again, even harder. "I'm going to be Superman, and she's going to be Lois Lane. I agreed on the condition that we go trick-or-treating only in her neighborhood."

"You won't be on Gardam Street?" Jane couldn't imagine Halloween without Tommy.

"Do you really think I'd show my face in my own neighborhood dressed in tights and a cape?" He hit the bag so hard Jane was almost knocked off her feet. "Ros—people would laugh at me for the rest of my life."

"Well, then, stay here and be something normal that doesn't include capes."

Moodily Tommy swung at the bag and missed.

181

Jane was getting frustrated with him—certainly this was no way for a hero to behave.

"You're not going to get her by moping around, you know," she said, abruptly letting go of the bag.

"Get who?"

"You know who. She needs action and valor. All girls do."

"Like that Cagney gave her, you mean?" Tommy tried to sneer when he said "Cagney," but instead looked pitiful. "What do you know, anyway? You're only ten."

"I'm a writer. Writers understand human emotions."

"Hooey," he said.

"Hooey yourself." She felt tears pricking her eyelids. "Go be Superman, then. I'm sure you'll do very well on some street that isn't Gardam Street. And certainly I, who am only ten, won't miss you."

She ran back across the street to grab the rake from her garage, realizing too late that she'd forgotten to ask Tommy if he wanted to help. But who wanted to rake leaves with a phoney Superman, anyway? Abandoning herself to the relief of tears, she pushed the leaves this way, then that way, then another, trying to build a big enough pile to crawl under. She was crying too hard to manage even that, though, so finally she simply lay down and pulled a few leaves over her face, and cried and cried until there were no more tears, but still she lay there, thinking that maybe she would stay forever, moldering along with the worms and the leaves, and at least she would help the lawn grow.

Moldering on Gardam Street turned out to be difficult. Before even one worm appeared, the leaves were being tossed aside by someone large and black, and then that same someone was licking her face.

"Oh, Hound," Jane said. It was nice to be looked for, even if only by a dog.

But it wasn't only a dog. When Hound finished cleaning her face, Jane sat up and saw that Iantha was there, too, with Batty hanging on to one of her hands and Ben the other, both in their secret-agent glasses.

"Are you all right?" asked Iantha.

"We thought you were dying," said Batty.

"Not dying, exactly. Just—" Iantha paused politely.

"Miserable," Jane finished for her.

"Yes, I thought you might be miserable, and wondered if a grilled cheese sandwich could help. We were just about to make some."

"With chocolate milk," added Batty.

To Jane's surprise, a grilled cheese sandwich with chocolate milk was exactly what she wanted right then, and by the time they were all back in Iantha's kitchen, her unhappiness was starting to lift. Then Iantha somehow burnt the grilled cheese sandwiches, and though Jane swore she liked them that way—and Batty and Ben were too busy smearing cheese on each other to care—Iantha was so apologetic that Jane decided to take her mind off it. So she talked about Skye going to Boston, the dreadful soccer game, and Tommy's boorishness, and Iantha was such a good listener that soon Jane was telling her about the Save-Daddy Plan and how worried Rosalind was.

"You're not worried?" asked Iantha.

"I suppose so, but not as much as Rosalind. She's worried beyond measure."

"Poor Rosalind."

Jane finished the last of her chocolate milk. "Too bad you're not awful, because you'd be a convenient date for Daddy, though Rosalind did say we shouldn't use anyone on Gardam Street because of the discomfort. You have no idea how much trouble we've had trying to find awful women."

Iantha smiled. Jane thought she was extra pretty when she smiled, like . . . who? Who did Iantha remind her of? The poor French governess in *The Enchanted Castle*, perhaps. She wondered briefly if Iantha spoke French.

Now Iantha's phone rang, and when she went into another room to answer it, Jane entertained herself by looking around the kitchen. It was nothing like the kitchen at home. It was warm and cozy like home, true, but it was also messy—delightfully so, thought

Jane—and it didn't look as though lots of cooking went on there. There was a laptop computer on the counter with duck stickers on it, the spice cabinet was full of Ben's toy trucks, and Jane couldn't spot a cookbook anywhere. This is the kitchen of a Thinker, she decided, and promised herself that she'd never bother with cooking, either.

Jane had been taught not to listen to private phone conversations, so when Iantha's voice in the other room got louder, she tried not to overhear. Ben and Batty were also trying not to hear by putting their hands over their ears, but Jane suspected that they were more concerned with the anger in Iantha's voice than with good manners. Iantha's voice was quite angry.

"No, Norman, that isn't appropriate," she was saying. "Keep this up and I'll have to report you. I'm hanging up now, Norman. Oh! *He* hung up on *me*!"

There was the crash of a phone being thrown to the floor, and Iantha strode back into the room. Her eyes were flashing, and Jane was sure her hair was curlier, perhaps electrified with anger. Ben took his hands from his ears.

"Duck," he said.

"Yes, darling." She picked him up and patted his back. "Jane, I'm sorry you had to hear me arguing. That Norman is a delusional ex-colleague who keeps accusing me of stealing his research, and no matter

185

how many times I explain that his research is so flawed no one would ever steal it—oops, sorry again."

"I don't mind. I'm used to temper, living with Skye."

"You're very kind," said Iantha. "Let's do something fun to make up for Norman. Batty, should we go on with our experiment?"

The experiment turned out to be an attempt to convince Asimov that dogs weren't evil creatures, and that Hound, in particular, could even be a friend. Iantha and Batty had been at it for a few weeks now, and had a chart on the side of the refrigerator to measure their progress. They'd worked slowly and systematically, first letting Hound into the front hall for two minutes while Asimov was safely locked in the second-floor bathroom, then letting Hound into the living room for five minutes while Asimov was in the second-floor bathroom, but with the door open, and so on. So far there had been no violent chases or battles, and today Iantha and Batty were ready for a big step—having Hound in the living room while Asimov was in the kitchen. Same floor, no restraints.

With a great deal of laughter and cajoling, Iantha and Batty dragged Asimov off his favorite pile of towels, carried him downstairs, and plopped him onto the kitchen counter. While Iantha and Ben guarded him, Jane and Batty opened the front door and invited Hound in, warning him with dire threats that if he didn't behave himself, his end was nigh. Eagerly he trotted in, and though he clearly knew where Asimov was—his nose pointed unerringly toward the kitchen—he settled down and lasted five whole minutes without once trying to leave the room. Iantha shouted "Time!" from the kitchen, and Jane and Batty took Hound back outside, and everyone congratulated each other heartily.

Now Jane realized that she'd been there for a long time. Her father might be wondering where she'd gone. "We'd better be going home," she said.

"And your misery?" asked Iantha.

"Vanished, thank you," said Jane, hugging Iantha good-bye without thinking first whether she should.

She floated home happily with Batty and Hound and, when she got there, discovered even more happiness. On the front step was a paper bag with JANE written across the front, and a battered helmet balanced on top.

"Oh, Batty, I'm going to be a football player for Halloween! Isn't that fabulous?"

"It's not as good as a dinosaur." Batty was a different dinosaur every year.

"That might be true for any old football player," said Jane. "But this one is much better than a dinosaur. You'll see."

CHAPTER FIFTEEN
Batty's Spying Mission

BY SUNDAY MORNING, Rosalind had picked out a sonnet to memorize for English class. Lying on her bed, she murmured the opening lines to herself.

> No, Time, thou shalt not boast that I do change:
> Thy pyramids built up with newer might
> To me are nothing novel, nothing strange;
> They are but dressings of a former sight.

Yes, that would work. No one would understand a word of what she was saying, let alone think she was talking about love. Still, though, she had a problem. It wasn't enough just to recite the poem—her teacher wanted her to recite with expression. And since she barely understood the poem herself, she didn't know

188

what expression to use. Solemn? Hushed, like she was imparting great wisdom to the other seventh graders? Like she could do that without looking silly!

Well, what then? Singsongy?

" 'No, TIME, thou shalt not BOAST that I do CHANGE.' " She stopped, appalled. Absolutely not singsongy.

She'd have to ask Anna for guidance. Anna had no such problems with her own poem, for she'd signed up for Lewis Carroll and *Jabberwocky*, which really *did* make no sense, and so could be recited any way the reciter wanted. And it was absolutely, definitely, not about love. Lucky Anna.

Rosalind closed her Shakespeare book and stood up. Yes, she'd go over to Anna's house to work on poem recitation. No one needed her right now—Daddy was home to watch Batty, Skye was still in Boston, and the last time she'd seen Jane, she was doing football drills by herself. This would be the perfect time to leave—she'd just have to find her father and make certain.

She found him in the kitchen, talking on the phone. Jane was there, too, doing deep knee bends.

Aunt Claire, she mouthed silently to Rosalind, pointing to their father.

Even if Jane hadn't told her, it would soon have been obvious who was on the other end of the phone.

"No, I don't need another blind date," he was saying. "Yes, I'm still dating Marianne. . . . This afternoon, as a matter of fact. . . . Yes, and it will be the second date. . . . Fabulous indeed, and suddenly I've remembered that it's actually a lunch date, and as it is almost lunchtime, I need to say good-bye and get ready to go."

He hung up the phone with a bang. "Here's some advice, daughters. Try to avoid having younger sisters."

"Too late for that, Daddy," said Jane.

"Right, of course. *Nemo mortalium omnibus horis sapit.* Or, in my case, not even frequently. Do not fret, my Rosy, for I'll translate it for you. 'No mortal is wise at all times.' "

"I'm not fretting." But Rosalind was fretting dreadfully, so much so that her hands were shaking. Since they'd gotten through most of the weekend without even a mention of a date, Rosalind had let herself hope that Marianne was gone from their lives. She'd even started to reconsider Valaria—the former Mary Magdalene, among others—as a possible blind-date candidate, maybe for that gala event at Cameron University in a few weeks. But now, without warning, the mysterious Marianne was back.

"You're going out, Daddy?" asked Jane.

"Yes, I'm taking Marianne to lunch, and I have to leave"—he glanced at his watch—"in fifteen minutes. Rosalind, do you mind being in charge for an hour or so?"

190

She minded very much. It didn't matter about not going over to Anna's house—Shakespeare could wait. But it mattered a great deal about this second date. A second date got one perilously close to a third, and then a fourth, and then how long would it be before that terrifying downhill slide to a stepmother?

"No, we'll be fine," she said.

"Good. You're my angels. And now—I'm off to primp and preen."

When he was gone, Rosalind threw herself into a chair. This was a nightmare. She said so to Jane.

"Well, Daddy certainly is acting oddly," said Jane, doing one last knee bend, then sitting down, too. "Could Skye be right about him going bonkers? But maybe she's wrong about it being the stress of dating. Could Daddy be driven mad by love? How long does it take grown-ups to fall in love, anyway?"

"I don't know; I don't know anything." Rosalind rested her forehead on the table. It was an uncomfortable position, which made it appropriate for the moment. "I don't even know anything about Marianne, except that she doesn't like flannel and does like going on walks."

"And that she's not listed in the phone book," said Jane. "No Marianne Dashwood anywhere around here."

"You looked in the phone book?" Rosalind lifted her head, impressed with Jane's ingenuity.

"Skye and I did one day, to give ourselves a break from rehearsing *Sisters and Sacrifice,* and we even called the phone company to make sure. We can't find a trace of her anywhere. Do you think she's an ex-con in the Witness Protection Program?"

"Probably not." Though the idea cheered Rosalind up slightly. Her father would never go so far as to marry an ex-con. "Listen, Jane, if Daddy's going to keep dating this woman, we have to find out something about her, or even—yuck—meet her. We can't fight against an unknown."

"A secret, a mirage, a will-o'-the-wisp." Jane swayed back and forth and waved her arms like she thought a will-o'-the-wisp would, but really it was more like Sirens on the rocks.

"So how do we do it?"

"Let me think." Jane stopped being a Siren and tried to come up with a plan.

But she couldn't. And neither could Rosalind, who said, "We'll just have to start asking Daddy questions."

"Tough, incisive questions, until he reveals all."

"Yes, we'll be tough!" Rosalind brightened up. "When Skye gets back from Boston, we'll make sure she's tough, too."

"Do or die?"

"For the Penderwick Family Honor."

And they shook on it.

Later, Batty tried to blame it all on Hound. And it was true that if he hadn't fallen asleep in the middle of hide-and-seek, she wouldn't have been stuck waiting for him in the kitchen broom closet. And if she hadn't been in the broom closet, she wouldn't have overheard the conversations that took place in the kitchen, especially the one between Rosalind and Jane.

She couldn't deny, however, that the actual stowing away in her father's car was her own idea. In fact, when she tried to load blankets—for hiding under—into the back of the car, Hound, now quite awake, grabbed hold of them, and no matter how hard Batty pulled, he wouldn't let go.

"You have to let me take these blankets," she said. "I'm going to hide under them and spy on Marianne for Rosalind and Jane. They're going to be impressed."

Hound, on the other hand, wasn't impressed. Maybe he knew that Rosalind wouldn't approve of such a scheme, or maybe he simply didn't believe in stowing away in cars. He took a firmer hold on the blankets.

Batty was desperate, for her father was going to show up at any moment. One blanket would have to do. In a sneak attack, she threw one over Hound's head, and he let go of the other one, as she'd figured he would. She grabbed it, leapt into the car, and closed the door, then watched out the window while he bucked and tossed until the blanket fell off. Free now, Hound whipped this way and that, searching for Batty. When he figured out where she was, he threw himself at the car, barking hysterically.

Batty tried burrowing under the one blanket she'd brought, hoping that would discourage him, but having her out of sight only made him bark louder. She huffed with annoyance—real secret agents didn't have dogs that gave away hiding places. Beaten, she opened the door again and told Hound to climb in. He whined and pawed the ground for a while, but when he realized that he had to go with her or let her go alone, he leapt in, dragging his blanket along.

"But we're being secret agents," she said, shoving him to the floor of the car and covering him. "So you must be quiet."

"Woof."

Now there was nothing to do but get into her car seat, fasten her seatbelt, cover herself, and wait. And think that if she brought back really good information about Marianne, maybe Rosalind would stop worrying so much about Daddy. Batty wanted it back the old way, when Rosalind was happier and never missed story time because she was on the phone talking about her worries with Anna, and then Daddy had to do story time instead, and he wasn't as good at the voices.

At last Batty heard her father opening the car door. She sunk down low under her blanket and nudged Hound with her foot to remind him to be quiet. But what was this? Daddy was walking away again. Where was he going? She waited and waited, and then, just before losing all hope, heard him coming back. This time he got in, and the engine came on, and the radio, and then the car was moving, and Batty was off on her first spying mission away from Gardam Street! She wished Ben were there. She'd have to tell him all about it later, and he would be amazed at her daring.

On and on they drove. Too soon Batty realized that she was hungry, and she hadn't brought along anything to eat, even cookies. Probably real secret agents had people who packed cookies for them to take along on their missions. To make things worse, it was hot hiding under the blanket. And dark, especially with her sunglasses on. She felt Hound stirring at her feet, but he kept quiet, and that gave her the courage to keep quiet, too, at least until a stray dog hair tickled her nose and she sneezed. Horrified, she clamped her hand to her mouth, but too late. Daddy must have heard her. But no, he only turned up the radio and kept on driving.

It was only when the car finally stopped that Batty realized this wasn't the best-planned mission. Her father could leave her locked in the car for hours while he visited with Marianne. Hound was grumbling—she was sure he was saying that he told her so—and she was getting more hungry all the time. What should she do?

For some reason, her father wasn't getting out of the car. He seemed to be just sitting in the front seat, still listening to the radio. And then he rolled his window down. Batty could tell, because drifting into the car came the most amazingly delicious smell. Oh! Oh! It was pizza! If Batty had been hungry before, now she was so hungry she thought she could die of it. Spying was terrible work. How did real secret agents do it?

Then her father started to talk. "Imagine that. I've parked right in front of Antonio's Pizza. I wish I had someone to share a pineapple pizza with me."

Now, of all the pizzas in the world, Batty's favorite was pineapple. Especially from Antonio's, where they put on lots of extra pineapple and extra cheese, so that the pieces of pineapple sank down into the cheese, and the cheese got all crispy around the sweet pineapple—oh! Her father started making the *mmm-mmm* sounds that people make when they're thinking about really special food, and Batty knew then that even if her mission failed, and Rosalind and Jane were not impressed with her, and Daddy got angry—even if all of that happened, she had to have some pineapple pizza. She threw aside her blanket.

"Daddy, it's me!"

196

"What a lovely surprise," he said, not at all angry, or much surprised, either.

"Hound is here, too, on the floor." She threw aside his blanket, too.

"Of course he is, for whither you go, there he usually is, too. Let's go get some pizza."

Since Antonio's was crowded that day, they had a picnic in the car, almost as big a treat as the pizza itself, and Batty spilled hardly anything, except for one piece of pineapple that got smashed on the floor of the car and never would come out again. When everyone had eaten their fill, even Hound, who was given the leftover crusts, and Mr. Penderwick had wiped down Batty with lots of napkins, he said, "Now we must talk seriously. Did you tell Rosalind you were stowing away?"

"No, it was a secret."

"So you didn't consider how worried she would be when she discovered you were missing?"

Batty pictured Rosalind frantically searching everywhere. "Maybe we should call her up and tell her I'm safe."

"Actually, I left a note for her before we left home."

"Thank you, Daddy. But how did you know I was in your car?"

"There was no other logical reason for a large mound of blankets to appear in the backseat."

Batty was disappointed. Her hiding skills were not as great as she'd hoped.

"Cheer up," said her father, cleaning one last blob of tomato sauce off her chin. "You'd have fooled me if I weren't so wise and all-knowing. But tell me, why are you here? Running away from home again? More rabbit trouble?"

He was referring to the time she'd run away from Arundel that past summer because she thought she'd murdered one of Cagney's pet rabbits. "No, no rabbits. I'm only here to spy on you—that is, on Marianne. Rosalind and Jane don't know anything about her, and I'm going to find out and tell them and then—" She stopped, suddenly remembering about honor.

"Then what?"

He sounded truly curious, not at all annoyed, and he *was* Daddy, after all. "Well, since they don't understand how you're acting, they wonder if you're going crazy."

"How about you? Do you think I'm going crazy?"

"No."

"How about now?" He made a face with his eyes rolling and his nose scrunched up and his mouth wide open in a loony grin, and Batty shrieked with laughter, and then he was tickling her, and she tried to tickle him, and everyone was laughing, and Hound was barking, and the pizza box and napkins were flying everywhere, until they all ran out of breath and flopped happily back into their seats.

Then her father said, "You want something to tell your sisters about Marianne? How about this: She's

198

sensible and clever, but eager in everything. Her sorrows and joys can have no moderation."

"I don't know that last word."

"Rosalind will. Maybe I'd better have you memorize it."

And so he did, until she could say it all the way through without hesitating.

"—can have no moderation!" she finished on a note of triumph.

"Perfect! And by the way, if your Aunt Claire asks, tell her, too. And you know what, Batty? You and I haven't had an adventure together, just the two of us, for a long time. Let's do that now. Where do you want to go?"

"Oh, Daddy, you know!"

He did know, and that's where they went.

"So where did you go?" asked Rosalind. She and Jane had pounced on Batty as soon as she got home, and dragged her away for questioning.

"First we went to the store for carrots, and then we visited Eleanor and Franklin," said Batty. Eleanor and Franklin were horses that lived on a nearby farm, and Batty had been visiting them with her father for as long as she could remember. "They were glad to see me and Hound, and Eleanor ate most of the carrots, but I picked clover for Franklin, and I told them all about Jeffrey."

"But what about Marianne?" asked Jane.

"She wasn't there."

"We realize that, honey," said Rosalind. "Jane meant, what happened to Daddy's date with Marianne?"

"I don't know."

"Did you hear him call her to cancel? Did he say anything about that?"

"No." Batty's happiness was oozing away. She'd forgotten about the date. What kind of a secret agent was she, anyway? But then she remembered that she hadn't failed altogether. She had the description of Marianne that Daddy had given her. She told the others.

"She's sensible and clever, but eager in everything?" Jane repeated. "Her sorrows, her joys, can have no moderation?"

"It doesn't sound like Daddy," said Rosalind. "Are you sure that's what he said?"

"He made me memorize it."

"Memorize it? Why?" Rosalind turned to Jane. "Does that make any sense to you?"

"No."

"We're in big trouble," said Rosalind.

"Yes, we are," agreed Jane. "Daddy's definitely going nuts."

CHAPTER SIXTEEN
In Between the Stars

Skye RETURNED FROM BOSTON that evening laden with gifts that Jeffrey had sent home for the family. There was a new eyeglasses case for her father.

"So you won't lose your glasses all the time," explained Skye. "I told Jeffrey you'd just lose the case, but he said we could only try."

"Very wise," said Mr. Penderwick, admiring the new case.

For Rosalind, Jeffrey had sent a pair of rose clippers. "For your Fimbriata bush. Oh, and Churchie said to tell you that Cagney's going to start teacher-training classes in January. She thought you'd be pleased."

"I am." Rosalind glowed, remembering long talks

on summer nights about Cagney's teaching, and how nice it had been to talk to a mature man instead of—well, instead of an immature boy.

Skye reached into the gift bag again and pulled out a gigantic bone for Hound, who shoved it under the couch for safekeeping. Next out was a great roll of neckties, which Skye handed to Batty.

"Jeffrey's mother is sending him a tie from every country she and Dexter go to on their honeymoon." Skye paused while everyone shuddered at the idea of Dexter and Mrs. Tifton—no, Dupree!—on a honeymoon, especially a honeymoon that covered lots of countries. "Since Jeffrey doesn't wear ties, he figured you might like to have them."

Batty did like having the ties—she was already smoothing them out and looking at the funny pictures on each. She chose one with tiny Eiffel Towers to drape across Hound's back.

Only Jane was left, but it was obvious to her that the gift bag was now empty, which meant that Jeffrey had sent everyone a present but her. She felt like crying. But did Rainbow cry when the priest pointed the knife at her chest? No. Well, she wouldn't cry, either.

Skye folded up the bag and pulled an envelope out of her back pocket.

"This is for you," she said, giving it to Jane.

Inside the envelope was a piece of sheet music.

The notes were all in pencil, and at the top was a title in Jeffrey's handwriting.

" 'Prelude to Sabrina Starr,' " read Jane without understanding what she was looking at.

"Jeffrey wrote you a piano piece." Skye didn't know she was pouring balm on a badly wounded heart. "If you'd visited instead of me, he would have played it for you. But since you didn't, he sent you the sheet music. I told him you can't read notes, but he sent it, anyway."

"I will learn to read notes!" Jane reverently clasped it to her. He hadn't forgotten her! "I will treasure it always!"

"Where's your present, Skye?" asked Batty.

Skye murmured vaguely, for she didn't want to share her present, yet didn't want to lie about it, either. No one noticed her evasion. They were all otherwise occupied, Mr. Penderwick with hunting for his glasses to put into the new case, Rosalind with actively not thinking about Tommy, Jane with trying to fathom the sweet mysteries of musical notes, and Batty with deciding which of her new ties was her favorite—the one with little tulips, the one with little pagodas, or the one with little cheeses.

Seeing her chance, Skye slipped out of the room and up the stairs. Her weekend in Boston had been wonderful, but she had missed her room, at least until she opened the door and went in. What the heck?—whole piles of Jane's flotsam and jetsam had drifted into Skye's side of the room. Someday she really would put a white line down the middle of the room, she swore it. For now, though, she shoved aside the worst of it, then resolutely turned her back on the mess.

"Now for my present," she said.

It was in her suitcase, wrapped carefully in a nest of tissue paper—a mug emblazoned with the name of Jeffrey's school, WELBORN-HUGHES. Skye gave it a quick polish with her sleeve, then opened her sock drawer, for she was going to hide the mug where no one else would see it, or worse, get any ideas about drinking from it. She wasn't even going to drink from it herself, not ever. She was going to keep it just to help her remember this weekend. Every minute of it—the ride on the subway, when they almost lost Churchie because Jeffrey kept daring Skye to switch cars. Her first-ever taste of potato pancakes, at that tiny delicatessen where Jeffrey ate five bagels with lox and cream cheese. The visit to the Museum of Science, where Jeffrey and Churchie patiently sat with her twice through the show at the planetarium. The pickup game of soccer in the hallway of Jeffrey's dormitory. And hiding with Jeffrey under his bed while his dorm master searched high and low for the rowdies who'd been playing pickup soccer in the hallway. What a perfect weekend it had been, the most perfect imaginable.

She slid the mug under the socks in her bureau, and just in time, too, for as she closed the drawer, Batty arrived with Funty, who was now wearing the Eiffel Tower necktie. Hound followed closely behind, with at least four more neckties trailing off his back.

"I'm enjoying my present very much," said Batty. "Did you tell Jeffrey how I am?"

"Yes." Skye started unpacking the rest of her suitcase.

"Did you tell him about my red wagon and how much Hound and I adore it?"

"Yes." Though not so much about them adoring the wagon as about how annoyingly underfoot it always was.

"Did you tell him about me and Ben spying on Bug Man?"

"Strangely enough, I didn't mention that."

"Did you tell him I'm going to be a dinosaur for Halloween?"

"It's much too early to talk about Halloween. It's a long time from now."

"It's not."

"Yes, it is. Now good night and thanks for stopping by." Skye firmly escorted Batty, Funty, and Hound out of her room and closed the door behind them.

Halloween! Rats on Batty for bringing it up. Skye's wonderful weekend in Boston was now truly over, for she'd just been yanked back into the harshness of real life. Why? Not because of Halloween itself. No, because of what was happening the night after Halloween.

"The Sixth Grade Performance Night," she groaned. She hadn't thought of it once in Boston, but now it was back, its horror undiminished.

Suddenly needing fresh air, Skye grabbed her binoculars, climbed out the window and onto her roof, and gazed woefully out over a dark Gardam Street. What was she going to do about *Sisters and Sacrifice*? She looked up at the moon, but no help was to come from that quarter. Despite what she'd said to Batty, Halloween and the awfulness that came after it weren't that far away at all. The Sixth Grade Performance Night was only two and a half weeks away—actually, nineteen days . . . actually, eighteen days and twenty-three hours—but she could have eighteen years and twenty-three days, and she would never be ready to get up on a stage as Rainbow. She'd already forgotten the lines she'd managed to memorize before she went to Boston, and even if she could re-memorize them, what about *point dramatically upstage* and *embrace Grass Flower* (Melissa!) and *gaze upon Coyote with love* (Pearson!) and *look noble while priests prepare for the sacrifice*?

"Stupid Aztecs. Stupid sacrifices. Stupid play," she said out loud. "Stupid Jane."

Skye knew it was low and cowardly to blame Jane.

It was her own fault, since she'd asked Jane to write the play in the first place. And if Jane wrote such a good play that it was chosen for Sixth Grade Performance Night? That wasn't Jane's fault, either. Just as it wasn't Mr. Geballe's fault that he'd chosen Skye to be Rainbow. Though Mr. Geballe probably was blaming himself for that, now that he was getting headaches at every rehearsal.

She screwed up her face in an imitation of Mr. Geballe with a headache. "Can't you put some emotion into your voice, Skye? Remember, you're about to sacrifice your life for your sister. Try to imagine how that would feel!"

How could she possibly imagine how that would feel? No one she knew had ever been sacrificed. And especially to sacrifice herself for Melissa Patenaude! And that wasn't even the most humiliating part of the play, for in the final scene she had to tell Pearson that he was the only boy she'd ever loved or ever would love, let the maize be her witness. True, she also got to tell him that since she had to devote her life to her people, he should go ahead and marry her beloved sister, Grass Flower, but even that wasn't enough to wipe out the shame.

"Beloved sister. Bah!" Skye glowered through her binoculars at the stars and reconsidered the falling-off-the-roof idea.

However, before she could once again weigh the

207

pluses and minuses of a broken leg, there was a thump beside her, and Asimov appeared out of the darkness, purring and butting his head against her knee.

"Silly cat, why don't you understand that I can't stand you?" she said, rubbing his ears. "Forget about me taking you home again. There aren't any football drills to avoid tonight."

But there was something else to avoid, for moments later Jane was leaning out the window. "Ready to dive back into rehearsals for *Sisters and Sacrifice?*"

"That would be just great, but I have to take Iantha's cat home."

"Maybe when you come back."

"Maybe." Skye hoisted Asimov onto her shoulder and inched her way over to the tree. She'd climbed down this tree a hundred times, but never with a hefty cat along for the ride. Well, maybe he'd scratch her on the way down, startling her so that she'd fall and break her leg without having to do it on purpose. That would solve lots of problems. Asimov wasn't in a scratching mood, though, and Skye made it to the ground with both legs intact.

"It's not too late for you to bite me and cause an infected wound. No one would expect me to be Rainbow with an infected wound," she told Asimov hopefully.

Unfortunately, he wasn't in a biting mood, either, and soon Skye was next door, gloomily unharmed, ringing the doorbell. Iantha opened the door, laden down with Ben in his pajamas.

"Here's Asimov," said Skye. "He was on my roof again."

"Oh, Asimov," said Iantha. "Ben, tell him he's a bad cat."

Ben had other ideas. "Pretty!" he said, pointing at Skye.

"I wish he wouldn't say that," said Skye, putting Asimov down and shooing him into the house.

"But you *are* pretty," said Iantha.

"Please don't," said Skye, then knew she'd been rude. "I'm sorry. I just don't think I am, and I don't care, anyway. I'd rather be amazingly intelligent."

"Martin—your father says that you are."

"He's biased, and I can prove it. What does he say about Batty?"

"That she has untapped creative genius."

"You see? Blindly biased." Skye sighed. How nice it must be for Iantha to already know she was amazingly intelligent. No one could ever force an astrophysics professor to be in an Aztec play.

Iantha must have heard the sigh, for she opened her door wider, inviting Skye to come inside. Which Skye did, for even having to look at Ben in his pajamas was better than going home to play practice.

"Did you have fun in Boston?" asked Iantha. "Jane told me you went to visit your friend Jeffrey."

"I did, thank you." Then, without meaning to, Skye burst out. "I didn't want to come home!"

"Oh, dear."

"Not because I don't like my family or anything, but because I have to star in a play in almost nineteen days, and I'm dreading it."

"The Aztec play," said Iantha. "Jane told me about that, too. She said it's quite well written."

"She *would* say that." Skye looked around for something to kick in frustration, but it's hard to find the right thing to kick in other people's houses. She should go home and kick some of Jane's stuff. "I'm sorry to be so grumpy. I'd better leave."

"Please don't. I have something I want to show you, if you don't mind waiting while I put Ben into his crib."

But Ben was thrusting out his chubby hands at Skye. "Duck," he said.

"Or, better, you can put him into his crib while I set up my something." Iantha plopped Ben into Skye's arms. "His room's at the top of the steps. Come into the backyard when you're done."

Horrified, Skye watched Iantha disappear into another room. She didn't know anything about holding babies. The only one she'd held in all her life was Batty when she was a newborn, and even that had been as seldom as possible, for Batty had always wailed when Skye picked her up. What would she do if Ben started to wail?

Gingerly, she shifted his weight until he rested against her shoulder. He snuggled in and made a gurgling noise that she hoped didn't mean he was throwing up, but when she checked, it seemed to have been a happiness gurgle. So everything was all right thus far, but she still had to get him upstairs without damaging him. Up the steps she crept, holding Ben like a bomb that could go off any second. At the top, she stopped and sagged with relief—they were almost to his room and the end of her responsibility.

His little room was bright blue, with constellations painted on the ceiling in gold and shelves piled high with ducks, big and small and in every color a duck could possibly be. Skye cared only for the crib in the corner, though, and got Ben to it as quickly as she could. Carefully—carefully!—she laid him down beside yet one more duck, a tiny white one who'd been waiting patiently for his master's return.

"Please don't take my dislike of you personally," she told Ben, thrilled to have gotten him into his crib without mishap. "I suppose you can't help being a baby."

He blinked at her, wrapped one fist around the white duck's bill, then closed his eyes. Now what? Skye looked around, lost, then figured that the yellow-and-red-checked quilt draped over the crib rail belonged on Ben, so she unfolded it and spread it over him. And realized that he was already asleep. Without thinking, she leaned over and—what was she doing? She jerked upright and took two steps backward, away from the crib. What insanity had come over her? She'd almost kissed Ben good night!

She turned out his light and ran downstairs, light-hearted despite the near kiss. For she was wildly curious about what Iantha was doing in the backyard. Whatever it was would be interesting. An astrophysicist was incapable of being boring.

Absolutely not boring! Iantha was setting up a telescope, an honest-to-goodness telescope on a tripod and everything. Skye pranced across the yard. "Oh, Iantha!"

"It's not really dark enough at this time of night, especially this close to town, but it'll do for what I want to show you."

"What?" breathed Skye. Not that she cared. Seeing anything at all through a telescope would be fascinating.

Now Iantha was pointing the telescope and adjusting it while looking through the eyepiece. She stood up and gestured for Skye to look.

Skye leaned down and peered in—how beautiful! The whole eyepiece was full of a glowing, glimmering disk.

"Venus," said Iantha. "The Aztecs called it 'Quetzalcoatl,' which means 'feathered serpent.' It was their symbol of death and rebirth."

"The Aztecs." It was the first time in weeks that Skye had been able to say that without a surge of dread. Why hadn't she ever thought about the Aztecs looking up at the sky, just as she did from her roof?

Iantha went on. "I wish I could show you the Pleiades, but they're hiding behind Quigley Woods now, down on the horizon. The Aztecs called them 'Tianquiztli,' and used their position in the sky to figure out when to hold the ritual sacrifices. Though not the sacrifice in your play, which Jane tells me is weather-related."

Skye watched Venus and its shimmering loveliness for a long time, then reluctantly straightened up. "Thank you."

"Does that make you feel better about the play?" asked Iantha.

"No." Skye was sorry to disappoint her. "I really appreciate you trying to help, but it's not actually the Aztecs I mind, it's the acting. And I don't exactly mind acting as much as it terrifies me."

Iantha was staring through her telescope again, moving it this way and that, then adjusting and refocusing. "When I was in the fourth grade, I was supposed to be a flower in my school play. I didn't even have any lines, and I fainted before I had to go on."

Skye tried to picture Iantha as a little girl—a sort of older Ben with long hair and a petal hat—fainting dead away.

"Is it hard to learn how to faint?"

"I think it has to come naturally," said Iantha. "Here, look now."

Skye bent to the telescope. This time there was no glowing planet to see. There was only blackness. "I don't see anything."

"Yes, you do. You're seeing dark matter."

Iantha started to explain, and though Skye understood only bits and pieces, she was enthralled, and wanted it never to stop. Terms swirled around her— 'ether,' and 'void,' and 'flux and flow,' and 'whirling gases,' and 'Big Bang,' and always this 'dark matter' thing, a theory of what filled the vast regions between stars. Then Iantha moved on to her own research, and how she'd discovered something important about dark matter and would soon publish an article about it in a scientific journal, and thus would add to the knowledge of astrophysicists all over the world, who were all trying to understand how the universe began, how it's expanding—

"And how it will end," said Iantha. "I've talked too much."

"No!" What Skye wouldn't give to be able to talk like that! "You were wonderful. And you *have* cheered me up. Who knows—maybe the universe will expand so quickly in the next few weeks that life as we know it will end, and I'll never have to be in the play."

"I suppose we could hope for that," said Iantha.

"I do, I do, I do, I do," answered Skye fervently.

Soon after that, Skye ran home, her terrible load of Aztec anxiety truly lightened. Sure, the universe expansion thing was a long shot. But, really, anything can happen in eighteen days and twenty-three hours—no, twenty-two hours. Anything at all.

CHAPTER SEVENTEEN
Halloween

MANY THINGS DID HAPPEN in the next eighteen days and twenty-two hours. Batty and Iantha brought Hound and Asimov face to face for a full minute without any fights breaking out. Rosalind finished memorizing the Shakespeare sonnet and recited it in class without anyone guessing it might be about love. The Antonio's Pizza soccer team played several games and won them all without Skye losing her temper. Batty got a bloody nose from climbing too high on the jungle gym at Goldie's Day Care, and then again when she tripped over her wagon during a spying mission on Bug Man. Rosalind, tired of cleaning up nosebleeds, told Batty never to spy on or mention Bug Man again. Jane ground out two more essays for Miss Bunda—one about Chinese ecology and one about the Erie Canal—without any mention of Sabrina Starr, though it almost killed her.

But one thing didn't happen—the universe refused to expand quickly enough to force the cancellation of *Sisters and Sacrifice*. Jane, never even hoping for such a rescue, dedicated herself to helping Skye survive the nightmare. Every afternoon she attended play rehearsals, taking copious notes for Skye, and every evening she went over the notes, and then Skye's lines, again and again and again—until Skye was reciting them in her sleep. She was still a terrible actress, but Mr. Geballe was no longer getting headaches during rehearsals.

And, oh, yes, another thing didn't happen. Though their father went on several more dates with Marianne, the sisters learned nothing new about her. They tried; goodness, how they tried. But the tougher and more incisive their questions became, the more vague were their father's replies, until no one could pretend he wasn't doing it on purpose. Rosalind then changed her plan of attack. They would no longer ask about Marianne, they would ask to meet her. So they did, using sly hints, polite suggestions, and, finally, direct requests. But their father always had excuses. Marianne was too busy. Marianne had a cold. Marianne was in London—that one really drove Rosalind crazy, and made her more determined than ever to meet the woman.

She decided to move on to outright demands.

Halloween was coming up, and the night after that was Sixth Grade Performance Night, and a few days after *that* was the gala event at Cameron University, the one where her father and Iantha were both featured speakers. Surely Marianne could be produced for one of these important occasions. If not, Rosalind didn't know what she'd do, but it might have to involve shouting. Fervently hoping it wouldn't go that far, she started asking about Marianne visiting on Halloween several days ahead of time, but when darkness fell on October 31, she still didn't have an answer.

Rosalind carefully lowered the dinosaur head onto Batty's shoulders.

"Can you see?" she asked.

"No," came the muffled answer.

Rosalind rotated the head half an inch. "Now?"

"No. Maybe I should be a lion instead, like Hound."

"We don't have a lion costume for you, and besides, you're always a dinosaur." Rosalind settled the head more firmly. "Are you sure you're looking through the mouth?"

The dinosaur head tipped up slightly. "Now I can see a little bit. Am I scary?"

"Terrifying. Come on, practice swinging your tail."

The small green dinosaur turned one way, then

the other, tentatively at first, then suddenly more energetically, banging her tail into Hound, who had been trying to remove the thick yellow fringe tied around his neck. Hound barked in protest, Batty gave out a dinosaur roar, and then they were tussling with each other. Within seconds, the dinosaur head was off Batty and on the floor, its nose slightly squashed.

"All right, that's enough practicing." Rosalind separated them and, for the dozenth time, adjusted the white bedsheet she was wearing. She and Anna were trick-or-treating as Roman goddesses, and Rosalind was already tired of being all trussed up. It seemed a waste to be a goddess if you could barely move without tripping.

She got Batty back into the dinosaur head, handed her a bag for candy collection, and led her carefully down the steps. Their father was in the hallway, lighting the jack-o'-lantern that glared out the window.

"My goodness," he said. "What have you done with my daughters?"

"Daddy, it's me," said the dinosaur.

"Who?"

"BATTY!"

"Why, so it is." Mr. Penderwick adjusted his glasses. "Who would ever have known?"

"Daddy." Rosalind nervously cleared her throat. "About Marianne."

Before he could answer, the doorbell rang. It was Anna, wrapped in another bedsheet. Batty lunged toward her, roaring loudly, but tripped over Hound before she got very far, damaging the nose even further.

"No more lunging," said Rosalind, picking her up.

"Yet another goddess," said Mr. Penderwick to Anna.

"I am Venus, goddess of matchmaking." She winked at Rosalind.

"*Omitte nugas,*" said Rosalind, not winking back, for the last thing she wanted was for Anna to make any more jokes, like about blind dates with skating coaches.

"What did Rosalind say, Daddy?" asked Batty.

"She told Anna not to speak nonsense," said Mr. Penderwick. "Quite impressive, Rosy."

"Mr. Smith says it whenever we make mistakes in Latin class. And speaking of mistakes—" Rosalind stopped herself, for that was no way to introduce Marianne into the conversation. "Daddy, what I meant is, did you invite Marianne over tonight?"

The front door burst open, and in came Skye and Jane, their bags half full of candy they'd collected from the streets on either side of Gardam Street. Jane was wearing a football uniform that was much too big for her, with a large red 86 on the jersey.

"Tommy!" exclaimed Anna. "How you've shrunk."

220

"I'm representing him tonight," said Jane. "During his unwilling and widely mourned absence from his home street."

"You're the only one mourning his absence." In Rosalind's opinion, anyone over the age of six who dressed up as Superman was beneath notice.

"What are you supposed to be?" Anna asked Skye, who was wearing black jeans, a black sweater, black sneakers, and a black hat.

"Dark matter, and don't ask me what it is. I'm tired of explaining to everyone."

"You can ask me," said Jane. "It's a mystery of the universe, like from *A Wrinkle in Time*."

"It's nothing like *A Wrinkle in Time*. You don't understand at all."

"Dark matter is Iantha's specialty," said Mr. Penderwick. "She's quite brilliant in her field, you know."

"We do know, Daddy," said Skye.

"At least that's what I hear," he said. "Well, goddesses and otherwise, are you ready to go?"

"Yes, but, Daddy—" Rosalind refused to leave without getting an answer from him. "What about Marianne? Is she coming over tonight to meet us?"

"I forgot to invite her, Rosy. I'm sorry."

"You forgot?" Rosalind felt herself getting dangerously close to the shouting stage.

The doorbell rang again, and with the look of a man rescued from near-drowning, Mr. Penderwick opened the door. Outside was an army of small ghosts, all shouting "Boo!" Anna took the opportunity to steer Rosalind and her sisters out of the house.

"He forgot?" huffed Rosalind when they'd gotten past all the ghosts.

"Maybe he doesn't want her to meet us," said Jane. "I read in a magazine once about how divorced and widowed men will keep their children a secret when they start dating again."

"Keep us a secret!" Rosalind had never considered such a thing. "Could he be worried about what Marianne will think of us?"

"Of course not," said Anna. "Maybe she'll come to Skye's play tomorrow night."

"Garghh." Skye sounded like she was choking to death, and looked almost that bad, too.

"Try not to mention the play," said Jane. "It's a sore subject."

Rosalind would have liked to ask how Skye was going to be in a play that no one was allowed to mention, but then she noticed that she was missing a dinosaur. "Where's Batty?"

Batty was still inside, saying a long and regretful good-bye to Hound. Despite his lion collar, he wasn't allowed to go trick-or-treating. Though Batty knew why—too much barking at other trick-or-treaters— she didn't like leaving him behind. But when Rosalind came back inside for her, she let herself be led away and out into the night.

Even without Hound, Batty was glad they were finally on the move. Halloween was not for worrying about Daddy and dates. Halloween was for candy and being out later than you usually were allowed, and for showing your new dinosaur costume to the neighbors. And now that she was outside, she was glad that she was a dinosaur instead of a lion. She liked being all wrapped up inside this costume, for it was warm and safe in here, even if she still couldn't see very well. She tipped the dinosaur head this way and that, catching peeks of carved pumpkins lit with flickering candles, dry leaves blowing in the wind, and—oh! what was that?—spooky figures flitting up and down Gardam Street. Batty shuddered happily. This was a scary night, just as Halloween should be.

They went first to Iantha's. Batty had told Iantha and Ben about her dinosaur costume, yet when Iantha opened the door and everyone yelled "TRICK OR TREAT!" she didn't know who they were. So Batty roared, because then Iantha would understand that she was a dinosaur and remember it was Batty, but Ben, who was dressed all in orange—he was a bag of Cheez Doodles—started to sob, and Batty had to tell him over and over that she was his own Batty until the tears stopped, and then Iantha gave everyone a candy bar and a dog cookie shaped like a pumpkin to take home for Hound. It was very satisfying.

It was just as satisfying at the other houses. Mr. and Mrs. Geiger were confused by the costumes—

they thought that Jane was really Tommy, and they didn't have any idea at all who Batty was, even after she'd roared. The Corkhills, on the corner, gave them homemade butterscotch brownies just like they did every year and told Batty she could eat hers right away if she wanted. The Tuttles had a ghost hanging in their tree that moaned, and Batty wasn't frightened at all—that is, she wasn't frightened after Rosalind showed her the tape recorder in the branches. And all of the grown-up Bosna sisters were home and made a tremendous fuss over Batty and each gave her an extra candy bar, until she figured she had enough candy to last her forever.

After that, it was especially satisfying when Nick Geiger and a lot of other big boys surrounded and teased them, though Batty wasn't impressed with their costumes, which were just regular old clothes and masks of some man they called "Nixon." Then Nick yelled "Switch!" and all the boys changed masks, and now they were some man called "Clinton," and then he yelled "Switch!" again, and Batty wasn't sure who they were this time. Nick said they could keep going back to the same houses with different masks, and Skye scolded them for taking all the good candy, and then one of the boys tossed Jane a football, and suddenly everyone was running around in the street playing football, though Rosalind and Anna had to hike up their sheets to do it.

This was less satisfying for Batty, since it's hard to play football in a dinosaur costume, and then one of the big boys tripped on her tail, so she got out of the way like he told her to. But she didn't go far, until a bunch of ghosts from another street came along, and as she was too shy to talk to them, she found a bush to hide behind. She could still hear Rosalind and the others playing football just a little bit away, so though it was dark behind the bush, she knew she was perfectly safe.

Which made it all the scarier when she swung her dinosaur tail and it bumped into something and that something turned out to be a someone, for it said "OOF," as though surprised to be bumped by a dinosaur tail. At first she thought the person would turn out to be one of Nick's friends, but then he started to talk in a grown-up man's voice, which was uncomfortable, and what made it even more uncomfortable was that his words didn't make sense. Frightened, Batty took a few steps backward and then managed to catch a glimpse of him through her dinosaur mouth. Now her heart was going like crazy, and she promised herself that she would never be a secret agent again, because there was just enough moonlight to show her exactly who the man was, even though he didn't have sunglasses on and somehow his ears had become pointed. As hard as she could, she hurled her bag of candy at him, then ran blindly in the direction of the street, shrieking and shrieking, until she was scooped up by someone, which made her shriek louder until he said he was Nick, and then she went limp, and her shrieks turned to sobs, and she kept sobbing while Nick carried her home and rang the doorbell, and she didn't stop even when Daddy carried her into the living room and put her on the couch and took off her dinosaur head. And still she sobbed, even when Daddy put a blanket over her and Hound licked her face and Rosalind ran in, looking so worried, and still she sobbed, and still and still.

Rosalind thought the sobs would never stop, but at last Batty wore herself out and just lay there with her face damp and her eyes closed. By then her father had sent Anna home and told Skye and Jane to go to bed. Nick, though, had insisted on staying. It was his friends who'd driven the little dinosaur off the streets and into the bushes, and he refused to leave until he knew Batty was all right.

Finally she stirred and opened her eyes.

"Hi, Battikins," said Mr. Penderwick. "How do you feel?"

"All right." One last tear slipped out. "I lost all my candy."

"You can have my candy," said Rosalind. "Oh, Batty, I'm sorry I didn't watch you every second."

"Can you tell us what happened, sweetheart?" asked Mr. Penderwick.

"Bug Man was hiding behind the bushes, and I bumped him with my tail."

Rosalind was too upset to mess around with Bug Man stories tonight. "No, really."

"It was Bug Man, it was, but his ears were pointed and he was a sock." Batty looked around now and noticed that Nick was there, too, and without any of his masks on, which was a relief.

"Hi, Batty," he said. "Excellent screaming."

"Thank you."

"Let's go back to the part about the man being a sock," said Mr. Penderwick.

Batty frowned with concentration. "He—Bug Man—said he was a sock and then something about a prize."

"That doesn't make sense," said Rosalind.

"Maybe it does, though, if you think about the pointed ears," said Nick. "I did notice some guy wandering around earlier dressed as a Vulcan."

"Batty, is it possible the man said that he was Spock?" asked Mr. Penderwick. "From the *Enterprise?*"

"Maybe."

"What else did the man say?"

"I don't know." Batty was drooping with fatigue. "He said he'd be vinchidated."

"Does anyone speak Vulcan? Rosalind?" asked Nick.

She shushed him, but not severely, for she was too relieved to mind his silliness. Batty had been badly frightened, it was true, but this man—whoever he was—sounded more odd than dangerous. After asking a few more questions, her father obviously agreed, and soon sent Nick home with strict instructions not to hunt Spock down to punish him. Then, while he carried Batty upstairs to bed, Rosalind went to Skye and Jane's room to let them know that the youngest Penderwick was safe and unscathed.

Before she could say a word, though, she stumbled over a football helmet.

"Bandits!" said Jane while Skye turned on the light.

"It's just me." Rosalind kicked the helmet out of her way, not as gently, perhaps, as she would have had its owner been on Gardam Street that night where he belonged. "Sorry to wake you. I wanted to tell you that Batty's okay. She was just startled by some man in a Spock costume."

"We weren't asleep, anyway," said Jane. "We're going over lines for the play tomorrow."

"Skye, I'm sure you know your part by now," said Rosalind with a confidence she didn't feel.

"Garghh."

"Come on, Skye, let's go back to where Rainbow tells Grass Flower she's going to take her place as the sacrificial victim," said Jane. "Grass Flower says *I cannot let you give your life for me,* and then you shed a tear and say . . ."

"I don't want to say it. Oh, Jane!"

"What good is my life, now that I know—go ahead, you can do it."

"What good is my stupid life, now that I know stupid Coyote loves you, even stupider Grass Flower?"

Shaking her head, Rosalind slipped away, leaving them to it.

CHAPTER EIGHTEEN
Sisters and Sacrifice

SKYE STOOD AT THE WINDOW in her bedroom, staring out into the rain. It was a cold rain, perfect for the coldness in her heart. And the coldness in her feet and her hands and everything except her stomach, which instead of feeling cold, felt seasick. All this discomfort was because soon her father would be driving her to school, where Jane would help her don the Rainbow costume and makeup. And soon after that, she would be walking onto the stage, where she would proceed to make a buffoon of herself. No, she would be worse than a buffoon. She would be pathetic. The audience, all four hundred of them, the teachers, her family—they would all feel sorry for her. Even the rest of the cast would feel sorry for her. Already, that afternoon at the dress rehearsal, Pearson, who knew nothing about acting and cared less, had given her tips on line delivery. And Melissa! Skye was sure she'd seen a hint of pity in Melissa's eyes. To be pitied by Melissa Patenaude was beyond mortification.

Skye turned away from the window and fell onto her bed. Well, at least one person wouldn't be there to pity her—Aunt Claire. A business obligation was keeping her in Connecticut that evening. She'd apologized on the phone to Skye, not understanding that Skye didn't want anyone there at all, then even sent a large basket of flowers with a note: *Sorry I'll miss your play. See you tomorrow for the soccer game.*

Skye thought longingly of tomorrow and that soccer game. Even though it was with Melissa and her Cameron Hardware team, it would be heaven compared to tonight. And after the game would be anything she wanted for the whole weekend, and nothing at all to do with Aztecs or plays for the rest of her life. If only time travel were possible, she thought, she would jump right now to tomorrow's soccer game, and to heck with the space-time continuum.

How could such a simple thing as a play terrify her so? She'd never been this frightened, not when she was five and rode Tommy's skateboard over the big ramps Nick had built. Not two summers ago at the beach when she took her raft so far past the waves that she had to be towed back to shore by the lifeguard. Not

231

even dangling off the Quigley Woods bridge last spring with Jane holding on to her ankles so that she could retrieve a soccer ball stuck on the rocks below. She would do any of those things a hundred times and more if it would keep her from playing Rainbow.

But nothing could keep her from playing Rainbow now. Unless—unless she lied and said she was too sick to go on. She did feel sick, after all. It wasn't as though the play couldn't go on without her. Someone could simply read the part in her place—they'd do a better job than she could, even after all her practice. Would it really hurt anyone if she stayed home? Would it be so wrong?

There was a knock on the door, and her father came in carrying a tray of food.

"I know you didn't want any supper," he said.

"I don't." Nor had she wanted any lunch or breakfast. She hadn't eaten since the night before, and felt so peculiar she thought she might never eat again.

"Nonetheless, you could use some food before your big performance as Rainbow. By the way, have I told you how much I like that name? In Latin, it would be *Pluvius Arcus*, *pluvius* being an adjective meaning 'rainy,' and *arcus* meaning, of course, 'curve' or 'arch.' *Pluvius*, by the way, also made it into our language, as *pluvial*." He stopped. "Sorry, you're not in the mood for an etymology lesson."

"It was interesting, though."

"No, it wasn't. Have some dinner, Skye. Food is good for nerves."

"I'm not hungry, honest."

"Then how about I leave the food here, and if you get hungry in the next few minutes, you try to stuff something down." He put down the tray and turned to go.

"Thanks, Daddy, but wait, I have a question. Is Marianne coming tonight?"

"No, she isn't. I hope you're not disappointed."

"No, I'm glad." This was the nicest thing she'd ever heard about Marianne. "I wouldn't want this play to be the first impression she gets of me."

"Skye, I don't think you're going to be as bad as you think you are."

"You have no idea how bad I am. But I have another question." She was grasping at her last straw. Her father was the most honest man she knew. If he would give her a loophole, however small, she would take it. "Is deceit always dishonorable, even a tiny bit that doesn't hurt anyone?"

"Heavens, daughter, that's a question for a philosopher, not a botanist."

"I'm serious."

"All right." He thought for a moment. "No, deceit is not always dishonorable. For example, lying to save an innocent life can be honorable. Is there an innocent life at stake here?"

"Besides mine?" She smiled to show she was kidding, but it wasn't much of a smile.

"Then I'd have to say, broadly, that even a tiny bit of deceit is dishonorable when it's used for selfish or cowardly reasons. Does that answer your question?"

"Yes, I guess it does." If the only loophole would be to act cowardly—and though, when it came to being Rainbow, she absolutely was a coward through and through—she wouldn't give in to it. "Could you please tell Jane I'm almost ready to leave?"

"That's my girl," he said. *"Audaces—"*

She interrupted him. "Daddy, I love you and I appreciate your advice, but I just can't bear any Latin right now."

"No, I don't blame you." He kissed her. "I'll get the car ready."

Skye stuffed her Rainbow costume and makeup into a bag and followed her father downstairs. Her fate was sealed, and from that moment her determination to go through with the play wouldn't waver. In the car, she clutched her bag and went over her lines and stage directions with Jane, speaking so quickly they finished the whole play and were starting again by the time they reached Wildwood. She kept it up, muttering maniacally as they dashed through the rain, into the school, and down the hall toward the auditorium.

"Thank you, Coyote, for your gift of food. Because the

234

rain will not come, we are close to starving. Ignore Melissa and look at Pearson. When he nods at me, point out toward the audience. *What news do you bring from the outside world?* Then he goes on and on about soldiers, and then I say—"

"Look, the programs!" Jane waved several red-covered booklets she'd snatched from a table in the lobby.

Mr. Geballe had mentioned there would be programs for that night, but Skye had been too anxious to worry about such details. Jane handed her one now, but Skye just stuck it into her costume bag and kept walking. "And then I say, *Surely the soldiers won't come to our little village looking for sacrificial victims.* Melissa gasps with fear, and Pearson puts his hand on her shoulder."

"But don't you want to see the *Sisters and Sacrifice* page?" Jane handed over another program, this one open to the middle. Here is what Skye read:

SISTERS AND SACRIFICE
An Original Play by Skye Penderwick

"Jane!" She stopped dead, in the middle of the hall. "They put my name right there as the author."

Several cast members rushed by, giggling. Jane stepped in front of Skye to keep them from seeing the look of dread on her face. "Of course they put your name as author. What did you think?" she whispered,

235

not adding that she'd give anything to have her own name there instead.

"I didn't think," moaned Skye. "I just didn't think. Deceit upon deceit, Jane. Deceit multiplied by the number of people who read this program. How much deceit does that make altogether? My honor will be lower than nothing. My honor will be in the negative numbers."

More cast members, including Pearson, appeared at the end of the hall. Jane looked around for a place to hide a disintegrating sister. There, just a few more steps and they could both disappear into the girls' bathroom. Half shoving and half pulling, she managed to get Skye hidden before Pearson could arrive and see the grievous state of she who was soon to be Rainbow.

Safely inside the bathroom, Skye slumped against the tile wall and dropped her bag on the floor. A black-yarn wig, crafted lovingly by the *Sisters and Sacrifice* costume committee, tumbled out onto the floor. Skye groaned at the sight of it and clutched her stomach.

"Do you want me to cross out 'Skye' in all of the programs?" asked Jane. "I could change it to 'Miss.' 'An Original Play by Miss Penderwick.' That works, right?"

"Even for you, Jane, that's a stupid idea. Sorry, sorry, sorry. It's not your fault. It's my fault. If I'd done my own homework, I wouldn't be in this mess. Swear we'll never switch homework again. Swear!"

Even in so dire a situation, Jane wasn't going to swear to that. There were still years of school to get through, and she was counting on Skye for at least trigonometry and physics. "Try to get hold of yourself. Maybe you'll feel better once you get to the dressing room and put on your makeup."

"The dressing room!" Skye grabbed Jane's arm. "Listen to me. I'll act in this play, which will possibly ruin my life, but I will not put on a costume and makeup in the same room as Melissa Patenaude. I'll do it here instead. Go tell Mr. Geballe where I am, okay? And then come back to help me."

"I don't know if I should leave you alone, Skye. You look a little weird."

"Of course I look weird. I'm close to a nervous breakdown. Now go! No, wait! I can't remember my first speech."

"*Yes, Grass Flower, though I wish we did not have to rush into marriage. Perhaps someday in the future, girls will be allowed to stay single—*"

"*—for many more years or even forever without social opprobrium.* I got it. Now go!"

Jane went, and Skye staggered over to the mirror. She looked like death. She didn't care. "*However, since that day is not yet nigh, I am glad that I have found a boy to love, for then I will be happy in my marriage. Then*

237

stupid Melissa says: *I, too, have found a boy to love. Who is yours?*"

She rummaged through her bag and pulled out a stick of red greasepaint. "I say, *You tell me first,* then Melissa says, *No, you tell me first.*" She drew a wavering line of red across her forehead. "Okay, I think I remember the rest of that scene. What is that line I have so much trouble with later? The one about innocent blood?" Another line of red, this one under her right eye.

Skye blinked, for her image in the mirror was a little blurry now. "*For I will spill my maize—*no*—I will spill my blood to bring the maize—*no, *the rain!*" She needed a line of red under her left eye, but the blurriness was getting worse, and she was having trouble seeing what she was doing. "*For I will spill my blood to—to—to . . .*"

Now there was a strange rushing sound in her ears. Suddenly dizzy, Skye clutched at the sink, but it managed to slip away from her. That's odd, she thought, I seem to be falling down.

Then all went black.

Rosalind pulled on an old sweater with a small hole in one sleeve. She could have worn one of the sweaters Aunt Claire had given her, but this one was good enough for the Sixth Grade Performance Night. No one there would be looking at her, unlike last year when she'd been the maidservant in *Dr. Jekyll and Mr. Hyde*. Of course, the maidservant hadn't had many lines, just lots of "Yes, sir" and "No, sir." Anna had much more to say—and a great chance to scream—as Mr. Hyde's first victim. Tommy had the most lines of all, for he was the star. What an excellent villain—

She stopped, frowning, unwilling to give Tommy any praise, even for something that had happened long before his Trilby phase. He was as pond scum to her now, just as, apparently, she was as pond scum to him. Since their Trilby argument, he no longer even looked at her, let alone said hello—not at school, not on Gardam Street, and especially not when he was with Trilby. Perhaps pond scum was too good for him.

Rosalind ran a brush through her hair, then headed downstairs. Her father, back from dropping off Skye and Jane, was helping Batty into her yellow raincoat and hat. Iantha was there, too, with Ben under one arm and his baby seat under the other, for they were riding along with the Penderwicks.

"I'm going to walk to the school, Daddy," said Rosalind, kissing Ben's fat cheek.

"Are we taking your spot in the car?" asked Iantha.

Yes, it would be a tight squeeze in the car with two car seats, but mostly Rosalind loved walking in the rain. Grabbing her raincoat and an umbrella, she left before anyone could argue with her, and swung cheerfully down Gardam Street, leaning into the wind, hearing the rain beat against the umbrella. By the time her father drove by a few minutes later, she was humming. What was it? Oh, yes. "Every time it rains, it rains pennies from heaven." Her mother had sung it whenever she walked in the rain, and she'd do this funny little dance—step, step, hop, hop, slide, step, step, hop, hop, slide.

Another car roared up beside her and stopped. The window was rolled down, and Nick grinned out at her. Rosalind wished she hadn't been hopping and sliding right then.

"Jump in," he said. "We'll give you a ride to the school."

Rosalind peered into the car—and there was Tommy next to Nick, staring straight ahead.

"I like walking," she said.

"Come on, it's pouring. As long as you don't mind a detour. We've got to pick up Trilby."

Only then did Tommy turn his head, but his eyes slid past her, as though the most fascinating thing in the world was just over her right shoulder. Oh! How dare he ignore her, just as if they hadn't known each other since they were in diapers! Rosalind angrily shook her umbrella, spraying rain all over Nick. "Why exactly is the magnificent Trilby blessing the Sixth Grade Performance Night with her magnificent presence?"

"Nice attitude, Rosy," said Nick, his grin getting

bigger. "You're not the only one with a sister in the sixth grade. Tonight you'll be treated to the smooth sounds of Elena Ramirez's saxophone solo."

"Oh." She wished she were dead.

"But you can still have a ride."

"No, thanks."

Rosalind watched the Geiger brothers drive away, then set off again toward the school, without humming and certainly without dancing. It seemed now like such a long walk to the school, and she wondered what was so great about walking in the rain, anyway. She thought, I am *lower* than pond scum, then at last there was the school ahead of her, and there—thank goodness—was Anna, waiting by the big front doors.

"Your family is saving us seats," said Anna. "Your neighbor looks pretty tonight, all sort of curly and wild."

"Iantha? I didn't notice."

Anna took a better look at Rosalind's face. "What's wrong?"

"I hate Tommy Geiger." Rosalind stamped her foot as she took off her raincoat, which is not easy to do. "I hate him, I hate him."

"You might want to keep your voice down."

A group of third-grade girls was hovering nearby, fascinated by the drama. Turning her back on them, Rosalind whispered, "And I don't care who he dates."

"Neither do I. Let's go sit down."

Rosalind allowed Anna to lead her into the auditorium. The last time they'd been there together was for their sixth-grade graduation ceremony. Tommy had worn one red sock and one blue sock—

"I really do hate him," she said as they reached the row where her family was sitting.

"I really do believe you." Anna pushed her into the seat next to her father, then sat down on the end.

Next to Mr. Penderwick was Batty, then came Iantha, with Ben on her lap, and then an empty seat waiting for Jane. Iantha, Rosalind now noticed, did have an air of trembling beauty that night—or maybe it was her halo of red hair. Rosalind savagely wished that she had red hair. Or green eyes. Or something different from what she had. Or maybe it was that she wished she lived somewhere else, like on another street, or even better, that Tommy lived on another street.

"You're soaking wet," said Mr. Penderwick. "We saw Nick and Tommy getting into their car and hoped they'd offer you a ride."

"They did," said Rosalind. "But I refused their offer."

"Oh? Have you and Tommy had a falling-out? I've noticed he hasn't been eating our food lately."

"I guess you could call it a falling-out."

"It isn't Rosalind, Mr. Pen," chimed in Anna. "It's Tommy who's gone off the deep end."

Rosalind wished that she'd kept her mouth shut about the Geigers being intolerable, for her father was still looking at her so kindly, and she wasn't in the mood to explain about Tommy and Trilby, especially since she'd just spotted them taking seats across the aisle and four rows back.

"Martin, you remember how peculiar twelve-year-old boys can be," said Iantha.

He swung away from Rosalind, distracted, and she sent Iantha a silent thanks for the rescue, then slumped down into her seat and stared straight ahead at the empty stage, determined not to set eyes again on the—yes—intolerable Tommy Geiger for the rest of the evening, if not for the rest of her life.

Which meant that she didn't notice Mr. Geballe coming toward them until he leaned over her to tap Mr. Penderwick on the shoulder.

"Martin," he said. "There's been a bit of a problem."

Mr. Penderwick was already on his feet. "Skye? Jane?"

"It's Skye. Unfortunately, she fainted while putting on her makeup."

"Fainted!" Rosalind grabbed Anna's hand for support. "Is she all right?"

"She's recovering, but is in no shape for acting tonight," said Mr. Geballe. "Oh, and Martin, she said to tell you that it wasn't deceit, but a real faint."

"Of course it was, poor girl. I'll go see her."

"Actually, she's asked for someone else," said Mr. Geballe, then turned to Iantha. "Ms. Aaronson? Skye says you've had experience with fainting, and wonders if you'd mind helping out."

"I'm happy to, if it's all right with you, Martin."

"Yes, of course, since she's asked for you, but I hate to impose—"

"Don't be silly." Iantha stood up and handed Ben over to him. "I'll send back word as soon as she's feeling better."

"Yes, thank you, Iantha, thank you. It's true that I know nothing about fainting."

"But what about the play, Mr. Geballe?" asked Rosalind. "Who's going to be Rainbow?"

"We're still working on that, but I believe we've found a substitute. Wish us luck."

CHAPTER NINETEEN
All Secrets Revealed

FROM THE MOMENT Jane found Skye crumpled on the bathroom floor to when she looked into the mirror and saw Rainbow looking back at her was one long blur of activity. Bits and pieces stood out—Mr. Geballe asking if she was certain she knew the whole play by heart, Iantha calmly kneeling beside Skye, Melissa's fury when she heard about the switch, and most of all, the sense that this was one of the most exciting things that had ever happened to her, Jane.

Then all at once she was on the stage behind the curtain with Melissa, listening to the last performance before the start of *Sisters and Sacrifice*, a band called Jesse's Wild Bunch. Jane danced along to their music, finding them as fabulous as everything else in her world that night. When they finished their song, and she heard the clanging and banging as they dragged their instruments and microphones off the stage, she knew the play was only seconds away.

She grabbed Melissa's hand and shook it, whispering, "Break a leg."

"Break your own leg," Melissa whispered back. "You'd better not mess up."

"*Never fear, Grass Flower. I cannot fail, for my whole life has led me to this hour.*"

"Oh, be quiet."

In front of the curtain, the narrator had begun. Jane silently mouthed the words with him. "*Long ago in the land of the Aztecs, there was great worry. The rain had not come for many months, and without the rain, the maize didn't grow, and without the maize, the people starved.*"

Next came the chorus with all their "Alas, alas"es, and then—

The curtain came up, and Jane turned to the audience, deliriously happy. They were out there, all wondrous four hundred of them, ready to love her as much as she loved them. And she gave them her best. From her first line, she was a Rainbow to end all Rainbows—through her brave switch with Grass Flower, her long march to the sacrificial table, her dramatic rescue by lightning, and all the way to the end of the play, which just happened to be Rainbow's most glorious speech.

"Dear Coyote, I am honored by your vows of love. But you must return to my beloved sister, who has nothing but you in this life. I, on the other hand, have a great destiny, to devote my life to my people. I will never forget you, and you must never forget me, either—Rainbow, who loves you, but loves duty more!"

The applause was intoxicating. Jane waved, and bowed, and didn't even mind when she bowed so low her wig fell off and everyone laughed. They were laughing with her! They adored her! If only it could go on forever!

Applause never does go on forever, but when the last curtain fell, still Jane's happiness went on and on. Behind the curtain was great celebration—Aztec maidens darting this way and that, shrieking with laughter, soldiers marching in and out of formation, priests gleefully reliving their gruesome deaths by crashing to the floor. Jane hugged herself with delight, for all this was the result of her imagination come to life. Then she saw Skye skirting a band of rampaging villagers.

Jane raced over to her. "Are you all right? Have you stopped fainting? Did you get to see any of the play?"

"I saw most of it from the wings, and you were terrific, Jane."

"Really? Because with all that applause I thought that maybe I was good, good enough that I could become an actress someday. I mean, I'm still going to be a writer, but in case I ever get writer's block, I could turn to acting. What do you think?"

But Skye wasn't listening. She was too busy steering Jane toward the exit, her only goal to avoid the crowds and go home. Fainting hadn't wiped out her horror at the deceit she'd perpetrated. Indeed, since then, the horror had only grown, for people had been so nice—Mr. Geballe, who hadn't scolded once, or even looked annoyed that his star was out of commission, and Iantha, bathing her forehead and feeding her bits of crackers she'd produced from goodness knew where. If only they'd known what a lying lowlife they were dealing with. *Sisters and Sacrifice* by Skye Penderwick—ha! She'd heard the applause. She'd even heard a few cries of "Author, author!" and had crouched behind a pile of boxes in the wings, terrified someone would spot her and push her out onto the stage.

The exit door was just up ahead, but before they could reach it, Pearson was suddenly in front of them, gawking at Skye with the intensity of a hungry frog.

"What's wrong with you?" she asked.

"Nothing." He shuffled his feet and turned into an out-and-out starving frog. "I'm sorry you didn't get to be in the play."

"I'm not. See you on Monday." She tried to maneuver Jane around him, but he stuck with them.

"It's only that I just tonight realized how good the

play is. When Jane said those words, you know, about life and death and love and stuff—well, I just thought about what a good writer you are, Skye, and how you know a lot about . . . stuff."

"Believe me, I don't know anything. Now get out of my way." This time Skye managed to dodge past him, still with Jane in tow.

"Are you sure you feel all right, Skye?" asked Jane, who would have greatly enjoyed a long conversation with Pearson about life and death and love. "You know, he was pretty good as Coyote, especially in that scene at the end, when I sent him back to Grass Flower."

"Shh," said Skye, for despite her efforts to escape, now it was Melissa blocking their path.

"You look okay to me, Skye Penderwick," she said, her hands on her hips. "I bet you two had the switch planned all along."

"We didn't, honest," protested Jane.

"Then, Miss Know-It-All Fifth Grader, why did you know the entire script by heart?"

Skye cut in before Jane could answer. "We're in a hurry, Melissa. I'm sorry if the switch made it hard for you."

"Oh. Well, I still don't trust either of you. Just wait until the soccer game tomorrow. I'll get my revenge."

While Melissa stomped off, Jane rounded on her

sister. "You apologized to your loathsome enemy? Did you hit your head when you fainted?"

"She expected to outshine me tonight, and instead you outshone her. I feel sort of sorry for her."

"You did hit your head. You must have."

"Maybe I did, but come on, Jane, please let's get out of here."

"Skye, Jane, wait!"

Rats! It was Mr. Geballe. Skye turned to him as though facing a firing squad.

"Good evening, Mr. Geballe," she said. "How are you?"

"How am I? For heaven's sake, Skye, how are you? Are you feeling better?"

"Much better, thank you."

"That's good," he said, smiling. "And, Jane, our savior, how do you feel?"

"Terrific, amazing, magnificent!"

"That's just what I was going to say about your performance. What a family for talent you are!"

"We are, aren't we?" Jane was aglow with his praise.

"Not particularly," said Skye, treading on Jane's foot to calm her down. "I mean, some of us are more talented than others in certain things."

"Well, you've got the writing talent, Skye, that's for sure," said Mr. Geballe. "And, Jane, you're certainly an impressive young actress. Are you a writer, too, like your sister?"

"I—um—am I, Skye?"

"Actually, Mr. Geballe, Jane's a much better writer than I am."

"Wow! I can't wait to see the play she writes next year. Who knows? Maybe another Penderwick will get a shot at Sixth Grade Performance Night."

"That would be great," said Jane, though even *her* enthusiasm was wilting under Mr. Geballe's unquestioning trust. She was as glad as Skye when he left to quell an uprising among the sacrificial maidens.

The sisters made it to the exit door without further interference. They emerged into the first graders' hall, hung everywhere with bright crayon drawings, bitter reminders of innocence lost.

"If only Mr. Geballe had been even a little suspicious of us. Or if I didn't care what he thought of me. Or if I weren't such a bonehead!" said Skye, glaring at one drawing in particular, in which stick figures cavorted merrily among green flowers and blue trees. "Jane, you know we're the biggest frauds in the universe."

"Not the universe." Jane was trying desperately to hold on to the last bits of Rainbow euphoria, but, alas, it was gone. She hated being a fraud.

"The solar system, then." All at once Skye knew what she had to do. "I need to tell Daddy I didn't write *Sisters and Sacrifice*. I can leave you out of it, though. I'll say I stole the play from a book."

Now Jane had to decide which would be worse—confessing to her father, or watching Skye confess to him all by herself, when half of it was her own fault. It took only seconds to work it out.

"That would be another lie," she said. "Don't leave me out of it. After all, you wrote my science essay about robotics."

"Antibiotics."

"I meant antibiotics."

"Are you sure, Jane? Because I really can do it alone."

"No, you can't. I *am* sure."

"Then let's tell Daddy tonight, and Rosy and even Batty, too, as soon as we're all home. Do or die?"

"Do or die." And Jane ran off to change out of her costume.

Later, with the whole family around the kitchen table—even Batty, whose bedtime was long gone—Skye and Jane came clean. They took no shortcuts, telling the whole story from beginning to end, leaving out no shameful detail, no evasion, no careless fib. They were lucid and concise—except while scrapping over which of them was more to blame—and made no excuses for their behavior. During it all, Skye stared fixedly at the ceiling, and Jane studied the floor as though she'd never seen it before. Only when they'd run out of guilty deeds to describe did they dare look at their father. He was twisting his eyeglasses this way, that way, and the other way, until everyone was sure they would break.

"All right," he said finally. "I want to make sure I have this straight. You two swapped homework because your own assignments bored you. And when Mr. Geballe decided to stage Jane's play, thus getting half of Wildwood Elementary caught up in your original deceit, it didn't occur to either of you to tell him—or anyone else—the truth. Is that correct?"

"Yes." Skye felt as small as a raisin, as small as a crumb that Hound would lick off the floor.

"Not even me. It didn't occur to you to tell me."

Skye, too ashamed to answer, could only shake her head no.

Now Jane tried to answer, but she'd started crying with such wrenching sobs that no one understood her. It was terrible to see. Rosalind pulled Batty onto her lap, needing comfort right then. Hound, just as affected, licked Batty's left sneaker.

Mr. Penderwick got up and poured a glass of water for Jane. Drinking it calmed her enough to let her choke out some words. "Not only have we sullied the family honor, we've hurt you terribly, Daddy."

"I'm disappointed, Jane, not hurt. I thought I'd taught you better than this." His sad smile made more than one sister think her heart would break. "At least you're telling me now, yes? That took courage. So let's figure out how to un-sully the family honor. Any ideas?"

Skye sat up straight. The hardest part was over now, and she could breathe freely again. "I'll confess to Mr. Geballe on Monday, and if he wants, I'll be his slave. I'll sweep the classroom floor and clean the blackboard and even the windows and his car. Of course I'll write an Aztec play of my own, even though I'll hate every minute of it and it'll be as poorly written as a play could possibly be. Oh, and I want to confess to Iantha, too. Is that enough, Daddy?"

"Add in a little slaving around here. I'll come up with a list of chores. What about you, Jane?"

Jane wiped away the last of her tears. "I'll write a new science essay, and I'll help Skye with home chores and Mr. Geballe's chores, and I'll send the *Cameron Gazette* a letter explaining what we did." She was already composing it in her head. *To my beloved town of Cameron, Massachusetts: It is my deepest sorrow to announce that it was not my sister Skye who wrote—*

"It isn't necessary to confess to the whole town, Jane. Only to your teacher."

"All right." Jane knew she'd rather face all of Cameron than Miss Bunda. But would Rainbow fear Miss Bunda? Would Sabrina Starr?

"Daddy, can you forgive us?" asked Skye.

"Of course I can." There was that smile again, though not as sad this time. "It occurs to me that I

254

might need forgiveness, too, for not paying better attention around here. Skye, how could I have believed you wrote that play?"

"Because she said she did," said Batty, though everyone had thought her asleep on Rosalind's lap.

"Daddy's right. We should have been more suspicious," said Rosalind. "Skye could never have written *I cannot live without the love of the boy I love*—what's the rest?"

It was one of Jane's favorite lines. *"Especially if I have to see him with Grass Flower."*

"I could have written that if I'd wanted to," protested Skye. She'd been through enough that night without having her intelligence insulted.

"But you wouldn't have wanted to," said Rosalind.

"No, I wouldn't have." One corner of Skye's mouth twitched. She'd almost smiled.

"How about this line, Skye?" said Jane. *"You must wed Coyote, dear sister. Bear him many children and name one of your daughters after me."*

"Nope, I wouldn't have written that one, either. Jane, say it the way I did."

With a look of mingled boredom and annoyance that was pure Skye, Jane did the line again. Then Skye took a turn being Jane as a madly emoting Rainbow, and Jane did Melissa as an upstaged—and furious about it—Grass Flower. Rosalind did Pearson stumbling through his love scenes with Melissa, Batty did the priests yelling "BLOOD!" and there was much laughter, for nothing is better for the spirits than unburdening a terrible load of guilt. Skye felt so much better that she inhaled a cheese-and-tomato sandwich, then started on a quart of fudge-and-caramel ice cream, which her sisters insisted on sharing.

In all the excitement of berserk mimicry and rattling bowls and spoons, only Rosalind noticed that their father wasn't joining in the festivities. After a while, she watched him leave the kitchen, then come back with the orange-spined book he'd been carrying around for weeks.

"*Sense and Sensibility*," she said, reading the title.

"Yes." He put it down in the middle of the table.

All the sisters were paying attention now. Consumption of ice cream slowed to a halt.

"Are you going to read it to us?" asked Jane, though she couldn't imagine why he would.

"No. Actually, yes, a few lines," he answered. "Sorry, I don't mean to be mysterious. It's just that I have a confession to make, too, and I'm not looking forward to it."

"What could you possibly confess about, Daddy?" asked Rosalind.

"Not murder or embezzlement, I hope," said Jane. "Skye, stop kicking me."

"Then stop being an idiot."

"It's not murder or embezzlement," said Mr. Penderwick. "Skye, earlier this evening, I told you what I believed about deceit. Something about being selfish."

She remembered it exactly. "You said that even a tiny bit of deceit is dishonorable when it's used for selfish or cowardly reasons."

"Ah. Well, lately I've been using more than a tiny bit of deceit around here."

"No," said Skye, adamant. "You never do."

"I wish you were right, Skye, but yes, I have been deceiving you girls about Marianne."

Jane gasped. "Have you secretly married her?"

"Jane!" This was Rosalind, close to kicking someone herself.

"Girls, maybe it would be best if you could let me tell the story without interruption." He ruffled Batty's hair. "How about you, pumpkin? Can you stay awake for a little longer?"

Rosalind took Batty onto her lap again. "We're listening, Daddy."

"I have to begin years ago, with your mother. Do you older girls remember how stubborn she was? Skye, you inherited more than blond hair and blue eyes from her. Sometimes when you narrow your eyes and tip your chin a certain way, I—I miss her so terribly."

Though Skye had been told hundreds of times about having her mother's hair and eyes, this was the first time she'd heard about having the stubbornness, too. She sat very still, trying not to explode with pride.

Her father went on. "I'm a little off the track of my confession already, but not really. Lizzy knew I'd miss her. She knew all about it—toward the end she seemed to know all about everything. She talked to me then about dating, and asked me to promise her I wouldn't be alone forever, but I couldn't promise anything like that. I couldn't bear even to think about other women, so I begged her to stop asking. I suppose it was then Lizzy wrote the blue letter and gave it to Aunt Claire. Girls, that letter was so full of love and caring—for all of you, and for me. It simply wasn't the kind of letter I could put away in a drawer and forget about. So I went on that first blind date, and it was about as unpleasant as a blind date could be." He stopped to shake his head at the memory.

"*Cruciatus*," said Rosalind. "I heard you tell Aunt Claire."

"Yes, absolute torture. But it was nothing compared to the second date, with that skating woman. She was—" He was interrupted by a flutter of embarrassment among his daughters. "What is it now? You all look as though you've been caught robbing a bank."

Rosalind thought that confessing to bank robbery would be easier than explaining the basics of the Save-Daddy Plan. But how could she be less courageous than her younger sisters? "Daddy, the skating coach was our fault. We decided—no, I decided, and made the others go along with me—that if we found you truly awful dates, you'd never want to date again, and then Anna suggested Lara."

"Anna set me up?" He seemed to find this amusing.

"She was just doing it because I asked her to. Don't blame the others, especially Skye. She said from the beginning it was all dishonorable."

"All right, Rosy, you may help Skye and Jane with the extra chores around the house. Still, though I can't approve of what you did, I'll give you credit for clear thinking. What you hoped would happen did, in fact, happen. My evening with Lara was so horrific that I never wanted to date again."

"Until you met Marianne," said Jane.

"Yes and no. This is where my confession comes in." He opened *Sense and Sensibility* and read out loud, " 'She was sensible and clever, but eager in everything; her sorrows, her joys, could have no moderation.' "

"That sounds familiar," said Rosalind, puzzled.

"Hold on, here's another passage: ' "With me a flannel waistcoat is invariably connected with aches, cramps, rheumatisms, and every species of ailment that can afflict the old and the feeble." ' And another: 'They gaily ascended the downs. . . . "Is there a felicity in the world," said Marianne, "superior to this? Margaret, we will walk here at least two hours." ' "

"Why, Marianne's in a book," said Jane with wonder. "She isn't a real person."

"Of course she's real," said Skye. "Daddy's been going on dates with her."

Rosalind felt like she was on a falling elevator, plunging into some dreadful unknown. "What are you saying, Daddy? What's going on?"

"I'm so sorry, but Jane's correct," he said. "Marianne is only a character in this book."

Skye couldn't believe it. "You haven't been going on dates?"

"No, though I did spend the time with Marianne. I told that much truth. I went to my office and read *Sense and Sensibility*. It's an excellent book."

Rosalind was in a tumult. She was upset that her father had been misleading them and yet was overwhelmingly relieved that since Marianne wasn't real, she'd never come to their home, never take over the kitchen, never marry Daddy—it would all be fabulous if it weren't so bewildering. "But why did you lie to us, Daddy? I don't understand."

"I'm ashamed to say that I panicked," he answered, and indeed he did look ashamed. "Claire was about to come up with another blind date, so I grabbed at the first crazy scheme that would get me out of it. Then I just kept going. I knew it wasn't fair to any of you, but I didn't feel ready to start dating for real again. I also couldn't admit that I wasn't doing what your mother asked of me—not to you girls, or maybe even to myself. Does any of that make sense?"

"Maybe," said Skye. "As much as anything about dating makes sense."

"I get it, Daddy," said Jane. "You made one false step, then found yourself mired in deception."

"I suppose that is what happened." Looking to see if Batty understood, he found that this time she *had* fallen asleep, her head on Rosalind's shoulder. "Another parental crime, keeping my youngest up past her bedtime to unburden my conscience, and she misses it. I'll explain it all to her in the morning."

"What about explaining it to Aunt Claire?" asked Rosalind, not yet ready to absolve him. "You fooled her, too. And other people."

"I'll make a full confession to Claire when she comes tomorrow," he said. "What other people?"

"Nick and Tommy," said Jane. "And Iantha. I told her."

"Iantha!" He sighed. "I'll explain it to her, too. One of you girls can straighten it out with Nick and Tommy."

"Not me," said Rosalind. "Jane, you do it."

"I'd love to." Jane beamed. "Daddy, despite your unfortunate experiences so far, do you think you'll ever date again?"

"No kicking, Skye," he said just in time. "It's a good question, but I don't know the answer. If I ever do date, however, it will be when and with whom I choose. No more interference. *Intellegitisne?* Do you understand?"

Three nods and a slight snore from Batty satisfied him. He went on.

"One more thing, and then we're all off to bed and badly needed rest. I solemnly swear on the Penderwick Family Honor—sullied, but not irreparably—that I'll never choose a woman you girls don't like and approve of. All right? Oh, Rosy, are you crying now?" Yes, she was, surprising herself as much as her father. He sorrowfully shook his head. "All this dating has been the hardest on you, hasn't it, sweetheart? Can you forgive me?"

She couldn't yet stop crying, but she could forgive him.

"And the rest of you?"

They all could. Had they ever not forgiven him anything?

"Though I'm not sure about forgetting," added Jane many hugs later. "The mystifying Marianne who hated flannel will long linger in my memory—Skye, stop kicking me!"

CHAPTER TWENTY
The New Save-Daddy Plan

MUCH TOO EARLY the next morning, Rosalind woke from a dream about having a big wet nose pressed against her face. When she pried her eyes open, she found that indeed she did have a wet nose in her face—Hound's. Her shocked gasp bothered him not at all, nor did it bother Batty, whose nose wasn't that far away, either.

"Everyone is still asleep, Rosalind," she said. "And Hound and I want someone to talk to, so is it okay if we visit Ben?"

Drowsily shoving Hound away, Rosalind checked her clock. It was before seven. "I don't think so, honey. Wait until later."

"But I already looked in their kitchen window and

Iantha invited me in, but I said I had to ask first. So now I asked. Good-bye."

Rosalind knew there was something wrong with that reasoning, but she was too groggy to work it out, and by the time Batty and Hound were gone from her room, she was once again asleep.

The second time she woke up, it was because Jane was sitting on her bed.

"Oh, good, Rosy, you're finally awake," she said. "I've been trying to lure you from your sleep with my intense gaze."

"I wish you hadn't." Rosalind yawned.

"Sorry, but Skye's ignoring me, and I just had to tell someone. Listen to this: *The archaeologist despaired of ever again seeing his dear home and his even more dear loved ones. He was trapped—hopelessly, horribly—in the ruins of an ancient Aztec temple, without food or water. But little did he know*—wait a minute." Jane scribbled furiously in a blue notebook.

"You're writing a new Sabrina Starr book," said Rosalind. Why did her sisters have so much energy this morning? She herself had none, for with so much to mull over and regret, it had taken her hours to fall asleep.

"*Sabrina Starr Rescues an Archaeologist.* I'm using all of my research on the Aztecs. The archaeologist gets trapped in the very temple where Rainbow was almost sacrificed, and then the ghost of Rainbow comes back to help Sabrina Starr rescue him. What do you think?"

264

"It's fascinating, though, honestly, I'd rather talk about it later."

"Okay." Jane got off the bed and almost left, then came back. "Do you think I should invite Iantha and Ben to today's soccer game?"

But Rosalind was asleep again, and the next thing she knew, there was a great SLAM, and Skye was tromping into the room. She'd thrown the door open so vehemently that it banged against the wall.

"Did you hear the phone?" she asked just as vehemently.

"I was asleep," answered Rosalind piteously. "Was it for me?"

"No, it was for me. It was Pearson." Skye scowled at Rosalind's dresser, which didn't deserve it. "He asked me to go to the movies this afternoon, and I told him to go soak his head."

"And?" asked Rosalind after a long wait for more information.

"And what?"

"And do you want to talk about it?"

"Of course not." Skye looked at Rosalind as though she'd suddenly sprouted an extra head or two.

"Then please let me go back to sleep."

"All right. It's time to begin my pre-soccer routine anyway. Oh, and Rosalind . . ."

Rosalind resisted the impulse to throw the bedside lamp at her. "What?"

"Iantha asked if we can take care of Ben tomorrow night. She has to go to that gala science wing dedication thing at the university, and her babysitter just canceled."

"Tell her yes. Now go away."

"I already did. That is, I told her yes as long as Daddy didn't make us have our own babysitter, but he said he thinks we've grown up enough lately, and as long as we start on our punishment chores—hey!"

Though the bedside lamp was still safe, Rosalind had launched herself out of her bed and, with one great shove, cleared the room and gotten her privacy back. She would be able to sleep now, for she'd run out of sisters. Gratefully, she snuggled back under her covers and slept, and slept, until she was woken up for the last time that morning by a polite knock on her door.

"It's me, Aunt Claire. Time to get ready for the soccer game."

At last someone worth getting up for! Rosalind leapt out of bed, threw open the door, and gave her aunt a giant hug.

"There's my Rosy," said Aunt Claire.

Rosalind knew what she meant. "I *have* been awfully grumpy lately. I'm so sorry."

"I wouldn't say grumpy, dear." Aunt Claire brushed Rosalind's stray curls off her face. "Just more private than usual."

"Did Daddy tell you everything? Are you angry with us?"

"Yes, everything, and no, I'm not angry. Do I look angry?"

No, she didn't. She looked just right, just like she always had all of Rosalind's life. Oh, it was wonderful to be done with the half-truths and fibs. Rosalind again hugged her own, dear aunt, squeezed her tight, full of love. But there was yet another question that had to be asked, one that had kept Rosalind tossing and turning the night before. "Do you think Mommy would be angry?"

"Angry at our plans and counterplans, with your father sneaking out in the middle of it all to read a book? No, Rosy. I think she'd be laughing herself into fits."

"Really?" But suddenly there it was, a memory of her mother laughing—roaring!—at one of Aunt Claire's silly jokes. How had she forgotten her mother's joyous sense of humor? Rosalind smiled up at her aunt. "Never mind. I think you're right."

"Of course I'm right. I always am, except when it has to do with your father and dating. Whoa, what a yawn!"

"I didn't get much sleep."

"And unfortunately there's no time to get more. Only ten minutes till departure for the soccer game."

A quick shower and the bagel Rosalind grabbed for breakfast did little to wake her up, and neither did the drive to the soccer game, though the rest of the family was lively enough, what with Skye, Jane, and

Batty chanting about annihilation and humiliation, while Aunt Claire kept making Mr. Penderwick laugh with ever more ridiculous ideas for dates out of books. Scarlett O'Hara! Miss Marple! Mary Poppins! It wasn't unpleasant, the sleepy, foggy feeling, as Rosalind described it later to Anna. Still, she was glad when they reached the soccer fields, for wandering vaguely was more suited to her mood than being with loud relatives. And after she wandered for a moment, she was even more glad, for she came upon Iantha and Ben, and Ben stretched out his chubby arms to her, and she took him and held him, and there's nothing less foggy than a warm, happy baby.

"Duck," he said quietly in her ear.

"I know," she answered, and wandered again until she found a bench to sit on during the game.

This final game of the season was the second matchup between Antonio's Pizza and Cameron Hardware, and thus a blood match. No one had forgotten the wild brouhaha that had broken out the last time they'd met on the field. And, too, whoever won this game would be league champion. Both teams knew it. The crowd—swollen today with half of Cameron Hardware's staff and all of Antonio's Pizza's staff—knew it. Even Rosalind knew it, though by the time the game started, she was barely awake, having slipped into a sleepy trance.

It all had to be described to her later—how Skye

calmly captained her team to perfection, and how she was strong and fast, and so completely owned the backfield that her goalkeeper had too little to do; this was the only complaint. And Rosalind had to be told that Jane, too, had played her best, combining the speed of a track star with the precise footwork of a ballerina, and though she did once or twice call on the Aztec gods for help, she never for a moment became Mick Hart, which was a great relief to everyone.

By the end of the first half, Rosalind had gotten herself off the bench and into a more comfortable position on the grass. Ben fell asleep in her lap, and she fell into a doze with him, barely taking in that neither team had yet scored. For Melissa Patenaude, refusing to be overshadowed yet again by Penderwicks, was playing better than anyone had ever seen her play—better than anyone had ever dreamed she could play—and her team was rising to her example, working in sync, like a purple-and-white soccer machine. One of the things they were doing best was making sure that Jane Penderwick couldn't score any goals. They stuck to her like shadows, and yet no one fouled her. It was brilliantly done.

All of this meant that the game could go either way, and the crowd—except for Rosalind and Ben—was in a state of wild excitement as the second half began. There were rumors later about Mr. Penderwick shouting Latin war cries, and Iantha and Aunt Claire teaching Batty how to lead cheers, though Rosalind only ever believed half of them. For surely, she protested, if there had been that much noise, she would have heard *some* of it.

All through the second half, the teams battled on, until there was so little time left that the specter of a scoreless tie rose up and hovered over the field. No one could have borne that, especially not Skye and Melissa, who would have had to share the league trophy, passing it back and forth between their homes. It was unthinkable. And since it was, Skye pulled one last, desperate stunt out of her captain's brain and, with only one minute left on the clock, shouted "SACRIFICE!" so loudly that everyone but Rosalind—and Ben—heard it. But though everyone heard, only one person understood what Skye meant, not because they'd discussed it or planned it, but because they were sisters and knew each other through and through. So when Jane next received the ball, she settled it, dribbling this way and that, crazily, fantastically, as one after another of Melissa's defenders came to her, surrounding her, making sure she couldn't get close enough to the goal to shoot. So intent were they on Jane that they didn't notice they were being maneuvered away from the goal while someone else was sneaking out of the backfield, taking a long route around the action, until, at just the right moment—

Wham! Jane crossed the ball past Melissa and directly to Skye, unnoticed Skye, cunning Skye, who in a move worthy of the greatest—a Pelé or a Hamm—danced past a startled defender, raised her arms in triumph, and neatly scored. Antonio's Pizza had won the game, and the season.

The roar of the crowd—and particularly of the Penderwicks—penetrated then even to Rosalind. She roused herself and looked down at Ben, who looked back up at her, smiling, for he was awake now, too, and then she looked out onto the field and saw that something odd was happening. Antonio's Pizza was on one half of the field, jumping up and down and screeching in triumph, and Cameron Hardware was on the other half, wandering around with their heads hanging in humiliation. That was all normal. But in the middle—where no one should have been—were the two team captains. They weren't beating each other up. They didn't even seem to be arguing. They were—talking? And if Rosalind wasn't mistaken, now Melissa was crying. And now—this was beyond imagining—Skye was putting an arm around Melissa. It was perhaps the briefest and most reluctant hug ever known to mankind, but it was a hug, nonetheless. If that really just happened, Rosalind thought, anything in this world can happen. She picked up Ben and joined her family and Iantha.

A moment later, Skye trotted off the field and graciously accepted everyone's proud congratulations and handshakes. Then Aunt Claire asked, "What happened out there with Melissa?"

"Oh, that." Skye looked disgusted. "She had some stuff to tell me."

"What stuff? That is, if it's private, you don't have to tell us."

"It's not private, it's just stupid." But Skye looked round at everyone, and it seemed that they'd all seen the hug and wanted an explanation, even her father, who usually didn't notice things like that, and Iantha, who was too polite to ask. Skye heaved a great sigh, then said what she had to say in a great rush. "Melissa said that she didn't hate me at all, but that she's been jerky to me because she's always been jealous of me because I'm so smart and pr—and a good soccer player. Oh, and because of stupid Pearson. She says she likes him. That's when she started to cry. So I told her she was smart, too, though she's not. Then I told her—and this was absolutely, totally true—that she could have Pearson, because I don't want him, and besides, I'd already told him to go soak his head, so I was sure he didn't like me anymore. And then she thanked me over and over, and so I hugged her to get her to shut up."

"That was very kind of you," said Mr. Penderwick when it was clear that she was done. He sounded like he was choking.

"Maybe you and Melissa could become friends now," added Iantha.

Skye looked as if Iantha had just suggested she take up needlepoint. "Holy bananas, I hope not," she said, then ran off, for now her team was calling for their captain.

Heavens, thought Rosalind, trying with great seriousness to take in this new version of Melissa. The three adults with her, though, didn't seem to be affected the same way. That is, they weren't serious. They were laughing. They were laughing so hard that they were all three leaning into each other to keep themselves upright. See them lean, Rosalind told herself, as time slowed down for her and the remains of her foggy trance started to lift. See Aunt Claire lean into Daddy, and see Iantha lean into him, too. And see him reach out to steady Iantha. See how gently he does it, and see how he looks down at her while he reaches out. And see—

Rosalind's world heaved up and shook itself like Hound after a bath. Now she was awake.

As soon as the Penderwicks got home, Rosalind ran upstairs to her room. As revelations went, the one she'd had at the soccer game was as huge as it was scary, and she couldn't act on it without help. She opened the bottom drawer of her bureau, and yes, there was the help she needed, the photograph she'd hidden away weeks earlier.

"Hi, Mommy, I missed you," she said, gazing hungrily at her mother's eyes, crinkled in laughter, her pretty blond hair framing her face, and her hands wrapped lovingly around the solemn, brown-eyed baby that was Rosalind once upon a time. "And I'm sorry I doubted you. I think I have it right now. Do I? Was *that* what you meant?"

There were no answers, of course, but asking the questions strengthened Rosalind's resolve. She put the photograph back on the bedside table where it belonged, then went to round up her sisters. It was time for an Emergency MOPS.

They were none too willing to come. Skye and Jane hadn't yet changed out of their dirty uniforms, and everyone was hungry for lunch. But since no one ever ignored an Emergency MOPS, all the sisters obediently gathered in Rosalind's room and sat in a circle on the floor. Settling down was another thing, though, because the excitement of the soccer game had not yet worn off, and Rosalind pounded on the floor over and over without getting their attention.

At last she had to shout. "QUIET! EMERGENCY MOPS—"

"We can hear you," said Skye.

"It's about time. Emergency MOPS come to order."

"Second the motion," said Skye.

"Third it," said Jane.

"Fourth it," said Batty. She knew better than to fifth it for Hound at an Emergency MOPS.

Rosalind put out her fist. "All swear to keep secret what is said here, even from Daddy and Aunt Claire—and actually from Iantha, too—unless you think someone might do something truly bad."

Marveling at the addition of Iantha to the oath, the other sisters put their fists on top of Rosalind's.

"This I swear, by the Penderwick Family Honor!"

It was now time for Rosalind to begin the meeting, but though she'd pounded and shouted to get to this point, she hesitated. The weight of what she was about to do almost overwhelmed her. For courage, she took the photograph of her mother down and put it in the middle of the circle.

"Ever since Aunt Claire gave Mommy's letter to Daddy," she said, "I've been mistaken, misguided, shortsighted, and selfish."

"Good grief, Rosy," said Skye.

"It's okay, Skye, because I finally figured it out at the end of the soccer game. What if Mommy was right about Daddy getting lonely and needing a grown-up woman to talk to besides Aunt Claire? What if it really is the right thing for him to date? What if— what if he even wants to get married again sometime? Would that truly be so terrible?"

"You said it would be," said Skye. "You were sure."

"You were positive," said Jane.

275

"I know, I know." Rosalind waved her hand as though to erase all that. "But what if he dates and then maybe marries someone really nice and kind and smart?"

"Rosalind, I'm too hungry for all these questions," said Skye. "Just tell us what you're thinking."

"All right, I will. I think Daddy likes Iantha."

Skye rolled her eyes in frustration. "Of course Daddy likes Iantha. We all do."

"That's not what I mean," said Rosalind. "I mean—Daddy *likes* her."

The first to understand, Jane leaned forward excitedly. "Does she like him back?"

"Yes, I think so."

"But—" This was Skye, who didn't know what she was trying to say.

"I know," said Rosalind. "It's perfect, isn't it?"

And Skye found, to her amazement, that it being perfect was just what she'd meant.

Only one sister hadn't reacted so far, and now the three older ones turned to Batty, who was flopped heavily over Hound, trying to untangle some of his neckties.

"Do you understand what we're saying, honey?" Rosalind asked her.

"You're saying that Daddy should date Iantha." She got one necktie free and started on another. "I said that a long time ago."

"She did, you know, at the last MOPS. I remember." Skye looked as disgusted as when she'd hugged Melissa.

"It's becoming clear to me," said Jane, "that Batty and I are the sensitive Penderwicks."

"Not now, Jane," said Rosalind before Skye could start an argument about sensitivity. "Lunch will be any minute, and we've got to decide what to do. Because if we think Daddy and Iantha should date, they're both going to the gala university event tomorrow night. They can simply go together."

"How thrilling!" said Jane. "How are we going to make them do it?"

"It's not like we can trick them into it," added Skye. "Not after last night. Daddy told us no interference, remember?"

"If we have to trick him, we will. We can always confess again," said Rosalind. "Now we need a plan, the new and improved Save-Daddy Plan. Everybody think until their brains fall out. We have less than twenty-four hours."

CHAPTER TWENTY-ONE
A Very Long Night

IT WAS JANE who thought of taking the battery out of the car—she'd read about it once while researching a Sabrina Starr book. Skye found out how to do it by going across the street and asking Nick to demonstrate on his parents' car. Rosalind wanted to be the one to do the actual taking out, since, as oldest sister, she should be responsible for the part that was sort of illegal. But when the whole schedule was written out, she realized that the battery removal and the fetching of Ben had to be done at the same time. And nobody thought that Skye should be sent for Ben.

"So Skye works on the car, Rosalind and Batty go next door to get Ben, and I make sure Daddy doesn't come downstairs before Skye's ready," said Jane. The plan was to be set in motion any minute—as soon as their father emerged from his study and went upstairs to get dressed for the gala event—and the sisters were going over the details one last time. There hadn't been much time for practice, as they'd had to lay low and look innocent until Aunt Claire went home, and Rosalind was afraid people would forget their parts.

"Skye, how will you let Jane know you're ready?" she asked.

"I'll go upstairs and tell her she'd better clean her half of the room or I'll kill her." Skye anxiously tugged at her sweatshirt. She had several essential tools tucked into the waist of her jeans, and she was worried that her father would notice the odd lumps.

Rosalind turned to Batty. There had been some discussion about Batty being the weak link, but she was needed. Besides, her future, too, was in the balance. "Now, Batty, remember that as soon as we get to Iantha's, you go to the window and watch for Daddy to come out of our house and get into the car. What's your spy code?"

"Bug Man."

"And you absolutely will not say 'Bug Man' until Daddy's really and truly in the car?"

"Even if I see Bug Man, I won't say so."

"There's-no-Bug-Man," Skye rattled off automatically.

Rosalind shushed her. "Bug Man" as the spy code

didn't please her, either, but it was one they could be sure Batty would remember.

"Anything else?" she asked. "Ready for Phase One to initiate? The oath, everyone."

The sisters formed a circle and joined hands.

"For the Penderwick Family Honor," they said in unison, just as their father came out of his study.

"Macbeth's witches, right here in my own living room," he said.

"There were only three of them," said Rosalind, wishing that she didn't look as guilty as she knew she did.

"Time to go get ready for the gala, Daddy," said Jane brightly. "I think I'll come up and talk to you through your door while you dress."

"Why?" He settled his glasses firmly on his nose and looked through them at her.

"To keep you company, of course," she said with a look of shock and sadness that almost fooled her sisters, even though they knew exactly what she was doing.

She did fool their father, who kindly put his arm around her and led her toward the steps. She'd be fine up there, Rosalind knew—they'd put together a list of topics for her to introduce as stalling techniques, including her new Sabrina Starr book. Jane could go on forever about Sabrina Starr without any effort at all.

Now it was up to the rest of them. They shoved

Hound into the kitchen with a bone to keep him quiet, then ran outside. The daylight had almost faded, which they hoped would give them enough cover—heaven forbid Iantha looked out a window and saw them stealing their own battery. When they reached the car, Skye popped open the hood.

"It doesn't look like the Geigers' car," said Skye, shocked. "Everything's in a different place!"

"Can you still do it?" Rosalind bit at her finger-nails, which she never did, while Skye poked around, muttering strange words like "alternator" and "fuel injector" and "electronic ignition."

"Yes, here's the battery," she said finally, then extracted an adjustable wrench from under her sweat-shirt. She looked less anxious now, and already had an impressive smear of grease across her forehead. "They really should teach us this stuff in school. Much better than the stupid Aztecs."

Rosalind wasn't going to get into any more discussions about the Aztecs for now and, she hoped, for-ever. She took Batty's hand and headed next door, abruptly realizing that she'd been so busy organizing everyone else, she hadn't planned how to keep Iantha from leaving her house too early.

"Please don't let her be ready," she said, ringing the doorbell.

But Iantha was ready, and—

"You look lovely," said Rosalind with a little gasp.

She was telling the truth. Iantha was magnificent—goddess-like, Rosalind told Anna later—in a flowing silk dress of a mysterious blue-green, the color of the sea just before sunset. Her hair, too, was stunning, swept up in an elegant twist, and she was wearing a heavy gold necklace with dark red stones.

"Thank you." Iantha's old shyness seemed to be back. "That is, are you sure?"

"Yes. Oh, yes."

"It's not too much for giving a speech? I loathe giving speeches. Thank goodness the speeches come first and I can get it over with. Oh, dear." She looked around her. "Have I lost Ben?"

"He's with Batty, looking out the window."

"Of course he is. Then I guess I'm ready to leave."

But since Batty had not yet said the spy code, Iantha had to be kept inside. So Rosalind made her go over everything that Ben would need that evening, even though they'd already discussed it that afternoon. What he could eat for supper, what time he should be put to bed, and what he should wear when put there. And how Iantha had packed his things in a little overnight bag, and that she would leave her front door unlocked in case she'd forgotten anything, but that Rosalind should be very careful not to let Asimov out if she did have to go into the house.

After they'd gone through all that, because Batty had still not said the spy code, Rosalind opened the overnight bag and slowly and carefully inspected every item it held: two jars of baby food, two pairs of pajamas, three diapers, a red duck, a yellow duck, an extra pair of socks—

"TOMMY!" shrieked Batty.

Rosalind rushed over to the window. Had Batty gotten the spy code wrong, after all? But no, it really was Tommy she'd seen, going into his house.

"Batty, you don't have to let us know every time Tommy comes home." Rosalind smiled sheepishly at Iantha, hoping it hadn't looked as though she were desperate for a glimpse of that most annoying boy.

"How is he?" asked Iantha.

"I don't know. He's not talking to me."

"I'm sorry. It's hard when you stop being friends with someone after such a long time. You must miss him."

Rosalind tried to summon an ironic laugh, as a polite way to tell Iantha that missing Tommy was a ridiculous concept. But somehow the laugh stuck in her throat, and before she had to wonder why, Batty screeched out "BUG MAN!" setting off a storm of cheers from Ben. Thank goodness. Phase One of the plan was complete.

"I'm all set, Iantha." Rosalind zipped up Ben's bag. "We can go."

Now for Phase Two, which would make removing a battery and stalling Iantha look easy. Bracing herself,

Rosalind opened the front door, letting out Batty and Ben first, who hopped down the steps quite pleased with themselves, then Iantha, who drifted gracefully behind them, looking even more lovely in the soft twilight of the evening.

One glance over to the Penderwicks' driveway, and Rosalind could see that everyone was exactly on schedule. Her father was in his car, the car's engine was not on, and Skye and Jane were lurking close by, pretending to look concerned. Good. Rosalind executed the prearranged signal—that is, she scratched the top of her head.

On cue, Jane waved and shouted, "YOO-HOO! DADDY'S CAR WON'T START!"

The sisters had discussed at great length how to get Iantha across her driveway and over to their own. Would Rosalind have to insist? But no, Iantha, without hesitation, glided in exactly the direction she was supposed to go. Rosalind followed with Batty and Ben, watching and holding her breath.

Now her father was getting out of the car. This was a crucial moment. If he looked under the hood, he'd see that the battery was missing, and he'd want to call the police to report a robbery, and all would be lost. Come on, Skye, thought Rosalind, still following Iantha, it's time for your next line.

Skye came through perfectly. She blocked her father's way to the front of the car. "Don't open the hood, Daddy. You'll get your suit dirty. Right, Jane?"

"Right, Skye, and besides, maybe what's wrong with the car is a computer glitch, anyway, and they're hard to see."

"Yes, a computer glitch is possible, like with a bad sensor."

Their father was still trying to get to the hood. "When did you two learn so much about cars?" He got past Skye, only to run into Jane.

"Magazines," she said wildly.

"What magazines?"

Rosalind, right behind Iantha, knew that Jane was close to breaking. Next she'd be nattering about who knows what and their father would get suspicious and the plan would fail. But Iantha was almost in place. If she would only speak before Jane got going. Say something, Iantha, prayed Rosalind, please say something.

"Hello, Martin," said Iantha. "What's the trouble?"

He turned toward her. The car keys fell out of his hand. Skye dove for them and shoved them deep into her pocket, but she needn't have bothered hiding the keys. As Jane said later, Daddy had stopped noticing anything but Iantha in her dress. And Iantha, seeing him notice her so completely, had gone so still and quiet that she might have been a statue.

"Daddy, is it true that the car won't start?" Rosalind gently hinted when the silence had gone on for too long.

"No. I mean yes," her father answered, like he was coming out of a dream. "The girls tell me it could be a computer glitch."

"Ah, a computer glitch," breathed Iantha, clearly having no idea what she was saying.

Rosalind tugged on Batty's hand. They'd given her yet one more line, even though it was a vital one, because fewer suspicions would be aroused if Batty said it.

Batty knew what the tug meant. She stood tall and spoke proudly.

"Iantha," she said. "Could you take Daddy in your car?"

Iantha murmured something, and their father murmured something else, then he held out his arm to her—like a true and honorable gentleman, his daughters agreed later—and she shyly took it. And then together, after only vague good-byes to their children, they drifted back over to Iantha's house and got into her car.

"Phase Two complete," said Rosalind, picking up Ben. "Let's get some supper."

When supper was over, and Rosalind was in the bathroom with Ben, washing applesauce off his face and hands and out of his hair, Batty went to her bedroom to get ready for her very first almost-sleepover. She wished Ben could stay the whole night, but even so, it was terribly exciting just to have him fall asleep in her room, and she wanted it to be just right for him. She took all of her stuffed animals off the bed and piled them in the corner, since no one likes sleeping with someone else's stuffed animals. She made sure the closet door was shut, just in case Ben was afraid of monsters. And finally, because it was a special occasion, she selected her favorite ties from the ones Jeffrey had given her and wrapped them around her waist, then wrapped several of her not-so-favorites around Hound's legs. In the meantime, Hound went on with his own preparations—unearthing the bone he'd left under the bed a week ago, just in case Ben was the type of boy to steal a dog's bone.

Now Batty and Hound were both ready. Side by side, they waited patiently until Rosalind carried in a clean and sleepy Ben, his red hair sticking up in damp spikes.

"Time for a story," said Batty.

"What do you think Ben would enjoy?" asked Rosalind.

Batty had thought long and hard about this, and had decided that he'd probably most enjoy a story about Batty. "Let's tell him about when Skye dropped me in the waves at Cape Cod and I almost drowned."

"I'm not sure that's the most soothing bedtime story for a little boy."

"He wants to hear it, don't you, Ben?"

"Duck."

"See, Rosalind, that means yes. Once upon a time there was a brave little girl named—"

"Duck," said Ben again. "Duck, duck."

"You mustn't interrupt," said Batty. "Once upon a time there was a—"

"DUCK, DUCK, DUCK, DUCK!"

"—BRAVE LITTLE GIRL NAMED BATTY—"

"Stop shouting, Batty," said Rosalind. "Ben's crying."

It was true. He was crying and rubbing his eyes with his fat fists. Rosalind rocked him, and Batty patted him on the head, feeling like her sleepover was getting off to a bad start. She felt so bad about it that she took—not Funty, because Funty didn't feel safe with anyone but Batty or Hound—Sedgewick the horse from the corner and handed him to Ben, but Sedgewick only made him cry more. So she tried Ursula the bear, but Ursula was no better than Sedgewick, and then at last Batty figured it out.

"He must want one of the ducks from his room."

Rosalind looked into the bag that Iantha had sent along and brought out the red duck and the yellow duck, but neither of them stopped his tears.

"Your white duck?" Batty asked him.

He nodded vigorously and clung to her as if to a life raft in a cold sea.

"He needs his white duck," she told Rosalind.

From long experience with younger sisters, Rosalind knew there was no point in arguing. If Ben needed his white duck to go to sleep, she had to go next door to get it. "All right," she said. "You two stay here. I'll send Skye in to help with stories."

But when she got to her sisters' room, Skye was out on the roof with her binoculars.

"Tell stories? Are you kidding?" she said when Rosalind leaned out the window and asked for her help.

"It's just for a few minutes. Anyway, you'll be the OAP, so you have to."

OAP meant Oldest Available Penderwick, and carried with it great responsibilities. However, Skye stated emphatically that she didn't consider storytelling to be one of those responsibilities.

Rosalind turned next to Jane, who was at her desk, writing.

"Jane, Jane," she said. "JANE!"

Jane tore herself away from her blue notebook. "Listen to this. *Rainbow and Sabrina Starr joined hands across the centuries, two brave and bold spirits sworn to—sworn to*—rats, what are they sworn to? Uphold something or the other."

"Jane, could you tell stories to Batty and Ben while I go next door for a duck?"

"All right." She stood, taking her blue notebook with her. "I'll read them my new book. They'll enjoy that."

"Thank you," said Rosalind.

She put on a jacket before going outside, for the daylight was long gone now, and Gardam Street was dark and chilly. It was the kind of delicious chilliness, though, that was good for thinking about how winter wasn't far away, and snow, and Christmas. Rosalind shivered pleasurably, and thought about all that, and thought, too, before she could stop herself, about how much fun it would be to buy Christmas presents for Ben. And then she did stop herself, for who knew what would happen with her father and Iantha. If tonight went badly, they might never speak to each other again, and then there'd be no Ben at Christmas. Oh, please don't let it go badly, she whispered into the darkness.

And back from the darkness came not an answering whisper but an orange cat streaking wildly across the grass before disappearing into the forsythia.

"Asimov!" she called, but she knew him well enough to know that if he didn't want to come, no calling would change his mind. Rosalind frowned, not from worry, for the silly cat always came home, but because it made no sense that he'd managed to escape. Had Iantha left a window open or had Asimov actually learned to open the front door? If Rosalind had been a nervous person, this would have made her nervous, but a moment later she'd forgotten about Asimov, because all of her attention was being used up on pretending she didn't notice the Geiger brothers driving up Gardam Street and pulling into their driveway. She pretended so well not to notice that she would have sworn it never happened, but all the pretending fell apart when Tommy ran across the street and stood in front of her. And looked at her, even.

She looked back at him.

Then he even talked to her.

"I want to tell you something. You don't have to listen, but I'm going to tell you anyway." He had a football with him, which he was anxiously tossing from one hand to the other—back and forth, and back and forth, and back and forth, and back and forth, until Rosalind took it away from him.

"I can't listen while you do that." She tucked the football under her arm. "Now what?"

"What?"

"Tommy!"

"Oh, sorry." He gulped a few times, then calmed himself by fixing his gaze on the football. "Trilby and I broke up today. That is, I broke up with her, because— never mind why."

"Why?"

"I said never mind why."

"Fine. I don't care anyway."

"Because she was boring. Unfortunately, I couldn't tell her that, so she may have gotten the idea that I broke up with her because of you, even though I definitely told her that you're just my neighbor, and even though you're prettier now than you used to be, I hardly ever notice and—"

Rosalind interrupted him. "You think I'm pretty?"

"I guess so, I mean, Nick says so. Actually, a lot of guys say so, and don't ask me what guys."

"All right. Good grief."

"So that's all I wanted to tell you. I'll leave now."

Rosalind was certain that she shouldn't let him go without saying something kind about Trilby and the breakup, though she didn't know why she was certain, and she didn't know what to say even if she knew why. She puzzled over it for what seemed a long time, while Tommy kept his gaze on the football. Finally she said, "I'm glad you broke up with her. I mean, not because I missed you or anything."

"You didn't miss me." It wasn't a question.

"Gosh, no. Maybe a tiny bit, but no, probably not."

"Of course, I didn't expect you to miss me."

"No, of course you didn't." Rosalind shook her head to emphasize how little anyone would have expected that of her. "I'm sorry, but I'd better go. I have to get a duck."

If Tommy had hoped for more than that, he didn't let on. He took his football and walked away, and Rosalind was once more alone in the chilly night. She shivered again, not so pleasurably as before, and reached for Iantha's doorknob. Before she could turn it, though, the door flew open on its own.

What was this? Was Iantha home already? How could that be? But no, it wasn't Iantha who had opened the door. It was a man Rosalind had never seen before. A not very big man, but a grown-up man nonetheless, with large glasses. He must be a friend of Iantha's, she thought, or why would he be coming out of her house? Oh!—and this explained about Asimov.

"Hello," she said pleasantly. "I guess it was you who let Asimov out."

"Who's Asimov?" he asked, shoving something under his coat as though to keep her from seeing it, but since it didn't fit all the way under his coat, she saw it anyway.

"Iantha's cat, of course," she said politely, because she still wasn't suspicious. "But why are you hiding her computer under your coat?"

"It's my computer," he said.

"With duck stickers on it?" The man looked scared, and for a moment Rosalind felt sorry for him, because he was a pathetic little person. But then, at last, she understood that this was no friend of Iantha's, and her pity turned to anger. People didn't steal from each other on Gardam Street, pathetic or not. "Give it to me."

"I won't."

"You have to."

She reached out, and he pulled the computer out of his coat as though he would comply. But it was a trick, for instead of handing over the computer, he thrust it at her so hard that she stumbled backward and fell, since even pathetic little men could be stronger than twelve-year-old girls. And then he was running away, taking Iantha's precious computer with him. Rosalind scrambled to her feet. She would rush after him, the creep, and exact her revenge—Iantha's revenge—though she wasn't quite sure how she would do that on her own.

But she didn't have to do it on her own, because here came sailing through the air a football, aimed not at a leaping wide receiver who would carry it triumphantly over the goal line but at the little man who was running for his life. Rosalind, delighted, watched as—touchdown!—the football made contact, and the man stumbled, slowing down just enough to be caught up to and tackled by Cameron Middle School number 86. For the second time in two days, Rosalind's world up and shook itself, and when it had settled down, everything was different again. She knew now how blind and stupid she'd been about Tommy. How could she have been so annoyed with him? He was old Tommy, always had been, always would be, and that was just right for her.

"Nice tackle!" she told him ecstatically.

He stood up and brushed off his pants. "Now tell me whether you missed me, Rosy."

"Oh, Tommy, I did miss you. I missed you this much," she answered, her palms six inches apart.

The man on the ground tried to sit up, and Tommy pushed him back down. "How much?"

"Okay, this much." She resisted throwing her arms as wide as they could go.

"Maybe you and I can date when we're older," said Tommy, trying to look nonchalant and failing horribly. "Like when we're fourteen."

Fourteen now seemed like a long time to wait. "Thirteen, I think. January for me, and April for you."

Now the man snorted sarcastically, but they didn't notice, for Tommy was too busy grinning like a fool at Rosalind, and she was too busy enjoying him doing it, and they were both ridiculously happy. They could have kept that up forever if eventually they hadn't begun to wonder what to do about their captive. Neither wanted to leave the other alone with him to go for reinforcements, and they had their first argument since their reconciliation, but it wasn't a true argument, and they made up just as the noise of the Penderwicks' front door slamming echoed through the neighborhood.

"My sisters are coming," said Rosalind to Tommy.

He leaned down and bravely kissed her on the cheek. "Don't forget. You're waiting for me until we're both thirteen."

She just as bravely kissed him back. "I won't forget."

And then Skye arrived. If she'd noticed the kisses,

she was for once diplomatic enough not to mention it. "I saw it all from the roof! Great pass, Tommy!"

"Thanks. I broke up with Trilby last night."

"Good work. Welcome home." Skye put her foot on the man's neck, for he'd made signs of trying to get up again. "Don't move, jerk."

Next to come was Jane, with Ben riding piggyback on her shoulders. "Who is this villain?" She looked with scorn on the fallen.

"We don't know yet. He was trying to steal Iantha's computer," said Rosalind, plucking Ben off Jane. He was wearing one of Batty's sweatshirts over his pajamas, and a pair of her kangaroo socks. Not only did he seem to have forgotten his missing duck, he looked delighted. He'd never had an adventure like the one he was having tonight.

Last came Batty and Hound, their neckties streaming. Hound took his natural place by the man's head and bared his teeth alarmingly. Batty crouched down next to Hound and looked at the man—and he looked back at her.

He spoke first. "You again! You're everywhere."

"Hello, Bug Man," she said.

"Batty, how many times do I have to tell you that there's no—" Skye stopped midsentence, her mouth open. Was it possible that Bug Man wasn't just a figment of Batty's imagination?

"Batty, is this really Bug Man?" asked Rosalind.

"He doesn't look like much," said Jane.

"He's scarier with his sunglasses on." Batty didn't want anyone to think she was a coward.

"Excuse me, I'm right here," said the man.

"Don't interrupt the ladies," said Tommy. Hound barked menacingly, too, for good measure.

"So this guy really is Bug Man." Skye was still doubting.

"Also Sock Man," said Batty.

"Spock, not Sock, you annoying child. But actually, I am Norman Birnbaum." He said it like he was saying "Albert Einstein."

The name Norman had caught Jane's attention. She turned to the others. "Now I know who he is! He's the nut that thinks Iantha stole his research! That's why he took her computer. He was stealing *her* research so that he could pretend it was his. Nasty thief."

"I am neither a nut nor a thief, and Iantha did steal my research, and I have been trying for weeks to find the right opportunity to take it back. I will be vindicated. You know nothing about it, so don't argue with me."

Skye leaned down and looked him full in the face. She understood now—this guy was just weird enough to actually be Batty's Bug Man. "We won't argue with you. I will simply tell you this. Iantha is a genius. She doesn't need to steal from pinheads like you. So not only have you been stalking my neighborhood and frightening my baby sister—"

"I'm not a baby!" interrupted Batty.

Skye plugged on. "—you're also making disparaging remarks about a woman who is on a first date with my father, a date that we worked very hard to make happen. I myself had to steal a car battery, and that's not as easy as people make it sound."

"You see, Mr. Bugbaum," said Jane. "Iantha is a Potential Penderwick."

"As is this handsome baby," said Rosalind, and kissed Ben's cheek for good luck.

Skye jerked her head up, for she hadn't thought of that, and grimaced at Ben, who waved happily back.

"So, team," said Tommy. "What are we going to do with Norman here?"

"Let me go, of course," he said. "I've done nothing wrong, and you are mere children."

"Mere children, ha!" said Jane. "I say we tie up the knave and then discuss his fate."

Since everyone thought this a good idea, Batty and Hound donated Jeffrey's neckties, and soon Bug Man, aka Sock or Spock, aka Norman Birnbaum, was bound hand and foot. Jane, Batty, and Hound then took a few minutes to be Aztec priests calling for blood, until Rosalind quieted them down. Norman was slime, but that was no reason to terrify him.

Then came a long discussion about what they should do next. No one wanted to interrupt the precious first date going on at the university, but, except for Skye, no one believed they should call the police all on their own. Jane's suggestion of throwing Norman into their basement so that he could dwell on his sins was rejected outright.

"We'd better call Daddy and Iantha," said Rosalind finally. "They need to call the police, not us. Their speeches came first, so we'll just be interrupting their dinner."

"Their romantic dinner together." Jane frowned at Norman, lying there in the neckties. "This is all your fault."

"All agreed, then?" asked Tommy.

Skye ran off to make the phone call.

Rosalind was perched at the top of the steps, waiting for her father to come inside. Her sisters had gone to bed, but tired as she was, she knew she couldn't fall asleep without hearing how it had all ended. With Norman and the police, and—with Iantha.

Now Rosalind heard the front door open and close and was about to call to him quietly, but he was already coming up the steps, for he knew right where she'd be.

"What's going to happen to Norman?" she asked.

"We don't know yet. Iantha told the police she

thinks he's more confused than dangerous, but lawyers will have to straighten it all out." He sat down and put his arm around her. "Did he frighten you badly?"

"Only for a second, until I realized he was more afraid than I was. And then, once Tommy was there, I couldn't be frightened anymore."

"Thank goodness for Tommy."

"Yes." She snuggled closer to her father. "We've decided to start dating when we're both thirteen. Isn't that good?"

"The best. *Optimus.* Tommy's a good person. He'll make a great son-in-law."

"Daddy!"

"Sorry."

She rested her head on his shoulder to show that the joke was forgiven, and there they sat at the top of the steps, father and oldest daughter, at peace with their world and with each other.

"I've missed this," he said quietly. "You do know how much I love you, don't you?"

"Yes, Daddy."

"And do you know—well, I know, anyway—that I've relied on you too much since your mother died? I've been remembering how concerned she was about you trying to fill in for her, and how I promised I wouldn't let you become too grown-up and responsible. I'm afraid I didn't keep that promise well enough,

Rosy. It's no wonder you hated the idea of me bringing a new woman into our lives."

As gratifying as this was—a few days ago Rosalind would have given anything to hear her father say these things—the conversation was going in the wrong direction. She and her sisters hadn't bothered to steal a battery and maneuver two oblivious adults into one car for it all to end like this.

"Maybe 'hate' is too strong a word," she said. "Or 'new.' Maybe 'new' is too strong a word."

"Sweetheart, you're so tired you're not making sense. Time for bed, yes?"

"No, wait." She was desperate. "You haven't told me yet whether you and Iantha enjoyed being together tonight. I mean, before we called you about Norman. No *cruciatus*, right? And you know how much we all like Iantha, right?"

"Excuse me?"

"Oh, you do like her, too, don't you?" By now Rosalind was babbling. "We were almost positive but don't have much experience with this kind of thing. And we're sorry about the car, but Skye thinks she put the battery back the right way."

He unwrapped her arms so he could look at her properly. "What are you talking about?"

"Why, you dating Iantha, of course."

"Oh." He stared off into space for a long moment. "But what was that about the car?"

"Nothing."

"Maybe I should look under the hood in the morning."

"Maybe you should, but please, about you and Iantha. You did enjoy being together, didn't you?"

"We did indeed."

"And?"

"Rosy, I'm lost here. Please speak slowly and clearly to help out your old father. Are you saying that you and your sisters won't mind if I date Iantha?"

"Will we mind? No, Daddy!" She wrapped her arms around him again, this time so tightly he couldn't get away. "We'll think it's *wonderful!*"

EPILOGUE

SEVEN MONTHS LATER

The sisters had decided together what they would wear on that most important day. Jane had asked for dresses with full skirts. Rosalind had picked out the color—a mysterious blue-green, the color of the sea just before sunset. Batty, with some guidance, had selected shoes with low heels and thin ankle straps. As for Skye, all she wanted was not to wear a hat with bows, or anything else on her head, for that matter. But when Iantha had asked if they would tuck yellow roses into their hair to match the yellow roses in her bouquet, Skye had agreed without a murmur, though she did tell Jane later that she would have drawn the line at pink roses, even for Iantha.

Now, on the day itself, the four were gathered in Rosalind's room, finishing their transformation from regular Penderwicks into bridesmaids.

"Hold still, Batty," said Rosalind. "Your rose keeps slipping."

Too excited to hold still, Batty was jumping up and down, trying for glimpses of herself in the mirror over the bureau. "I look beautiful, Hound," she said in between jumps, though Hound was ignoring her, being too busy trying to bite off the yellow bow around his neck. "Beautiful, beautiful, beautiful."

"As do we all." Jane put her hands on Batty's shoulders and held her down, letting Rosalind pin the errant flower firmly in place.

"I think that will hold," Rosalind said, then turned to Skye, who was almost as green as she'd been the night of *Sisters and Sacrifice*. "Are you all right?"

"I've forgotten my speech again." Skye plucked at the skirt of her dress and wondered if there was time to escape to the roof for some solitude. But from the roof, she'd be able to see into Iantha's backyard, where there was a flowered arch and an altar and dozens of chairs set in rows, and, worse, the already arriving guests. That would make her more nervous.

"It's not actually a speech," said Rosalind, not for the first time.

"Just a line," said Jane, who'd written this part of the ceremony. "Rosalind says: 'For a long time we didn't know what we wanted.' Then Skye, you say: 'And when we finally knew, we realized that what we wanted was right next door.' And then I say, 'Her name was Iantha, and magically, she wanted us, too.' Then Batty says—"

" 'And so did Ben,' " finished Batty.

" 'And when we finally knew,' " muttered Skye. " 'And when we finally knew, and when we finally knew'—"

Now Aunt Claire was calling them from downstairs. "Girls! The groomsmen are here!"

All worries about roses and speeches vanished as the girls flew out of the room and down the steps. Aunt Claire was at the bottom, flushed with excitement and lovely in dusky lavender. She gave them each a quick inspection and a quicker hug, then shooed them into the living room to greet the groomsmen.

There were three, splendid in dark suits. The tallest had a big smile and eyes only for Rosalind. She was across the room and hanging on his arm in a flash, certain that Tommy looked more grown-up and handsome than ever, and she may have been right, though she'd been thinking the same thing every day for the last seven months. The second boy, with freckles and green eyes, was not as tall but just as handsome, and was joyously attacked by Skye and Jane almost before he knew they were in the room.

Batty and Hound, too, needed to show their great devotion to this boy, for, after all, he'd been far away in Boston for months and months.

"Jeffrey, I love you so!" Batty cried, flinging herself at his knees, while Hound barked in agreement.

"I love you, too, Battikins," he said, picking her up in a fierce hug.

The third groomsman was quite short, and his red hair was combed and flattened to within an inch of its life. Bewildered by the unfamiliar clothes and all the noise, he was thinking about crying, but before he could get started, Skye had torn herself away from Jeffrey and was kneeling beside him.

"Hey, Ben." Though she still didn't like babies, she'd decided to make an exception for this one. "How are you?"

"Not good."

"Me neither, but it'll all be over soon and then we'll have cake. Okay?"

This reminder of cake cheered him greatly, and he was now happy to quietly pluck at Hound's yellow bow until it came undone, earning him even more love from Hound than he already had.

In the middle of all that, Aunt Claire had melted away, but she came back now, and with her was—

"Oh, Daddy," said Rosalind. "You look—you look—"

"Gorgeous," said Jane.

"Nonsense," protested Skye, though her breath, too, had been taken away.

It wasn't the suit, of course, or the starched white shirt, or even the tie that didn't clash with anything. It was the happiness that had settled in every part of him, the pure and solid happiness that he'd longed for and deserved, and now was his.

"My princesses," he said, and all four rushed to him and hugged him until he gently pulled away to pick up Ben for a hug of his own. Then he nodded to the other two, man to men. "Tommy, Jeffrey, thanks for being here."

They nodded back, suddenly serious and adult, until Jane tickled Tommy, and Skye tickled Jeffrey, and everyone became themselves again.

Now there was a knock on the front door. It was Nick and Anna, come to say that it was time to go next door.

"She's ready?" asked Mr. Penderwick, and no one had to ask whom he meant.

"Yes, she is, Mr. Pen," said Nick. "And the minister."

"And all of the guests are here," said Anna gleefully, for she loved weddings when they weren't her own father's.

Mr. Penderwick handed Ben over to Aunt Claire, then gave each of his daughters one last hug. "Well, girls, are we ready to get married?"

Married. Was it possible? But yes, astoundingly, miraculously, all of the Penderwicks were absolutely, positively, indisputably, and without a shadow of a doubt—ready to get married.

And so they did.

When Jeanne Birdsall was young, she promised herself she'd be a writer someday—so she could write books for children to discover and enjoy, just as she did in her local library. *The Penderwicks* was her first novel, and it won the National Book Award for Young People's Literature.

Jeanne lives in Northampton, Massachusetts, with her husband and an assortment of animals, including cats, a snail, and a dog named Cagney. You can find out more about Jeanne (and her animal friends) at her Web site, www.jeannebirdsall.com.